McCARTER'S MOUTH FELL OPEN AND HIS BLOOD RAN COLD

How could he have missed seeing the tank?

He leaped across the dead Iraqi, hit the back doors running, tumbled from the APC and landed on his face. Adrenaline was pumping through the Briton's veins as he got to his hands and knees in a desperate scramble, putting ground between himself and the preliminary target of his enemies.

The muzzle blast was loud, a clap of thunder, but it was nothing compared to the explosion generated by an armor-piercing round that ripped through the crippled APC. The shock wave picked up McCarter, throwing him into an awkward somersault, then slamming him into the ground thirty feet distant.

At first the Phoenix Force warrior thought he was dead, then he realized that the blast had merely deafened him. But moments later sound penetrated the ringing silence.

He could hear the tank advancing, its engine growling, big treads finding traction in the sand. The juggernaut was coming for him, bent on finishing the job and grinding him to bloody pulp beneath its tracks.

Other titles available in this series:

STONY MAN II
STONY MAN III
STONY MAN IV
STONY MAN V
STONY MAN VI
STONY MAN VII
STONY MAN VIII

DON PENDLETON'S

MACK BOLAN®

STONY MAN™

STRIKEPOINT

A GOLD EAGLE BOOK FROM

WORLDWIDE®

TORONTO • NEW YORK • LONDON
AMSTERDAM • PARIS • SYDNEY • HAMBURG
STOCKHOLM • ATHENS • TOKYO • MILAN
MADRID • WARSAW • BUDAPEST • AUCKLAND

First edition March 1994

ISBN 0-373-61893-X

Special thanks and acknowledgment to Mike Newton for his contribution to this work.

STRIKEPOINT

Printed In U.S.A.

STRIKEPOINT

PROLOGUE

Petrograd, Russia
Tuesday, 2215 hours

Deciding to leave was the hard part. The rest of it, once he made up his mind, was relatively simple. More or less like stepping off a cliff.

Conditioned by a lifetime of repressive discipline and rules that bore the strictest consequences for a minor breach, Vasili Nabakov had questioned his ability to make the change. No, more than that. To the climactic moment, Nabakov was certain in his mind that he wouldn't—couldn't proceed.

It was a relatively simple matter, when he thought about it. Over two-thirds of his life—three decades, give or take a year—he had been mass-producing death in the support of a political regime that tolerated no defiance or dissent. From early adolescence, when his aptitude for science first revealed itself in structured tests, he had been chosen for the life that he would lead. The choice was made by total strangers, men and women he would never meet, but Nabakov knew better than to question their decision. When the faceless masters spoke, deciding his curriculum, directing his career, Vasili heard the stern voice of the state.

He had performed his duties well enough. No cause for any of the system's countless watchdogs to complain about his work in thirty years. How many men in any field make that claim? A year ago, it would have been a point of pride with Nabakov, but he was different today.

Vasili Nabakov had changed.

The world had changed.

Perhaps the warning signs were visible to others, but Vasili was a man of narrow focus, concentrating on his work almost to the exclusion of what others called a private life. He had no family on earth, had never married, never truly loved.

He thought about the Change as if it were a concrete object, a machine that rolled across the landscape, grinding men and institutions into pulp. The air was cleaner when it passed, the sun shone brighter from the heavens, but conformity had always carried comforts of its own.

Before the Change, Vasili never had to think about his future: it was etched in stone, much like the marker that would someday decorate his grave. He went to work five days a week, sometimes on weekends if a crisis should occur, and he enjoyed the privileges that came from working in a "special" occupation, shoring up the state's security. Without his contribution, who would hold the line against the Germans, the Americans, or the Chinese? If he was privileged to have a car at his disposal, shop in special stores, enjoy young women on the second Friday of the month, it was Vasili's just reward.

Or so he had believed, before the Change.

These days, he wondered if his life had all been wasted. Worse, instead of helping to prevent a global war, had he done evil in the name of state security? Chernobyl came to mind more frequently, of late, and he was forced to keep the images at bay with alcohol. At times, it almost worked.

If anyone had asked him, six months earlier, about the prospect for upheaval in his life, Vasili would have thought that they were mad. The only change his mind had been conditioned to accept was the inevitable triumph of the People's Revolution over capitalism, and logic told him that must be a long way off. He never really doubted that the revolution would succeed, but Nabakov wasn't inclined to think in terms of how or when. Perhaps a generation in the future, when the West caved in beneath the weight of so much decadence.

But now, he knew the truth. There was no People's Revolution, never had been. It was all a lie—or, to be charitable, a bizarre mistake—perpetuated over three-quarters of a century by men who profited from maintenance of the facade. Without the revolution as their guiding principle, the military to support them, those in power would be cast aside, eliminated by the very people they professed to serve.

In fact, the Change had taken everybody by surprise and turned the whole world upside down. In place of fifteen united socialist republics, there were now fifteen independent nations, ten of which formed the Commonwealth of Independent States. After seventy-four years of dominance, communism—the sacred state—was suddenly a discredited concept, swept into the dustbin of history. Its memory was reviled, and the system's former subjects were exercising their well-known talent for erasing unpleasant aspects of the past.

Even the city in which he stood had been stripped of its name and given a new one...or, more properly, an old name restored. Leningrad was Petrograd today, an echo from the dark days of the czar. The bitter monuments to Hitler's three-year siege wouldn't be swept away—not soon, at least—but there were other changes underway. The KGB was gone, he understood, in name and spirit. Their stronghold in the Polustrovo suburb was deserted, no more muffled screams or black sedans arriving with their trussed-up human cargo in the middle of the night. It was a brand-new day.

Except that for every change there was resistance, someone furious at being stripped of privileges and honors he had cherished through the years. The party had been good to some while crushing others underfoot, and it was difficult for those in powerful positions to relinquish their authority without a fight. Still, when the Change swept over them it had been so complete, so unexpected, that the vast majority of diehard Communists were taken by surprise. One moment they were riding high, albeit forced to smile and feign support for *glasnost;* blink your eyes, and suddenly an empire lay in ruins at their feet. The military coup was a pathetic disappointment. In Romania the fate of Nicolae Ceauşescu gave them food for thought. Discretion was the better part of valor. Watch and wait. The world keeps turning, and their time might still come around again.

And in the meantime, they could always give a little boost to history.

The sudden rash of offers had amazed Vasili Nabakov. In all his life, while working for the state, it never once occurred to him that he possessed intrinsic value. There was never any question of free agency or going public with his knowledge and his talent. He was simply not at liberty to entertain such thoughts.

Until the Change.

Today he understood what millions of foreign nationals had understood from birth. There was a world outside the boundaries of Mother Russia where a man could sell himself for cash, the same way others dealt in crops, commodities and livestock. Men of expertise and insight were in short supply. It was a seller's market, most particularly where the oil-rich Arab nations were concerned. The going price was more important than a buyer's race or ideology.

At first the numbers dazzled Nabakov. He scarcely understood what they were saying when his new friends spoke in terms of millions, numbered Swiss accounts, the rest of it. He might have let himself be cheated, but he listened to an agent who, as luck would have it, represented others like himself. Incredibly the price was even higher for a package deal. If Nabakov had no objection to a desert climate, he could live like royalty, practice his profession in a country where his skills would be appreciated.

Once he understood that he was rich—or would be, soon—it had been easy saying yes. He knew the other men involved, two of them personally, one by reputation, and it reassured him, knowing they would be together once the deal was struck. A foreign land wouldn't be quite so strange with two or three acquaintances from home.

The doubts came later, after the arrangements had been made, his numbered Swiss account established with a fat down payment on his fee. At first, Vasili's second thoughts had been so vague and ill-defined that he couldn't pick out their meaning. Over time, as he made ready to leave from Moscow, Nabakov began to realize that there was something wrong.

With him.

With the arrangement.

With his life.

For thirty years he had constructed weapons for the state, in service of a cause that seemed correct, ordained by history. Without the state, without that cause, Vasili started questioning himself, his motives and morality. If he continued building weapons for a different master, someone who had shown himself aggressive, brutal—possibly insane—wouldn't he share the guilt for all that followed from his private choice? Could he, Vasili Nabakov, escape eternal judgment if his skills and expertise were put to evil use?

Religion was as foreign to his life experience as, say, communion with a race of men from Mars, but Nabakov wasn't amoral. Right and wrong had been ingrained in him from birth: the state was right and just; its enemies were wrong and dangerous. But late events had shown those teachings to be false, and once the basic underpinning of his mind-set had been swept away, Vasili doubted every "truth" that he had ever known.

And so, he had decided it was time to leave.

A rather different trip than his employers of the moment had in mind, that is. He would be leaving Petrograd a day ahead of schedule—the next day, as it happened—and his destination would lie westward. He wouldn't be going to the desert after all. Of course, it meant that he wouldn't be rich, but there was still the money waiting in his Swiss account. With any luck at all, by Wednesday afternoon he would have cash in hand, and if the buyers felt like suing him...well, they would have to find him first.

Vasili's smile reflected bitter irony. His innocence in terms of politics and world affairs didn't extend to thinking that the people he was dealing with would ever think in terms of lawsuits. They had other means of punishing duplicity, but they would still be forced to track him down. It was the very reason he had spent a portion of his meager cash on bogus documents, to let him leave the city unobserved.

Alone, he passed the Varsovskij Vokzal, walking briskly with his head down and his hands filling the pockets of his overcoat. This far north, adjacent to the Gulf of Finland, spring evenings were cold. A sturdy coat was mandatory if you meant to move about in comfort, but Vasili Nabakov was barely conscious of the chill. His mind was on tomorrow and the tumult that his disappearance would produce in certain quarters.

It was something, after all these years of living by the rules, to flaunt them so outrageously. The very risk itself was thrilling, like a pint of vodka lying warm beneath his belt.

From Zurich, it was on to Paris for a rest stop, then across the broad Atlantic to a Latin climate. Someplace where his cash would last awhile and let him live in comfort. Nothing ostentatious, mind you, but a far cry from his suite of rooms in Moscow.

He had chosen Petrograd to leave from on the basis of a whim. His parents had been natives of the city, and their graves were found in Lenoj, to the north. Vasili had no trouble in persuading his associates he needed time to say goodbye before he put the motherland behind him. He was in demand, a millionaire-to-be, and no one questioned his intentions for a moment.

Had they?

Sudden doubt assailed him, causing Nabakov to glance across a shoulder, searching for a tail. It was his own imagination, he decided, thinking that he had been followed all the way from Moscow. He wasn't a suspect. It was madness to believe that he would throw away a fortune on a whim, to salve his conscience, when the world was bound to self-destruct in any case. A wise man recognized the signs, and he would profit while he could.

Another backward glance, for safety's sake, before he stepped inside the entrance to the underground. Broad marble steps descended to a spacious platform, bright as day. Fluorescent fixtures lined the ceiling, yards above his head, and banished shadows to the low ground, tucked away beside the tracks. Instinctively Vasili checked the platform, sizing up the travelers who had arrived before him.

Nearest on his left was a dumpy woman with a scarf wound tight around her head. Except for ballerinas, figure skaters and selected whores, Vasili found most Russian women squat and thick. The Latins also ran to fat, he understood, in older age, but Nabakov preferred them young.

The other travelers were men, and there were only two of them, both dressed in business suits beneath their stylish overcoats. They talked in quiet tones, ignored him absolutely, and he let himself relax. The paranoia would recede with time, once he was safely out of reach.

There was a time, not long ago, when running from the KGB had been the rankest sort of fantasy. No place on earth was small or dark enough to hide once agents were on your trail. Now the dreaded agency of death was no more than a footnote in the textbooks. Nabakov could stand right there, in Petrograd, and thumb his nose at men who would have made him tremble short weeks earlier.

The train was coming. He could hear it first, before a distant headlight pierced the tunnel's gloom. Vasili turned to face it, waiting. When the businessmen stepped up behind him, one on either side, they caught him unaware. The hands that gripped his biceps felt like clamps of steel, constricting muscles, cutting off the flow of blood and feeling to his hands. Vasili tried to struggle, but they held him fast.

In front of him, the dumpy woman turned and stepped in close, one hand emerging from her shoulder bag. The contents of the small syringe were clear, like water, but Vasili knew it must be something else. He tried to kick her, knock the deadly needle from her hand, but one of the men who held him saw it coming and reacted with a swift kick of his own. Vasili's legs were cut from under him, knees sagging, and the woman had a clear shot at his jugular as she stepped closer, reaching out with the syringe.

It might have been a wasp's sting but for the immediate response of numbness spreading through his chest and shoulders, down to his waist. Vasili's vision blurred, and he wasn't aware of drooling on his captors as his mouth fell open, muscles going slack. He understood that he was dying, had perhaps a minute left to live, but there was nothing he could do.

The one sensation Nabakov retained, beyond a hopeless anger deep inside, was the vibration of the train as it approached the platform. He was moving now, his two supporters rushing closer to the edge. Below him silver rails lay arrow-straight on beds of filthy concrete. He was looking at an open grave.

His own.

It would have been appropriate to scream, Vasili thought, but he couldn't dredge up a sound from lungs and vocal cords that felt like solid wood. He had a sense of falling, watched the silver tracks rush up to meet him, but the train was there before he ever reached the ground. The engineer was braking for the station, but it still took time, almost a quarter-mile of track before the engine came to rest. The engineer would describe the two men and a woman for police, as best he could, but it was foolish to assume they would be found.

And what was one life, more or less, compared to all the other wonders of the Change?

CHAPTER ONE

Blue Ridge Mountains, Virginia
Friday, 0950 hours

A thousand feet above the narrow track of Skyline Drive, the Beech King Air C 90 cut a path through wispy cirrus clouds, its Pratt & Whitney turboprops maintaining a steady air speed of two hundred miles per hour. The cabin seated six at full capacity, but this run was a special outing, with a solitary passenger. He sat amidships, on the starboard side, forehead touching the cool windowpane as he watched the highway and the mountain forest slip away below.

Mack Bolan never tired of forests, in the abstract. Whether tropical or temperate, montane or marsh, they made up fascinating ecosystems, teeming with life. A woodsman from his youth, Bolan could lose himself among the trees given half a chance, emerging hours or days later with fresh, unique observations on the operation of the food chain.

The summons had been couched in terms of Bolan's personal convenience. It was always so, polite with strident undertones of urgency. The warrior wasn't under contract to the government and so couldn't be ordered to report. He came when called, most times, because he felt a sense of duty, recognized that no one would attempt to reach him in the first place if the situation wasn't desperate.

At that, despite the shadow of disaster and potential death that darkened every visit to the Blue Ridge Mountains, Bolan still enjoyed the trip. It felt like coming home, a luxury that he hadn't allowed himself for years, since the destruction of his family propelled him into never-ending conflict with the savages. Even so, his life-style was a matter of selection, Bolan's conscious and deliberate choice. He didn't feel ill-used, or put-upon.

Reporting to the Farm was something that he did because he could. It was within his grasp to hear the problem out, discuss a possible solution and participate in that solution if it fell within his means. On rare occasions, there was simply nothing he could do. Most times, he found a way.

Of course, he had no inkling what the latest problem was. An invitation to the Farm didn't contain specifics. There was too much risk of interception, even with the various security precautions used at Stony Man. Experience had taught them all to minimize their risks whenever possible.

The Beech King Air was circling westward, into its approach. The flight from Washington had taken less than half an hour. Below him, virgin forest was replaced by cultivated fields and orchards. Stony Man Farm was a working operation in more ways than one, its cover solid enough to pass inspection by a team of experts on the ground. Officially it was experimental agriculture, all hush-hush, but there was nothing strange or futuristic about the crops produced from one year to the next. The orchards yielded peaches and pecans. The other crops were subject to rotation: this year, beets and beans; next season, squash and sweet corn. Produce from the Farm was eaten by its staff, with surplus sold at the prevailing rates.

It made the perfect cover, overall, with nothing to excite suspicion. Motorists or hikers had to veer well off the beaten track before they would encounter signs attached to barbed-wire fences, warning them of their approach to a restricted area. In the event of any questions, programmed answers were available from spokesmen for the U.S. Department of Agriculture. The spokesmen were as ignorant of Stony Man's true function as were accidental drop-ins. They could answer any routine questions from the public, deal with business propositions, junk mail and the like. Persistent queries were referred to Justice and a special three-man team that made the FBI's crack SWAT contingent come off seeming soft on crime. One visit from the Justice agents nipped ninety-nine percent of any problems in the bud.

On-site security at Stony Man was high-tech, multilayered and lethal. Infrared technology and motion sensors backed up listening devices, fiber-optic cameras and patrols by men and dogs. The "farmhands" were adept at their routine assignments; they were also members of the U.S. Army Special Forces, and they kept their weapons out of sight but close at hand. In the event of an attack they were prepared to take all necessary measures to annihilate their enemies.

Intruders—and there had been several through the years—could be divided into "innocent" trespassers and hostile adversaries. The former were detained, identified, interrogated and cautioned that a public reference to the incident would doubtless lead to prosecution on an epic list of federal charges. Hostile prowlers would be taken alive, if possible, but their debriefing was a more aggressive matter. Damage was anticipated, the results inevitably fatal. When the necessary questions had been answered, leads pursued beyond the Farm, a tract of forest in the northern quadrant swallowed up the dead.

Three graves, so far, and with a bit of luck there would be no more added to the toll.

"We're making our approach," the pilot's disembodied voice informed Bolan. "Please prepare for landing, sir."

His belt was fastened, and he didn't bother checking. Certainty of detail was a hallmark of survivors. When you had to check and double-check the same thing countless times, you didn't know your job.

The airstrip was constructed to accommodate a jumbo jet if necessary, but a casual observer couldn't tell it from the air. Instead of sweeping off the longer east-west runway as an airport would, the team at Stony Man applied fine layers of dust from time to time, to complement the camou paint job that they touched up every other month. Descending from an altitude of 750 feet, the east-west runway looked like so much dirt and grass. A short strip—the one the Beech King Air would use today—bisected it from north to south.

The buildings helped, of course. Across the near end of the longer runway, planted in a bed of artificial turf that hid its wheels, a battered mobile home appeared to have been squatting forever, bargain paint and shingles suffering from too much sun and rain. In fact, a tractor could remove the trailer on a moment's notice, when arrivals were expected and approved. In the event of unexpected airborne visitors, the roof and walls were hinged, spring-loaded. Six or seven seconds' warning was enough to prime the battery of 7.62 mm GEC miniguns on 360-degree swivel mounts.

South of the main runway, a smaller, equally dilapidated building was occupied by two lookouts around the clock. In addition to standard infantry small arms, the watchmen were equipped with FIM-92B Stinger surface-to-air missiles, a last-ditch response to any surprise callers from outside the Farm.

Bolan heard and felt the landing gear lock in position. He was ready when the Beech Air touched down, a single jolt immediately followed by deceleration. From his window seat he saw a Chevy Blazer rolling toward the tarmac, braking to a halt with room to spare. A moment later he was on the ground and shaking hands with Calvin James, one-fifth of Phoenix Force.

"You beat me in," Bolan said.

"Didn't have as far to come, for once. Survival exercises in the 'Glades. If you catch a whiff of Spanish moss, that must be me." The black man's smile was comfortable, his handshake firm.

"What's shaking?" Bolan asked him as he walked around the car and took the shotgun seat.

James slid behind the wheel. "I haven't got a clue, so far. You know the way Hal plays it when it's need-to-know."

"Okay, I guess I've kept him waiting long enough."

"He did look anxious, now you mention it."

The Phoenix Force commando put the Blazer through a tight U-turn and powered toward the house, five hundred yards away.

"HE'S DOWN," Aaron Kurtzman announced. He cradled the telephone receiver, feeling Hal Brognola hovering at his elbow.

The big Fed checked his watch and frowned. "Some kind of hang-up at the airport, maybe."

"Actually," Kurtzman replied, "they made good time."

"You're saying I'm on edge?"

"It never crossed my mind."

"Well, shit, you're right," Brognola groused. "I wish we had this business cleaned up yesterday."

"No turning back the clock."

"Too bad."

"We've still got time," said Leo Turrin, seated to the left of Kurtzman.

"You *hope* we've still got time," Brognola answered, looking glum.

Just then, the coded access door sighed open to reveal the form of Yakov Katzenelenbogen. Entering the War Room, Katz circled the conference table to reach his favorite chair. Behind him, Phoenix warriors Rafael Encizo, Gary Manning and David McCarter moved in single file to take their seats. Barbara Price was nowhere to be seen, and Kurtzman reckoned she was waiting for the new arrivals on the floor above.

"Is this the lot, with Cal and Striker?" Manning asked of no one in particular.

"Grimaldi's on a loan-out to the DEA," Kurtzman said. "Able Team is mopping up a job in California."

Kurtzman made no reference to the regulation that restricted Able Team to work on U.S. soil. The rule was known to every person in the room, and he had said enough already to suggest that they were outward bound. The rest was for Brognola to deliver in his own inimitable style.

And the big Fed was right. It felt like longer than the forty minutes, give or take, since Bolan's flight had lifted off from Washington. A thing like this, you always felt an urge to move immediately, but it was rarely practical. The worst thing you could do in crisis situations was to let the first instinctive fear or anger take control and push you into rash, disorganized response. A prompt response was one thing; rushing into action with a half-assed plan—or no plan at all—was something else again.

By now they had the plan, or most of it, but there was still a matter of transmission to the troops. At that, twelve hours wasn't bad for pulling Phoenix Force off their survival exercises in the Everglades and catching Bolan in between two private strikes. With everyone on-site, the wheels were turning now, and Kurtzman felt the old excitement coming back, replacing simple apprehension and disquiet with a sense that they were getting something done.

If only it wasn't too little and too late.

At times like these, the wheelchair felt confining, but he knew that there was no percentage in lamenting fate. His frontline days were over, granted, but the man they called The Bear was still in action, standing firm against the enemy.

Today, with any luck at all, they were about to strike another blow against the savages.

God willing, they would all survive to see it land.

HE RECOGNIZED Barbara Price from a distance, standing on the front porch of the farmhouse, and Bolan felt his pulse quicken. The Blazer rolled to a halt and James switched the engine off, leaving the keys in the ignition as he stepped out. A farmhand in faded denim waited by the porch to take the car away.

"Good flight?" Price asked. She and Bolan didn't touch, but it was there between them, like a crackle of electric energy.

"Air pockets over Arlington," the warrior told her, putting on a smile. "The rest of it was smooth."

"Well, buckle up," she cautioned, leading him inside. "We've got more turbulence downstairs."

"That bad?"

"I wouldn't want to spoil it for you."

"Thanks."

They entered through steel doors, James bringing up the rear, and crossed a spacious entry hall to reach the basement stairs. The Executioner watched Barbara's gently swaying hips as she descended, let his mind drift free for just a moment from the Farm and all its military trappings.

Downstairs, they passed a silent office, pausing at the entrance to the War Room. Price pressed her palm against the glass of an illuminated screen and let the camera do its work. A heartbeat later, she had cleared the threshold, James and Bolan on her heels.

"The gang's all here," Leo Turrin said, rising briefly from his seat to clamp a grip on Bolan's hand. The warrior sat beside his oldest living friend and nodded to the others one by one, while Price settled on Brognola's left.

"I'm glad you had a chance to join us," said the man from Washington.

"It sounded urgent."

"Make that critical." Brognola turned to Kurtzman with a frown. "Let's do it."

The computer whiz keyed a switch and brought the lights down, no preliminaries. The hidden slide projector hummed into life, and a man's life-size image appeared on the screen to Bolan's left, at the far end of the room. The man was average height and weight, with salt-and-pepper hair receding from a prominent forehead. Wire-rimmed spectacles had the effect of magnifying limpid eyes. Bolan mentally pegged the guy somewhere in his early to midfifties, an academic of some sort, perhaps a minor politician.

"Vasili Nabakov," Brognola told the room at large. "Until recently he was one of Russia's top nuclear physicists. By now you've all heard the rumors about Russian brains jumping ship. For some time now they've been in the process of cutting their nuclear arsenal by sixty-odd percent, and new productions in the Twilight Zone. With emigration restrictions wiped out overnight, no more KGB to keep tabs on the flock, it's free-agent time all around. According to Langley, we've got a couple dozen active bidders in the game, mostly third-world revolutionary or reactionary types."

"Terrific," Katzenelenbogen muttered. "Any crackpot with an oil well or a gold mine can afford a stock of warheads now."

"It's funny you should mention oil wells," Brognola said.

"The Iranians?" James asked.

"Iraqis. According to our best reports—including confirmation from inside the Commonwealth—they're bidding high and meeting with a positive response. All those years of state ideology, the profit motive comes as a pleasant surprise. So far, they've picked up four brains we're sure of. Nabakov was one of them."

"You make that past tense?" Bolan asked.

"Affirmative. On Tuesday night he had a little accident in Petrograd. Went off a subway platform as the train was pulling in. What's left of him would fill a sandwich bag."

"You said an accident."

"Officially, that is. Our private sources, which include the Russians now, inform us he was pushed. The engineer saw something, I suppose. In any case, no clear ID and no arrests so far. It's still an accident to anybody from the media, but Petrograd and Moscow are proceeding with a homicide investigation."

"What's the angle?" James inquired.

"They tell us Nabakov was sitting on a phony passport, airline tickets in a different name, the usual. Thing is, his destination wasn't Baghdad. He was booked to Zurich Wednesday morning, with connections on to Paris in the afternoon. From there, who knows?"

"Cold feet?" McCarter asked.

"I wouldn't rule it out. The guy has second thoughts about his future in the desert. Maybe he's just sick of building warheads and reactors. It can happen, I suppose. I understand that he was mixed up in Chernobyl somehow, but we can't get any details. Say he wanted out or suffered an attack of conscience, either way. With an investment running seven figures, the Iraqis would be mad as hell at anybody backing out."

"Especially if they contemplated splitting with the cash," Katz said.

"Especially then."

"You think Iraqis dusted Nabakov?" James asked.

"They wouldn't have to do it on their own. Word is they've got a broker on the deal, some kind of go-between. We're working on it, but the Russians don't have much to share."

"Or so they say." McCarter's voice was frankly skeptical.

"There's always that."

"So, we've got one brain down," Manning said. "What about the other three?"

On cue another face filled up the screen, replacing Nabakov. This man was four or five years younger, with a perfect sunlamp tan, and he paid more attention to his hair. If Bolan had to guess, he would have said the teeth revealed by that effusive smile were capped, perhaps expensive dentures.

"Vladimir Polyarni," Brognola informed them. "Child prodigy, nuclear physicist, the nearest thing covert weapons development ever had to a superstar. What I hear, he was designing viable reactors in his early teens. Deuterium-tritium fusion, it's all Greek to me. Anyway you slice it, he's the man...or one of them, at least. I'm told the going rate was seven million just to bring him over, plus a million-five per year as long as he's in Baghdad."

"Where is he now?" Bolan asked.

"Somewhere in Iraq. The northern part, we think. They took delivery last week."

"That still leaves two."

The third face up was long and slender, lined with years of work and worry. Bolan thought it might have been a passport photograph or something similar. The man made no attempt to smile. Behind his horn-rimmed glasses, flat gray eyes observed the world without a hint of curiosity.

"Piotr Serpukhov," Brognola said. "An engineer in charge of warheads and delivery systems. Over the past ten years he's broken new ground in multiple alternative-targeted reentry vehicles—MARV for short—to defeat our ABM systems. We show him crossing into Iraq from Syria eight days ago."

"He's with Polyarni now?" Katz asked.

"We think so, but the confirmation's hard to come by. As you're all aware, we know Saddam's lied through his teeth about reactors, warheads and delivery systems. That's a given. But we don't know how much progress has been made since Desert Storm."

"In a week, ten days," James said, "these two bozos couldn't build him anything too fancy."

"That's the hope in Washington. If we can break the party up in time, we might prevent Hussein from nuking Israel or Iran and moving on from there."

"Delivery's still a problem," McCarter said, "if his Scuds are any indication."

"Maybe not."

Brognola gave a nod to Kurtzman, and a fourth face flashed onto the screen. The man had gray hair, and light blue eyes beneath a set of heavy brows. His chin was deeply cleft, his jaw square-cut and strong.

"Hey, Katz," James said, "you take a righteous picture, man."

There *was* a fair resemblance, Bolan realized, but it wasn't Katz on the screen. A Moscow street scene in the background canceled any fleeting doubt.

"Meet Ivan Baranovich," Brognola said. "Top of his field in rocketry, propulsion systems, you name it. He's worked on the Soviet Gammon, Grail and Acrid systems. The Sandal, Scarp and SS series of strategic missiles owe more to Baranovich than any other single designer. If anyone can put Iraq on the map, delivery-wise, you're looking at him."

"Should I ask?" McCarter sounded glum, discouraged.

"That's the bright spot," Brognola replied. "They haven't got him yet. As of this morning, he was still in Budapest."

"Why Hungary?" Katz asked.

"Some kind of farewell visit. As a child, he lived there with his parents, father in the diplomatic service. I suppose he's kept in touch with friends. Besides, word is he wants a break before he goes to work for Baghdad. Flying's out. Baranovich is traveling to Turkey on the Orient Express. A pickup team's supposed to meet him there and see him through the last leg to a border crossing."

"We seem fairly well-informed," Manning said.

"Thank the Russians. They've got problems as it is, without a handful of their people running off somewhere and starting World War Three. I gather that they've been in touch with Langley right along."

"So, let them clean it up," James suggested. "It's not like they're exactly inexperienced at making people disappear."

"You keep forgetting that the KGB is out," Brognola said.

"Or so they'd like us to believe."

"In this case I'm inclined to think they're playing straight," Brognola said. "If anything, the hard-core types that used to hang around Dzerzhinsky Square would love to see a deal with the Iraqis go ahead. Embarrass Yeltsin's government no end, turn up the heat on Israel, maybe start another shooting war between Iraq and the United States. If it's a shooting war with nukes involved, no matter who starts throwing warheads first, America comes out the loser. We can either watch our Mideast allies fry or blitz Saddam back to the Stone Age—which would make us just about the biggest bully on the block, in third-world eyes."

"So what's the plan?" Rafael Encizo asked. "They've already claimed two members of the team, and number three is dead."

"Which leaves Baranovich."

"You want to lift him?" McCarter asked.

"Not exactly."

"So?"

"The thought is to replace him," Brognola said. "Send a ringer in his place."

"A ringer?"

"Someone fluent in the language who could pass a cursory inspection. Long enough to get inside, at least."

Mack Bolan glanced at Katz and found the gruff Israeli frowning.

"Did you have someone in mind?" Katz asked.

"We voted you most likely to succeed."

"A little something might have slipped your mind." As Katzenelenbogen spoke, he tapped the conference table lightly with the stainless-steel pincers he used for a right hand.

"In fact, that's our ace," Price said, speaking for the first time since they all sat down. "Baranovich likes mountain climbing... or he did, until four years ago. He had a fall in the Pamirs, got hung up in the rigging somehow. He sustained major damage to his right arm, and the nearest doctor wasn't much on reconstructive surgery. They couldn't save the hand. Gangrene."

"I don't believe it." James was grinning wickedly at Katz. "This guy's your freaking clone."

"Coincidence," Brognola said. "It happens now and then. This time, it works to our advantage."

"Superficially," Katz said. "You're ignoring the fact that he must have a watchdog by now, in light of what happened with Nabakov."

"We know he's got a shadow. Former KGB, now free-lance."

"So?"

"It's being handled. We've arranged for you to have some company outside the shop."

Katz clearly didn't like the sound of that, but he had other problems on his mind. "Another snag."

"Which is?"

"I'm no rocket scientist."

"You're going back to school. The basics, anyway. Crash course."

"It won't fool anyone for very long."

"You're not supposed to make it a career," Brognola told him. "A foot inside is all we need."

"And there's the other thing," McCarter said.

"*Two* other things," James said.

Manning spelled it out. "The other Russians. One look at Katz, and they'll blow the whistle loud enough to hear it back in Moscow."

"If they have a chance," the big Fed replied.

"Why wouldn't they?"

Brognola glanced around the conference table, facing Bolan first, eyes moving on to sweep the members of the Stony Man team.

"Because," he said, "he won't be going in alone."

CHAPTER TWO

Stony Man Farm
Friday, 0130 hours

It was his second shower of the day, and this time Bolan let himself enjoy the steamy heat, relaxing with his head thrown back, eyes closed, the water drumming on his chest. No rush until tomorrow morning, when he caught the Concorde out of Dulles for the first leg of his journey east. He understood the plan, and there was nothing to be gained by worrying about his prospects in advance.

The risks were obvious for all concerned, but he had never let the odds determine a response to any challenge where inaction would be tantamount to failure in itself. In a job like this, once having recognized the enemy and his intent, retreat wasn't an option for the Executioner.

He would proceed and damn the risks, take any reasonable measure that he could to minimize potential danger, but the mission took priority above all personal concerns.

"I should have known you wouldn't wait."

His eyes snapped open at the sound of Barbara Price's voice, her golden body blazing at him as she stepped into the shower stall and closed the sliding door behind her.

"Sorry. I was trying to unwind."

"That's my job."

"If you put it that way..."

She moved into his arms, her body melding tight against him with the water flowing over both of them. She raised her lips to kiss him, and he felt her firm breasts flattening against his chest, her nipples standing out like exclamation points.

They separated moments later, Price standing in the circle of his arms and reaching for the soap. He felt an urge to speak, but she stopped him with a gentle index finger pressed against his lips.

"Not now."

And so he stood in comfortable silence while she worked up mitts of lather on her hands and started bathing him, beginning with his chest and shoulders, working downward, finally kneeling at his feet. Her fingers took their time, and Bolan concentrated on the warm sensations they evoked, his mind as close to blank as it would ever be. He braced himself with one hand flat against the tile, the other cupped behind her head as Barbara took him in her mouth.

Another moment, and he bent to slip both hands beneath her arms, lifting her to face him, feeling her thighs clamp around his waist like a velvet vise. He pressed her shoulders back against the sweaty tile, and she opened for him like a flower, closed around him like a strong, hot fist.

"Oh God!"

A primal atavistic sound erupted from Barbara's throat, somewhere between the realms of pain and pleasure. "Hurry, Mack!"

Bolan hurried, knowing they would still have time to try again before he left for Dulles. More than once, if they were lucky and the final briefings didn't eat up too much time.

She clung to Bolan's neck when they were finished, legs still wrapped around his waist, half drowned in steaming water and sensation. Neither felt the urge to separate and break the bond between them.

"I think I need a shower," Bolan said at last.

"You did work up a sweat, at that." She smiled into the hollow of his shoulder, nipping at his flesh.

"Whose fault is that?"

"No fault involved."

"I still need somebody to scrub my back."

Her smile went dreamy. "Mmm. I thought you'd never ask."

Much later, in the double bed, there would be time for talk, but neither one would raise the subject of his mission. It wasn't for private time, this talk of death and danger in a foreign land where every man—or most them, at least—would be his enemy. The private times were meant for solace, binding wounds and sharing tenderness.

The pain and killing would distract him soon enough. They always did.

Tomorrow would be soon enough for that.

In the meantime there was peace.

ON FRIDAY AFTERNOON, Yakov Katzenelenbogen went back to school. His tutor was a thirty-one-year-old rocketry expert named Jane Piersall, on loan from the Pentagon to Stony Man Farm at Brognola's urgent request. Their classroom was a vacant office in the northeast corner of the farmhouse basement level, where she set up charts and diagrams on a folding easel.

With more than thirty years of military service behind him, Katz was familiar with rockets from first-hand experience. He had witnessed the destruction they wrought on a battlefield and in the urban killing grounds where terrorists conducted hit-and-run campaigns. He had been personally targeted on more than one occasion by Soviet RPG rockets, and he was proficient in the use of such portable launchers as the American LAW rocket, M-47 Dragon, and the Stinger, the British Blowpipe and the German Armbrust. Still, as he listened to his dark-haired, blue-eyed coach, there was obviously much remaining to be learned.

They started off with the basics of solid fuel versus liquid, with a discussion of thrust levels and fuel configuration in solid-propellant missiles like the Poseidon C-3 and the Minuteman III. Liquid propellant, as used in the Titan II, led them into fuel feed systems and the relative merits of pressure feed versus the turbo-pump. Cutaway drawings revealed the various missile subsystems, starting at the lethal business and with warheads, moving on to the propulsion systems, guidance and control systems, and mission-specific systems, including command destruct mechanisms for aborting launches prior to impact. Katz learned about thrust vector control, essential for guidance of missiles traveling outside the earth's atmosphere, and he took mental notes on the difference between inertial and command guidance systems, with the latter including passive, active, or semiactive homing mechanisms.

The mechanics took an hour and a half. His mind nailed down the basics, but Katz knew that he would never pass for expert if the questions moved beyond a very basic stage. He caught himself at that, remembering Brognola's words about a foot inside the door and realizing that the other Russians—Polyarni and Serpukhov—would blow the whistle on him at the moment they beheld his face. In essence his new expertise was a cover designed to fox any Iraqis or others who plied him with questions en route to his final destination.

And from there, it all came down to timing after all. Katz simply had to trust the other members of the team. Without them he was dead.

A coffee break gave way to military applications of the new technology he had acquired that afternoon. Jane Piersall covered the difference between tactical weapons, used in the context of a military engagement, and strategic launches aimed at targets such as enemy population or industrial centers. They ran through the various ballistic missile types, from short-range to intercontinental. Tactical missiles were ground-, air-, or sea-launched, with the sea-launch variety further divided into surface or submarine. Nuclear warheads included multiple reentry vehicles—designed to saturate one target, multiple independently targeted reentry vehicles—MIRVs—for widely separated targets, and multiple alternative-targeted reentry vehicles—MARVs—wherein each warhead carried its own rocket and computer, designed to change course for preselected alternative strikes that would defeat an enemy's ABM system. With treaty reductions in progress, the Commonwealth of Independent States would still be sitting on some 8,200 ballistic missiles equipped with an estimated 14,000 nuclear warheads.

All dressed up with nowhere to go.

The briefing's final hour was consumed by data on specific Russian missile systems, filling gaps in Katzenelenbogen's knowledge of the former enemy. The Snapper and Sagger were antitank weapons designed for use by the infantry. Gammon, Ganef, Gecko, Gainful, Grail and Goa were all air defense missiles, with the latter model suited for launches from land or surface vessels. Acrid was the standard air-launched tactical missile of the Russian air force. Land-based tactical missiles in the IRBM and ICBM range included Sandal, Scarp and the SS series, ranging from SS-16 to SS-20. The litany of apocalyptic hardware left him enlightened . . . and vaguely depressed.

Katz knew from Pentagon briefings that Iraq already possessed short-range ballistic missiles in the Scud B class, but the Scud's reputation for poor accuracy had been borne out in the Desert Storm conflict. Ivan Baranovich would presumably go to work on the problem if and when he reached Baghdad, coaching the Iraqis in construction of bigger and better killing machines, while Polyarni and Serpukhov got busy with warhead delivery systems.

Correction. Polyarni and Serpukhov were already at work in Saddam Hussein's stable, earning their seven-figure salaries in some covert laboratory, whipping up nuclear nightmares for the rest of the world. Would taking out Baranovich defeat the plan? Could Katz or any other member of the Stony Man team get close enough to pull the plug?

Brognola's plan looked fairly simple on the drawing board. Katz was going into Budapest with McCarter as his shadow. Once on-site, he would be met by his connection—someone from the Russian camp—and it was there he saw the program start to fray around the edges.

Katz was all for progress and democracy, regardless of the setting. He could sympathize with Russians who had labored underneath the yoke of communism all their lives, at last set free—in theory—to pursue their destinies without directives from the state.

But a lifetime spent in the defense of Israel, standing firm against a host of Arab enemies with backing from the Soviets, inclined Katz toward a certain cynicism where the Russians were concerned. He had no doubt that Yeltsin and his comrades in the Moscow leadership were more or less sincere about reform, but there were thousands more whose rank and privileges were stripped away with communism's swift decline. Some would adapt, no doubt, but many others would inevitably bide their time, expecting the tide of reform to reverse itself in a few months or years. Eight decades of dictatorship weren't wiped away with the stroke of a pen. The KGB might not exist these days, officially, but its die-hard officers had to have gone somewhere, along with the bureaucrats who had once relied on the party for their limousines, their houses and their privileged shops.

In some respects, Katz knew it was a lot like postwar Germany, where dedicated Nazis vanished overnight, replaced by "innocent" men and women who saw nothing, heard nothing, never suspected the worst. These days, the children of those "rehabilitated" fascist goons were on the march again in a united Germany, and Katz wasn't prepared to trust the Russians yet, by any means.

But he would follow orders. If that meant flying into Budapest, connecting with a former agent of the KGB and taking an excursion on the Orient Express, so be it. He would carry out his duty like a soldier, even if it cost his life.

Which very probably would be the case.

He had his orders; he would do his job.

But there was nothing in the book that said he had to like it.

"YOU'RE SURE about this contact?" Leo Turrin asked.

"As sure as I can be," Brognola told him, "from eight thousand miles away."

"A year ago, I would have said it was impossible."

"A year ago it *was* impossible. Things change."

"I heard that rumor."

They were seated in the office next to the War Room, several doors from the cubicle where Katz was learning the ins and outs of Russian rocketry. Brognola had allowed himself a rare cigar in the tension of the moment.

"All things considered," he said through a screen of smoke, "I thought they took it fairly well."

"You mean Katz took it fairly well."

"All of them. You think the past few months have shaken up a lot of old-line politicians, think about the impact on the military. All these years of squaring off against the Soviets as enemies, and now we're allies. Hell, they aren't even Soviets anymore."

"You hope."

"I'm covering the angles, Leo, but we have to let our guard down somewhere, or we might as well resign ourselves to living in the past. I've been around the horn with Langley on this thing, and no one has a clue what Minsk or Moscow has to gain by dreaming up disinformation on a deal like this. If they were setting out to screw us, they'd be working hand in glove with the Iraqis."

"What about Mossad?"

"They hate it," Brognola admitted. "Old habits die hard, all around. But where's the choice?"

"They're in?"

"The last I heard. They've got an agent set to rendezvous with Striker when he gets to Belgrade. Nothing heavy, but they want a pair of eyes on-site, in case it falls apart."

"I have to say it makes me nervous, splitting up the team that way."

"Beats sending six men into Hungary," Brognola said. "We know the handlers are keeping close watch on Baranovich. It stands to reason they'll be looking out for strangers in the neighborhood, as well. With the conditions as they are, it's not exactly tourist season in the heart of Budapest."

"If it's a setup—"

"Then we lose one man or two, instead of six."

Brognola's tone was gruff, unyielding, but concern was written on his face. Whatever risks or problems Turrin thought of, the big Fed had been there first, examining the angles through a sleepless night before he called the meet at Stony Man. If there was any other way to go, he would have tried it, but the risks involved with sitting back and doing nothing were horrendous.

Grim silence stretched between them for a moment, broken once again by Turrin's cautious voice. "You think we've covered everything?"

Brognola scowled at his cigar. "Hell, no. The Concorde might go down tomorrow, or the Red Chinese might hop across the border from Mongolia. The President might have a stroke or get pissed off and change his mind. There's no way anyone can cover all the bases. We just do the best we can and hope it's good enough."

"When you put it that way, it comes off sounding pretty lame."

"You're telling me?"

He understood what Brognola was going through, the doubt that came attached to any choice he made. Both men had been involved with Bolan's one-man war almost from the beginning, Turrin even longer than Brognola. Each would have taken Bolan's place if that had been an option, but they lacked his front-line skills and expertise. It was a case of the job choosing the man, and there was small consolation in the knowledge that Phoenix Force would be backing him up this time out. Eastern Europe and the Middle East could swallow armies and digest their bones; six warriors on a holy quest would barely constitute an appetizer if their luck ran out.

And any way he tried to slice it, there was still no choice. The options were unthinkable.

But if they failed...

Turrin blocked that train of thought before it left the station. Failure was a possibility, of course, but he would focus on the downside of the job another time. Right now, Bolan and the others needed firm support from every member of the Stony Man team, without exception. There was no place for distractions on the firing line.

"They'll be all right," he said at last, surprised and then embarrassed that the private thought had passed his lips.

"I hope so," Brognola said, tapping ash from his cigar. "I surely do."

MCCARTER SANK the nine ball with a swift, clean stroke and watched it disappear. The cue ball stopped dead on its mark, waiting for the Briton as he straightened up and chalked his cue, circling the table to line up a shot at the ten.

He was alone inside the combination den and recreation room, adjacent to communications on the ground floor of the farmhouse. Katz was downstairs, boning up on rocketry, while Manning, Encizo and James sat down to something from the mess hall's microwave oven.

As for McCarter, he had lost his appetite.

The job could do that to you, if you let it. Under normal circumstances, the former SAS commando rode close herd on his feelings, holding emotions in check and dismissing his doubts when they got in the way. At the moment, however, he had the luxury of time. Twelve hours and a little more, before he joined Katz on a flight to Paris, and from there to Budapest.

Too late for backing out, but that had never been McCarter's style in any case.

He didn't fear the job, per se, but he had grave misgivings. Eastern Europe was a part of it, so recently liberated from the thrall of Moscow and the KGB. Old enmities and habits had a way of hanging on despite the fact they were no longer welcome, and he wondered how their new "friends" in the East would take to having Western agents on their soil. Of course, there was a chance that the Hungarians and Yugoslavians were ignorant of what was going on. In that case, they would neither hinder nor cooperate...unless their agents stumbled onto something quite by accident and moved to intervene.

It grated on McCarter's nerves that he was playing watchdog, leaving Katz to work the front line with a former member of the KGB while he, McCarter, lingered in the shadows, watching like a hired voyeur. If anything went wrong, he would attempt to bail Katz out, but there was only so much one more could do.

As for the others, Bolan and the bulk of Phoenix Force, they would be waiting for the Orient Express in Yugoslavia. Not boarding, mind you—that would raise too many eyebrows, multiply the risks involved—but rather running parallel in separate cars. Whatever happened on the train, if there was trouble anywhere along the route from Budapest to Ankara, Turkey, it would be McCarter's game.

He sank the ten ball in the corner pocket, nearly scratched but saved it at the final instant. Pure dumb luck, the kind you couldn't count on in a killing situation, when your life was riding on the line.

A part of him was challenged by the mission, pleased to take it on. McCarter's training in the British SAS had primed him for the moments such as this, when he was called upon to make the life-or-death decisions, scratching for survival with the odds against him, winning through by means of skill and guts combined. Another part foresaw disaster if he missed a single cue along the way—not merely for his friends and comrades, but for all the world at large.

And it was true, the hoary joke that every silver lining had to have a cloud attached. At first, the news from Russia and her satellites had been mind-boggling, too good to be true. Overnight democracy, with communism in ruins. Gone was the Berlin Wall, the hammer and sickle, KGB "reeducation" camps that formed the Gulag. Fear and loathing had been wiped away, as if some cosmic master artist had decided it was time to change his theme and lean the slate to start from scratch.

Iraq was something else. Unfinished business there, in spite of Desert Storm and all that followed after. McCarter made no bones about his skepticism when it came to leaving Saddam Hussein in power, permitting a demented dictator to claim "victory" and continue his defiance of UN peacekeeping forces. McCarter had no expertise or aspirations in the realm of politics, but he could spot a bad idea from miles away.

When surgeons went in after a milignant tumor, they didn't remove only three-fourths of the offending growth. Firefighters didn't douse a blaze and leave the embers glowing red. You didn't wound a rabid dog and leave it thrashing in the gutter, snapping at the legs of passersby.

A job half-done had really not been done at all. If anything, the consequences of such negligence were often worse, more dangerous for all concerned.

Like now.

From Desert Storm and rank humiliation, the Iraqi strongman had reorganized his act to the extent that he was buying talent from the Russians, building up his prewar arsenal with brand-new weapons that would give him greater range and striking power than his former arms. For all McCarter knew, it might already be too late for a last-minute save.

But they would have to try, and that meant Budapest. The watchdog's job.

He tried for the eleven ball and clipped it at an awkward angle, missing the selected pocket by a good six inches. Rolling on, his cue ball kissed the bumper and rebounded with sufficient force to set the eight ball rolling toward the nearest corner pocket. Scowling down the slim shaft of his cue, McCarter watched it go, the traditional symbol of bad luck blazing a trail across the green baize. For just a heartbeat he was confident that it would miss the pocket, but the eight ball knew its way, homing on the trap as if a hidden magnet were beaming a signal it couldn't deny.

McCarter watched it drop and disappear from sight. Strike three.

CHAPTER THREE

Budapest, Hungary
Saturday, 1255 hours

Yakov Katzenelenbogen had lifted off from Dulles International at 8:29 on Saturday morning. The Concorde was nearly full, 123 of its 128 seats sold out for the transatlantic flight, and Katz wondered now many of his fellow passengers were on their way to some secret rendezvous, perhaps a life-and-death encounter on the other side. There were two that he knew of—himself and David McCarter, sitting farther back—but it was possible that there were others in the crowd, as well. A spy or two, perhaps the CEO of some conglomerate whose vote of yea or nay on some proposal from his European counterparts would rock Wall Street on Monday morning.

Katz made a point of relaxing on the two-hour flight from Dulles to Orly. Given the hour, he drank no alcohol, but allowed himself four cups of rich, dark coffee. Perversely the caffeine soothed his nerves, where it would have had another man biting his nails. Katz sipped the brew in silence, staring out the window at a solid floor of clouds two thousand feet below.

They had an hour on the ground in Paris, waiting for the scheduled flight to Budapest. Katz ignored McCarter, killing time in the transit lounge once he'd overseen the transfer of luggage to Air France. The passport check was perfunctory at best, the immigration officer bored and distracted.

At 11:40 a.m., Katz boarded the Air France 727 and took his seat in coach. McCarter sat two rows in front of him, on the aisle, but they avoided any contact beyond the briefest meeting of eyes. From Dulles onward, they were traveling as total strangers, one British and one Israeli, both with passports listing bogus names. In Budapest McCarter would be Katzenelenbogen's life insurance, unknown even to his contact from the Russian side. If anything went wrong, McCarter would at least be able to observe what happened, even if he didn't have an opportunity to intervene. From there the other members of the team might salvage something from the mission, extricate themselves if nothing else and live to fight another day.

The flight to Budapest used up another hour and fifteen minutes, leaving Katz with ample time to run the drill again and sort through any problems in his mind. The immigration officers at Ferihegyi airport had the harried look of border guards in any land where sudden change has swept away the status quo and left the natives on their own to look for solid ground. In 1956 the fathers of these men and women had declared themselves in violent opposition to the Soviets, and they were crushed by sheer brute force. Today, another revolution had achieved the goals of that frenetic moment almost overnight. The rules and regulations of a lifetime had been swept away, and it would take some getting used to in the ranks.

Budapest was, in fact, two cities—Buda on the west bank of the Danube, Pest upon the eastern side—and that division typified the country as a whole. East of the river lay Hungary's fertile plains, the Alföld, while rugged hills dominated the west and north. Historic antipathy to eastern invaders had prompted Hungary's pact with Nazi Germany in World War Two, but it was a losing bargain, leading to Soviet dominance after 1945. Old wounds were slow to heal in such a land, where some still hated the Turks for massacres inflicted in the latter 1600s, but most Hungarians looked forward these days, imagining a future without the hammer and sickle.

Katzenelenbogen caught a taxicab to the Hotel Gellert, a popular establishment with tourists for its fine view of the Danube. Ironically his sixth-floor room faced eastward, toward the National Museum, but he didn't mind. If he felt any sudden, overwhelming urge to see the river, he could always step outside.

McCarter would be following, a gap of several minutes orchestrated to disrupt surveillance or at least preserve the fiction of two men traveling separately. If they were blown already, somehow, then the effort would be all in vain, but Katz relied on Stony Man to keep their cover solidly intact. Once they were on the ground, all bets were off, and he would have to play the cards as they were dealt.

A shower first. The hours of traveling had left him feeling grimy, and Katz was anxious for a change of clothes. When that was done, he would behave like any other tourist in a new, exotic city, waiting for his Russian contact to make the first move.

And from there...well, they would have to see what happened next.

Unarmed and on his own, he was a sitting duck right now if anyone had reason to suspect him, a desire to take him out. As there was nothing he could do about it, Katz decided he should do precisely that.

Nothing.

He thought about the possibility of listening devices in the room and forced himself to whistle as he padded naked to the shower. Let them listen if they wanted to, whoever "they" might be.

Katz was committed now, and there could be no turning back.

He was booked to the end of the line.

Belgrade, Yugoslavia
Saturday, 1320 hours

TWO HUNDRED and fifty miles south, Mack Bolan checked his single bag through customs in the capital of Yugoslavia. His passport in the name of Michael Belasko raised no eyebrows, and his suitcase wasn't opened once he told the customs officer that he had nothing to declare. Thirty minutes later, after displaying his international driver's license and signing the mandatory rental forms, he was seated in a dark blue Porsche 944, his suitcase safely locked inside the trunk.

So far, so good.

From the airport he motored north and west along Bulevar Revoiucije, making his way into Old Town. He had the best part of twenty-four hours to kill in Belgrade, while Katz was waiting for his contact in Budapest and boarding the Orient Express at noon the following day, putting wheels in motion that could change the course of history. Meanwhile Bolan was registered at a small hotel on Visnjiceva, a block from the ancient Bajrak Mosque. It would be there, or somewhere in the neighborhood, that he made contact with his counterpart from the Mossad.

His transatlantic flight had been a classic exercise in misdirection, just in case there was a problem with security. With Gary Manning, Calvin James and Rafael Encizo, he had traveled on the Concorde into London at the crack of dawn. From Heathrow he had flown with British Air to Rome, and on to Belgrade via Alitalia. The men of Phoenix Force, meanwhile, had flown Swissair to Zurich, finishing the last leg of their trip to Belgrade on Malev Hungarian Airlines. Barring some unforeseen mishap, Bolan wouldn't see his comrades again until he reached Turkey and they regrouped for the crossing into Iraq.

His first stop, before going to his hotel, was a pawnshop on Georgi Dimitrova, not far from Tasmajdan Park. The ancient proprietor didn't know him from Adam, but Bolan's password, provided to Stony Man by a friendly contact at Langley, seemed to do the trick. Without a second thought, the old man locked his door, reversed a hanging sign to indicate the shop was closed, and beckoned for Bolan to follow him behind the display counter.

The back room was small and cramped, piled high with crates and cardboard cartons of secondhand merchandise. One corner of the room was dominated by a giant safe, some six inches taller than Bolan himself. The old man turned his back and bent to spin the dial, his body blocking Bolan's view of the combination as he worked the knob from left to right and back again, repeatedly.

It took the best part of the old man's strength to move the massive door once it was opened, and he stood aside to let his guest inspect the special items stored within. There was a cash box on the bottom shelf, but all the rest was military hardware, weapons stacked three-deep in places, with grenades and loaded magazines in boxes, labeled with a felt-tipped pen.

Browsing, Bolan first selected a Beretta Model 92 automatic, its muzzle threaded to accommodate a silencer. His backup weapon was an Uzi submachine gun with a folding metal stock, plus half a dozen extra magazines for each of the selected arms. Four boxes of spare 9 mm parabellum rounds extended his firepower, and Bolan topped it off with four British L2A1 antipersonnel grenades. A shoulder rig for the Beretta made his shopping list complete, and the old pawnbroker supplied a leather athletic bag to carry the rest of the hardware.

Bolan took a roll of dinars from his pocket, ready to pay for the weapons, but his contact raised both hands in protest, shaking his heads in a vigorous negative. With a combination of sign language and broken English, the old man made it clear he would be compensated in a different manner for his merchandise. Bolan took him at his word, shook hands in parting and returned with his selected weapons to the waiting Porsche.

Beyond this point, he was in violation of the law, beyond such trivia as traveling on bogus documents. Possession of the bag that sat beside him on the empty shotgun seat could earn him several years in prison, anywhere from Belgrade on through southern Yugoslavia, Greece and Turkey. Once inside Iraq the niceties of law would scarcely matter. "Justice" in the territory of Saddam Hussein was something else entirely, and especially so for an American engaged in hostile moves against the state.

So be it.

He put the Porsche in gear and checked out his rearview mirror, merging cautiously with traffic as he picked up speed. His stomach growled, reminding him that it was hours since he had eaten anything of substance. After checking in at his hotel, he meant to remedy that situation with dispatch.

And after he had eaten, he would settle back to wait.

Novi Sad, Yugoslavia
Saturday, 1600 hours

DRIVING NORTH from Belgrade in a rented Citroën sedan, approaching the Hungarian border at a cautious sixty-five miles per hour, it occurred to Calvin James that they could count on language problems, at the very least, before they reached the last stage of their mission in Iraq. His fluent French and Spanish complemented the linguistic skills of Gary Manning—bilingual in French—and Rafael Encizo—a native Spanish-speaker—but James's working knowledge of Korean and Vietnamese would do them no good whatsoever on their trek. None of the Phoenix Force warriors spoke Serbo-Croatian, Macedonian, Slovenian, Greek, Turkish, Kurdish or Arabic, the offical languages of four nations they would be traversing within the next few days.

In short they had to be cautious at every moment, avoiding any complications that arose from failure to communicate.

So far, of course, the mission had been relatively trouble-free. He didn't count the fat Italian seated next to him on board the flight from Switzerland to Belgrade, wheezing garlic all the way and spitting into a silk handkerchief every few moments, examining the product at length before it was stowed away in his pocket.

Traveling light was the worst of it, winging halfway around the world without a weapon more substantial than the fiberglass "letter opener" tucked away inside his jacket. In a pinch, at close range, the needle-pointed blade would suffice, but James felt naked pulling away from the Belgrade airport, painfully aware of how vulnerable he and his comrades were just then, on foreign soil, without a gun between them.

Once again, Brognola's contacts with the CIA resolved the problem. Crossing the Sava into New Belgrade, they continued on for fifteen minutes, stopping in a suburb where they introduced themselves to the proprietor of a machine shop, swapping passwords back and forth until the man was satisfied. When they departed half an hour later, they were armed with three SIG-Sauer P-220 autoloading pistols, manufactured in Switzerland and chambered for the classic 9 mm parabellum round. They had also acquired a Beretta Model 12 submachine gun and two Vz.58 assault rifles—Czech versions of the Soviet AK-47 with 30-round magazines and folding metal stocks.

Feeling better, the three warriors continued on their way, James taking his turn at the wheel. The plan was relatively simple, when he thought about it. They would meet the Orient Express when it crossed the border at Subotica, verify Katzenelenbogen's presence with a prearranged signal, and then keep track of the train as best they could, watching for any trouble, until he disembarked in Ankara. Call it two thousand miles, give or take a hundred; roughly two days on the rails, when you included stops for fuel, unloading passengers and so forth.

Naturally they wouldn't be keeping track of Katz day and night. You had to figure that the Orient Express was relatively safe, at least while it was moving. Any kind of serious assault on the train would raise hell in the media from London to the Bosporus, with Interpol and countless local agencies involved. It was enough for Phoenix Force to be available at major stops, and in the Citroën they could race ahead to keep a rendezvous.

The rest of it, whatever happened on the train itself, was up to Katz, McCarter and their Russian contact. Something else that Calvin James had trouble with was the notion that a lifelong enemy was suddenly their bosom friend. It brought to mind the various alliances of World War Two, their ever-shifting status, and the way that wartime "allies" wound up facing each other down for almost fifty years, once they had finished mopping up the Nazi threat.

James opted for a wait-and-see approach, securely founded on a base of cynicism. If his orders called for him to work with Russian agents, he would do so. But directives from the brass didn't require that he let down his guard or give their newfound "friends" a chance to stab him in the back. If anything went sour between Subotica and Turkey, anything at all, he was prepared to kick some righteous ass.

And if it all went smoothly, that was fine with James. He didn't mind a milk run now and then, just so the easy jobs were balanced out by something with a bit of challenge to it. Anytime it got too easy he'd know that there was something wrong.

No sweat, he told himself.

The warrior's instinct told him that the job at hand would offer all the challenge he could handle, by and by. For now he simply had to keep his deadline with a train and see what happened next.

He settled back and focused his attention on the road.

"WE'RE ALMOST THERE," Manning announced, checking his road map for a mileage report. "I'd estimate another fifteen minutes at our present speed."

"'Bout time," James said. "These funky highway signs, I might as well be driving on the dark side of the moon."

"I haven't let you down so far."

"We've got a long way yet to go."

The tall Canadian put on an injured look. "O ye of little faith."

"I got your faith right here."

"Another time, perhaps."

They reached Subotica on schedule, rolling through the streets of a typical Slavic border town, James watching the posted speed limit and signaling his turns well in advance. The last thing they needed was a traffic stop with a carload of illegal weapons.

"Man, I'm telling you," James said, "I never felt so black before. You notice any brothers on the street?"

"You're a minority of one," Encizo told him, grinning in the back seat.

"Make that two," James replied, "unless we passed a barrio I didn't notice, coming into town."

"For all they know," the Cuban said, "I could be Arab or Castillian."

"Sure, until you open up your mouth."

"You don't think I could pass for Spanish?"

"Spanish Harlem, maybe."

"Never mind," Manning said with a crooked smile. "Just let me do the talking. I make the railway station up ahead."

They parked and locked the Citroën, keeping it casual on a walk around the depot, checking out the posted schedule for the Orient Express. There were some uniforms around the customs office, but no one appeared to give the strangers a second glance, taking their presence for granted at a border crossing.

Manning knew that Yugoslavia had never discouraged tourism, as most of the Soviet satellite nations had done throughout the Cold War. Americans and residents of western Europe were free to drop in and leave their money behind, as long as they kept their political opinions to themselves. A certain number of Western spies were tolerated in Belgrade and environs, on the assumption they were more interested in Soviet than Yugoslavian affairs. If anything, that sometimes grudging quasi-friendship with the West had helped insure Yugoslavia's independence from Soviet domination through the years.

Their present mission was a different story, though. While it didn't affect the Belgrade government directly, any conflict with Iraq would certainly be viewed as hazardous, perhaps beyond the pale of "normal" cloak-and-dagger work. The CIA would gladly wash its hands of all responsibility for mapping out the plan, and Manning understood that capture meant the men of Phoenix Force were on their own.

As always, right.

It was a given in their covert war against the savages. Permission might be granted at the highest levels of the government—in this case Washington and Minsk—but "plausible deniability" remained the rule of thumb for politicians interested in preservation of their own careers. The White House was committed, for the moment, to a course of diplomatic pressure in the Middle East, and Russian leaders would be even less inclined to claim responsibility for hostile moves against Iraq. The Commonwealth of Independent States had problems of its own, without inviting terrorist attacks, petroleum embargoes and the like.

"We'll need to double-check tomorrow," James said to no one in particular. "Make sure the train's on time."

"With Katz on board, it wouldn't dare be late," Encizo stated.

"That's if he gets on board."

"He'll be there," Manning said. "Now, we'd better see about a place to sleep."

CHAPTER FOUR

Belgrade
Saturday, 1930 hours

After supper Bolan took a walk through Old Town, keeping up his facade as a typical Western tourist. At that hour the Ethnographic Museum and the Bajrak Mosquc were closed to visitors, but he walked five blocks to the historic Kalemegdan Fortress and circled its perimeter, winding up near the zoo on Donjoggradski Boulevard. Inside, the cats seemed restless, or it might have been that dusk aroused their predatory instincts, causing them to pace their pens and bellow as the night came on.

He knew the feeling, marking time and waiting for events that you couldn't control with any certainty. At first he had considered staying in his room and waiting for the call or knock that would announce his contact from Mossad, but it occurred to Bolan that a tourist on his first night in the capital of Yugoslavia wouldn't retire without some effort to behold the local sights. He wore the new Beretta in its shoulder rig, two extra magazines in armpit pouches on the right, but he had left his other weapons in the Porsche's trunk in case someone should search his room.

Walking south along Pariski Tadeusa Koscuska, the Executioner made a point of checking out the traffic and pedestrians. If he was being tailed, the shadow was a pro who didn't give himself away with careless moves. No sudden stops or jerky turns when Bolan changed his mind and doubled back along his course. No screeching brakes or rubbernecking from the driver of a passing vehicle.

Which could mean he was clean...or that his adversaries had him marked and knew he had to return to his hotel. Surveillance might be hit-or-miss, a lookout watching his hotel and car, reporting when the mark went off on foot.

But who would care to shadow him at this point in the game? The Russians might decide to take out some insurance, just in case the Americans messed up and dropped the ball. There was Mossad, of course, well-known for double-checking every move before they would commit an agent in the field.

And there were still his enemies.

Who were they? The Iraquis, for a start, intent on making sure Ivan Baranovich arrived on schedule to complete their lethal brain trust. Based on past performance, they would stop at nothing to insure success, but Bolan saw no reason to believe Iraqi agents would be conscious of his mission or his presence in the neighborhood. Right now, their full attention would be focused on Baranovich, in Budapest, and that put Katzenelenbogen on the firing line.

The Russians were another problem. Not the government in Minsk or Moscow, but the diehards who would profit from disruption of the fragile Mideast status quo. Brognola was convinced that certain past or present politicians were involved with former members of the KGB to close the brain sale with Saddam Hussein, and KGB—"retired" or otherwise—meant agents skilled in every nuance of evasion and surveillance, death and double cross. Again, however, Bolan thought the main attention of his enemies would be directed northward, toward their man in Budapest. If they concerned themselves with Yugoslavia at all, it would be later, once the phony Baranovich was aboard the Orient Express.

And if surveillance teams had staked out his hotel, well, there was nothing he could do about it at the moment, even if he made their watchdogs on the street. A confrontation in the heart of Old Town wouldn't help his case, and it might well prove fatal if he found himself outgunned.

With that in mind, the Executioner deliberately gave up on looking for a shadow in the last two blocks before he entered the hotel. He couldn't make out any watchers in the lobby, unless someone had bribed the registration clerk or bellboy to report his movements.

He passed the elevator out of habit, briskly tackling the stairs to reach his third-floor room. The key was in his left hand as he reached the door, his right hand free for the Beretta.

Just in case.

He caught a whiff of the intruder as he crossed the threshold. Subtle, aromatic, a perfume that had no place on bargain counters or on hotel maids. He palmed the automatic, moving from the narrow entryway to scan the room at large, his progress frozen as he saw the slender, dark-haired woman watching from a seat beside the window.

"Hotel locks," she said by way of introduction. "Never trust them."

"Thanks. I'll make a note."

"You won't need that," she told him, glancing at the gun, "unless you always shoot your friends."

"I've met my friends," the Executioner replied. "For all I know you're just a thief."

"Not quite."

The lady rose to meet him, fluid grace in motion, curves that were surprising and impressive on a body barely five-foot-four. She risked a smile and offered him a manicured hand with crimson nails that matched her lipstick.

"Sascha Lentz," she said. "You were expecting me?"

"I wouldn't go that far." He shifted the Beretta to his left hand and shook her right with his. Her grip was firm and dry.

"I hope you don't make judgments based on sex," she told him flatly.

"Just survival."

"Fair enough. I've managed to survive so far."

"I guess that makes you all of twenty-five."

"You flatter me." Her green eyes swept the room at large. "Are we alone?"

He shrugged and put the gun away. "It was a random choice, no reservation. If they've planted anything, it's been since dinner."

"Then we're safe enough," she said. "I've been here since you left."

"Feel free to make yourself at home."

Her gaze was frank, appraising him. "Another time, perhaps. We still have business to discuss."

"Your interest in the job, for starters."

"That should be self-evident. If the Iraqis finally perfect a warhead and delivery system, who is their most likely target?"

"These days, take your pick."

"I think you know the answer well enough. In Tel Aviv there are no doubts."

"So much concern, I would have thought Mossad would run the show themselves."

"It was considered...and rejected, as an act of provocation."

"Even so, you're here."

"To safeguard Israel's interest in the outcome."

"Ah."

"It is too early, yet, for us to trust the Soviets."

"You mean the Commonwealth."

Her smile was almost mocking. "But of course."

"Where are you staying?" Bolan asked her.

"Two floors up."

"Coincidence?"

"I checked in after you arrived."

He thought of asking how she knew where he would be, but kept it to himself. The lady wouldn't give up secrets easily, and at the moment it was more important to cooperate in the pursuit of common goals.

"Well, then, shall we get down to business?"

This time there was more warmth in the smile.

"Why not?"

Budapest
1945 hours

WAITING WAS the worst part, but a soldier soon became accustomed to delays, the downtime that was part of any field campaign. A veteran of the British army and the SAS, David McCarter had done his share of waiting from Belfast to Hong Kong and the Falkland Islands. Phoenix Force offered more of the same, but with greater rewards—chief among them a feeling of accomplishment that rule-bound military service seldom managed to afford. As part of Phoenix Force, he had a chance to strike his enemies—the enemies of civilized mankind at large—without the constant hindrance of negotiations, treaties and diplomacy.

But first, before the strike, he was required to watch and wait.

Like now.

His room at the Hotel Gellert was on the same floor occupied by Yakov Katzenelenbogen, at the far end of the corridor. The quaint, old-fashioned elevator was between them, and McCarter's ears pricked up each time he heard the car begin to groan and rattle in its shaft. Each time, he thought it might be Katz's contact making the approach. So far each time he had been wrong.

Surveillance would have been a problem if McCarter was required to crack his door and peer outside each time the elevator stopped on number six. He got around the difficulty with a compact jeweler's drill and fiber-optic lenses that permitted him to scan the hallway from the safety of his room. Inside, the eyepiece was concealed behind a hanging lithograph of Budapest by night. To any casual observer in the corridor, his tiny fish-eye lens would simply be another flyspeck on the wall.

The drill and optical equipment had come over in his suitcase, but the guns were something else. A quarter-mile from the hotel, on Rudas Laszlo, he had found the shop identified by Hal Brognola's Langley contacts as a friendly source of military hardware. He obtained a Model 61 Skorpion machine pistol with suppressor and extra magazines, plus a squeeze-cocking H&K P-7 automatic chambered for the same 9 mm parabellum rounds. McCarter tucked the pistol in his belt and hid the other gear inside a paper shopping bag, walked back to the Hotel Gellert and shut himself inside the sixth-floor room to wait.

Katz had a password for his contact, if and when the agent showed, but they were otherwise completely in the dark. No photograph, approximate description—nothing. For all McCarter knew, they could be waiting for a midget or the bearded lady from a sideshow. He would have to cover everyone who stopped on six, and that meant frequent checks to make sure there was no one sneaking up the stairs.

The worst scenario involved a double cross, some kind of setup by the Russians he couldn't begin to understand. A short time ago, the very thought of joining ranks with Russian agents would have been absurd.

Assuming that the meet wasn't a trap, they still faced major risks. Vasili Nabakov had been eliminated when he tried to back out of his bargain with Iraq. Someone—and it was too much to suspect Iraqi killers—had observed his moves in Petrograd and slammed the door before he had a chance to bolt for freedom. To McCarter that meant Russian agents, probably alumni of the KGB, and with the Nabakov example fresh in mind, it stood to reason they would also keep a close eye on Baranovich. McCarter knew of one man baby-sitting their intended target, but there might as easily be others standing in the shadows, waiting for an enemy to show himself. And if they bowled Katz out, it stood to reason they would try to take him down.

Another possibility involved some kind of glitch or double cross between the Russians. Dismissing officers and changing names for an intelligence-collecting agency didn't erase old debts or friendships overnight. In times like these, when everyone at Stony Man was justly paranoid, it made no sense at all to think the former Soviets were totally secure against potential leaks, betrayal and the like. The man assigned to meet with Katzenelenbogen might be dead and buried, maybe weighted down and rotting in the Danube. At the moment there was no way Katz could even double-check.

And if the Russian contact never showed, then what? They had a good fix on Baranovich and his companion, but they needed two Russian-speakers to make the plan work. If Katz turned up alone in Turkey, the Iraqi buyers would retreat like scalded cats. McCarter couldn't even help Katz run a bluff without the necessary language skills. The best that he could do was hang back on the sidelines, ready to jump in if Katz was threatened by an enemy.

McCarter heard the elevator coming, scrambled off the bed and took the Skorpion with him, just in case. The hanging lithograph had been removed and laid aside, so there was no obstruction as he leaned into the eyepiece, scoping out the empty corridor. Another moment and the elevator stopped on six, its ornate door slid open and a well-dressed man stepped out. Caucasian, middle thirties, an athletic build beneath the stylish business suit. He glanced both ways along the corridors, saw nothing to concern him and proceeded to his left.

Toward Katzenelenbogen's room.

McCarter thumbed the safety off his machine pistol, waiting. He couldn't afford to make a move without some demonstrated danger to his comrade, and it gnawed the British soldier's gut to know that by the time the new arrival tipped his hand—produced a weapon, for example—it might be too late for any help. At this range, if the stranger drew a gun and opened up on Katz, the best McCarter had to hope for was revenge.

He watched the man stop short in front of Katzenelenbogen's door and glance along the hallway again before he raised his hand to knock.

McCarter's knuckles whitened as he gripped the Skorpion and kept his eye pressed to the peephole, waiting for the gesture that would tell him it was time to kill.

YAKOV KATZENELENBOGEN was sipping his second glass of claret when he heard the elevator stop on six. He set the glass aside and waited, facing the door. In front of him the remains of a steak dinner occupied a low-slung coffee table.

Footsteps sounded in the outer hallway, drawing closer to his door. Katz leaned forward, took the sturdy steak knife in his left hand and wiped its blade clean on his napkin. It was a meager weapon, but for now it was the best that he could do. If he got close enough...

The footsteps stopped outside his door, and there was a moment's hesitation while the unseen stranger thought about it, making up his mind—or was he reaching underneath his jacket for a weapon, maybe screwing on the silencer?

McCarter had him covered. Fifty feet away, but it was close enough, assuming David had been able to acquire the necessary hardware. In the well-lighted corridor, with no obstructions, it would be an easy shot.

But could he make that shot in time?

The knocking almost came as a relief. Katz rose and crossed the open space between the couch and door, released the chain and turned the knob. A younger man with light brown hair was staring at him from the hallway, working on a smile. His hands were empty and his jacket buttoned, no apparent threat.

"What is it?" Katz inquired, remembering to speak in Russian.

"You have been expecting me, I think."

"I didn't order flowers," Katz responded, falling back on the password.

"But some roses bloom best at night."

"Come in."

Katz stood aside to let the stranger pass, then closed the door behind him, turning the lock.

"You won't need that," his visitor remarked, glancing pointedly at the steak knife in Katzenelenbogen's hand. "In fact I think this suits you better."

As he spoke, a Browning FN Hi-Power automatic appeared in the stranger's fist, the butt extended toward Katz. It was a decent trick, smoothly executed, and Katz was impressed. He put down the steak knife, took the Browning in his left hand and pulled the magazine, confirming it was loaded. Almost as an afterthought, he whipped the slide to put a live round in the chamber, lowering the hammer gently with his thumb. He tucked the pistol in his waistband.

"I am Nikolai Tyumen," said the Russian operative.

"Ivan Baranovich."

"Of course." There was a measure of amusement in the stranger's smile. He glanced at Katzenelenbogen's right hand, checking out the metal claw. "I frankly had my doubts about a decent match. The Company outdoes itself."

Katz saw no reason to argue the point. If Tyumen thought he was CIA, so much the better. "We do our best."

"Of course, it helps us that Baranovich has never met with the Iraqis face-to-face."

"His escort?"

"No." Tyumen shook his head. "Arrangements were made through a third party, ex-KGB."

"Like yourself?" Katz inquired.

Tyumen shrugged and found himself a seat. "I served in various capacities," he said. "It was a job, much like your own."

"And now?"

"You read the news, my friend. There is no KGB today, but the collection of intelligence goes on, by any name."

"I had a feeling that it might."

"Is this so strange?" Tyumen asked. "Did you expect the Commonwealth to leave itself defenseless in a hostile world?"

"We aren't here to discuss philosophy," Katz pointed out.

"Indeed. You are prepared to do your part against our common enemy?"

"I'm here," Katz answered.

"Baranovich and his companion have a suite at the Grand Hotel Royal on Lenin Korut. You have seen it?"

"No."

Tyumen shrugged. "It makes no difference. They have tickets for the Orient Express tomorrow morning, with departure fixed at ten o'clock. We shall surprise them over breakfast and relieve them of their duties, yes?"

Katz touched the pistol at his waist. "This might be somewhat noisy for a grand hotel."

"Of course."

This time, he watched the Russian's hand as Tyumen reached inside his jacket and produced a compact silencer. He placed it on the coffee table next to Katzenelenbogen's dinner plate. Katz left it there.

"You mentioned a companion. Is there only one?"

"As far as we can tell."

Katz didn't like the sound of that. Uncertainty in combat was the kiss of death. "And if you're wrong?"

"Then we shall know tomorrow."

"No offense intended, but it sounds like you've got problems with communication in your own backyard."

"A revolution always leads to difficulties, even when it is accomplished at the ballot box. Some of our finest operatives opposed the move toward *perestroika*. I believe it is a safe assumption that some others might have shared those views but kept their feelings to themselves."

"Which means you can't trust anyone," Katz said.

"I'm trusting you," Tyumen countered. "In another time and place, this meeting would have been unthinkable, an act of treason at the very least."

"Let's hope we don't regret it."

"As you say."

"Once we're aboard the train, what happens?"

For the first time since he entered Katzenelenbogen's room, Tyumen looked uneasy. Sitting with his fingers laced across his stomach, frowning, he replied, "For that I have no answer. We were fortunate to learn about this plot at all. Its finer details, sadly, are unknown."

"Terrific."

"Even so—"

"You don't know if Baranovich is being met en route," Katz persisted, cutting him off. "For all we know there could be an Iraqi waiting on the train, or anyplace along the way from Budapest to Ankara. No matter how you break it down, we're flying blind."

"Not quite," Tyumen said. "In Moscow an associate of those involved in the conspiracy was known to us. He was interrogated vigorously over several days. The information he possessed is now at our disposal."

"And?"

"We know Baranovich has never met with the Iraquis, as I said. His escort is a minor functionary specializing in deliveries. He also has no personal connection with Iraq."

"The man in charge?"

"Is unavailable," Tyumen said.

"How's that?"

"He has already crossed the border to Iraq."

"And he'll be waiting for us when we get there. If we get there."

"I have every confidence," Tyumen told him with a smile.

At least one of them was, Katz thought, but he resisted the impulse to speak. Instead he spent a moment pondering the odds, deciding there was no way he could even make a decent estimate. They might have other enemies at large in Budapest, or waiting on the Orient Express. They could be watched or ambushed anywhere along the line of travel, some 2,200 miles by rail, with Katz and his companion locked up in a sleeping car like stationary targets. At the other end they would be met by hostile Arabs and escorted to Iraq, identified as ringers from the moment they arrived.

It was a perfect setup... for their enemies.

And there was nothing Katz could do but forge ahead.

He faced Tyumen squarely, swallowing the apprehension that he felt inside.

"So, what time's breakfast, anyway?"

CHAPTER FIVE

Al Mawsil, Iraq
Saturday, 2015 hours

Leonid Glazov struck a wooden match with his thumbnail and held it to the tip of his Cuban cigar, playing the flame back and forth as the tobacco caught, finally drawing the aromatic smoke deeply into his lungs. When hc exhaled, a smoke cloud rolled across the spacious desk in front of him and made his male companion grimace at the smell.

"Is it so gratifying to pollute your body?" Amal Mashhad asked.

"It pleases me. What other reason do I need?"

The slender Muslim frowned and let it drop. He knew from long experience that there was nothing to be gained from argument with this one, even on a minor subject like the evils of tobacco. They had more important business to discuss in any case.

"The preparations have been made?"

Glazov nodded, amused by the question. His Iraqi counterpart was always nervous, always questioning. It made no difference if his doubts were laid to rest at ten o'clock and once again at noon; by half-past one he would be back again, demanding reassurance. Glazov recognized the lack of confidence, translated it into a cultural weakness, and decided the Iraqis would never be a great world power, regardless of the weapons they possessed.

No matter.

At the moment it would serve his purposes to help them to raise a little hell.

"All ready," Glazov answered, permitting himself a thin smile. Mashhad would interpret the expression as a sign of friendship, missing the contempt that Glazov beamed across the desk in radiating waves. "Less than twelve hours now, before Baranovich is on his way."

"I quite agree, but what are we to do with childish fears? A rocket scientist afraid of flying!"

Glazov chuckled to himself and shook his head, amused as always by the quality of personnel he was forced to contend with in field operations. If only his superiors—

He caught himself and felt the corners of his mouth turn down. Those days were gone, at least for now. He didn't take his orders from Dzerzhinsky Square these days, but rather from himself. There was exhilaration in the fact of being self-employed, but there was also doubt, akin to fear, which he acknowledged only to himself in private moments. Demonstrating weakness to another person, whether friend or enemy, was still the quickest way that Glazov knew to end an otherwise productive life.

It wasn't merely being cut off from official rank and privilege that dismayed him, though. Leonid Glazov was a Communist by choice, committed to the prospect of a People's Revolution that would change the world. His choice of a career within the KGB was therefore natural, predestined. Where else could he make such worthwhile contributions to the cause?

Each time he took the field against the British or Americans, the French or Austrians, he felt that he was fighting on behalf of revolutionaries everywhere. Their cause was his, and Glazov wouldn't let them down while he had strength to stand and fight.

At last it was the state that let *him* down, and Glazov didn't count forgiveness on his list of virtues. *Glasnost* was a joke—or worse, a madman's fantasy—and it would turn the clock back to an age when czarist autocrats communed with God in cloistered churches, passing on His word to peasants trembling in fear of lightning from the clouds. Dismantling the revolutionary state was a mistake and a catastrophe for all mankind. Without the steadfast leadership of Moscow, who could bring about the move toward global liberation under Marxist principles?

He ran the mental list in seconds flat and came up short of candidates. Fidel was nearly senile, penned up on his jungle island with the populace deserting him in droves. The Red Chinese were more concerned with birth control and silencing the children in their universities. As for the North Koreans and Vietnamese...

No, any leadership would have to come from Mother Russia, but the torch had been allowed to sputter out. It would be Glazov's duty—and his privilege—to rekindle hope among the faithful, strike a spark and fan the brand-new revolutionary flame to life.

Beginning, as it happened, in the Middle East.

It was ironic, Glazov thought, that the Americans should make it easy for him, keeping up their pressure on Saddam Hussein, demanding more and more concessions from a man of brittle and unyielding temperament. From Glazov's point of view Saddam was a buffoon, the ultimate big frog in a small pond, with echoes of Idi Amin in his personal life-style. All the same, he was a useful puppet, one manipulated best by letting him believe he was the source of great ideas that came instead from others brighter than himself.

Which left the field wide open to a multitude of candidates, Glazov thought, smiling to himself.

"You are amused?" Mashhad inquired.

"It's nothing."

"Please to tell me," the Iraqi prodded. "I appreciate the Western sense of humor."

Glazov smiled at that in turn, to hear himself lumped with the West, but he didn't remark on his companion's faulty choice of words. Mashhad was sensitive to criticism at the best of times, and this wasn't the moment to excite him by issuing a correction. Better to provide him with a smile and send the weasel on his way.

"I was imagining the shock in Tel Aviv and Washington the day your missiles fly," Glazov said.

"Ah."

In fact, such thoughts hadn't been far from Glazov's mind since he conceived the shift of Russian scientists some months earlier. He wasn't banking on a global holocaust, per se, but sometimes fire was necessary to eliminate dead wood and clear the way for newer, vital growth. Another flare-up in the Middle East this soon would embroil the Western powers, this time faced with weapons they weren't prepared for in the field. When mushrooms blossomed over Tel Aviv and Haifa, Washington would blame the government in Moscow from established habit. It wouldn't take long for politicians in the spineless Commonwealth to recognize their danger and return to a position that would keep their homeland safe.

The party would be waiting when its various defectors realized their grave mistake and came to call with hats in hand. Some of the worst offenders would be sacrificed, of course, but others stood a chance at being rehabilitated, once they understood the error of their ways.

When vital revolution had been reestablished in the nation of its birth, the fire would spread to every corner of the globe. And it would need a leader, someone with a strong hand at the helm.

Leonid Glazov still believed in revolution, but he saw no reason why the coming change should cost him anything. With any luck at all, he just might turn a handsome profit on the deal.

Amal Mashhad was smiling with him, all in ignorance, as Glazov threw his head back and began to laugh out loud.

West of Nineveh, Iraq

"I'M HAVING second thoughts about the desert," Piotr Serpukhov said.

"So soon?" There was a mocking tone in Vladimir Polyarni's voice, not all of it the vodka.

"It will be a month tomorrow," Serpukhov replied. "That's long enough to know the weather doesn't suit me."

"You spent too much time in Kazakhstan," Polyarni said, sipping the vodka in the heavy tumbler in his hand. "But think, Piotr. What about the pay? The women?"

Serpukhov thought about Yasmina and the special talents she possessed, remembering that there had never been a girl like her in Russia. Not for him, at any rate. His wife was in Kiev, and she could stay there. What use did a man of his obvious value to society have for an aging, overweight cow who was frigid at best, and shrewish at worst?

Of course, Serpukhov knew he wasn't getting any younger. He was losing hair on top and gaining bulk around the middle, sagging down below. It didn't take a genius—which he was, by any standard—to recognize that Yasmina was an actress, playing a role when she came to his bed. Simply put, the beautiful young woman was a whore, one of the pleasant fringe benefits built into his arrangement with the shrewd Iraqis. First and foremost was the cash, deposited on his behalf in a numbered Swiss account, with enough on hand for him to live like minor royalty while he did his job.

"The desert has its compensations," Serpukhov allowed, half smiling, as he poured himself another glass of vodka.

"So," Polyarni said, "you see the light."

"I only wish there could be more."

"You are a greedy man, Piotr."

"And why not? The leaders of our homeland bask in profit now—or would, if they could ever learn to manage the economy."

"Forget the homeland," Polyarni said. "Our economy is doing very well, right here."

But it was more than cash or sex, though Serpukhov had trouble spelling out exactly what he felt was missing in his life. The truth was he missed living in a city, even one like Moscow, where the working class lined up in early morning for a loaf of bread or pair of shoes. He missed the theater, the ballet, sporting contests, stylish restaurants—in short, the sense of living in a civilized society. Iraq was primitive, a hand-to-mouth society outside of Baghdad, and the capital wasn't much better since the ravages of Desert Storm. Between the strictures of a Muslim background and the ruthless tactics of Saddam Hussein's totalitarian regime, Iraq impressed Piotr Serpukhov as a cultural wasteland, devoid of light and gaiety. It was ironic, thinking back to Moscow and the Communist regime as an oasis of refinement, but there it was.

Piotr Serpukhov wasn't exactly homesick—any major city would have satisfied his needs—but he had come to feel confined, much like a lab rat in a cage. It was almost enough to make him regret his decision.

Almost.

"Baranovich is on his way," Polyarni said. "Tomorrow, I think."

"He's flying?" Serpukhov was visibly surprised.

"Don't make me laugh. He's traveling by train."

"From Budapest?"

Polyarni nodded and sipped his vodka. "He should be here in a few more days."

For Serpukhov the news was neither good nor bad. He knew Baranovich, of course, but they weren't close friends. When it came down to cases, Serpukhov had no real friends of any consequence. Polyarni was the next best thing, a certain closeness bred of working side by side for years, but Serpukhov would gladly have deserted him for life in Paris, Rome or London.

What about New York?

The weapons expert frowned and took another swig of vodka. The Americans were still an unknown quantity for Serpukhov. He had been raised to view them as his enemies, devoted half his life to building warheads that could turn their decadent society to smoking rubble. Now, as if by magic, they were allies and potential saviors of the troubled Commonwealth.

It was a strange, perplexing world these days.

Perhaps, once Ivan had arrived, they could accelerate their pace. When he was finished building rockets for Hussein, the warheads would be simple, frosting on the cake.

And once the job was finished, Serpukhov could find himself a European city to retire in, living out his days in well-earned luxury. Unless . . .

He shook his head and drained the vodka glass. No point in turning paranoid. It was a little claustrophobia and nothing else. Yasmina would erase the problem when he went back to his quarters.

Still, he couldn't shake the vague sensation of a rodent in a trap.

The sense that he would never be allowed to leave Iraq alive.

AMAL MASHHAD WAS GRATEFUL to be rid of Glazov for the evening. Working with the stuffy, self-important Russian was a curse, but one didn't ignore directives from the high command. In one respect, of course, it was an honor, working on the project that would ultimately give Iraq the means to dominate her neighbors, punish the Iranians for the atrocities endured in eleven years of warfare, wipe the Jewish state of Israel off the map. As for the smug Americans . . .

Mashhad believed he was a child of destiny, selected by the hand of God for a leading role in the upheaval that was shortly coming to the Middle East. Some nights he dreamed about jihad—the holy war in which loyal Muslims would unite and drive the infidels from Palestine, North Africa, and back across the Caucasus. Once that was done, the troops of God could proceed to claim their due in Western lands. They only lacked technology, the weapons built for mass annihilation of their enemies, and that small deficit would soon be remedied.

It was a pity, Mashhad thought, that Russians were required to make the project work, but native experts had been struggling to build such weapons for over a decade, without success. In June 1981 an Israeli air strike had destroyed Baghdad's prized nuclear reactor, and American warplanes nearly finished the job ten years later. Still, Saddam had managed to outfox his enemies, obstruct UN inspection teams, conceal the precious ore and laboratory gear that had survived the latest villainous attack. With some assistance from the Russians, it wouldn't be long until the missiles flew again.

And this time, they wouldn't be landing harmlessly around the suburbs of Jerusalem.

One day, when all had been prepared and suitable technicians trained from the Iraqi population, it would be Amal Mashhad's distinct and lasting pleasure to eliminate the Russian pigs. Their scientists were one thing, huddled in the lab all day, content to swill their vodka and consort with prostitutes by night, but Glazov and his second in command, Gregori Berdichev, were something else again. They had a predatory quality about them, sizing up Mashhad, his people, and his homeland with their hungry eyes, as if Iraq were simply one great meal to be consumed at leisure.

It occurred to him that Glazov and the others were involved in some conspiracy to damage and humiliate Saddam Hussein's regime, but when Mashhad reported his suspicions back to Baghdad, he was told to mind his business. It wasn't for him to meddle in the realm of tactics and diplomacy. As a member of the Iraqi secret service, it was Mashhad's job to observe, report and follow orders without question. Individual initiative wasn't encouraged or rewarded by Saddam Hussein.

So be it.

But the day was coming, Mashhad could feel it, when Glazov and Berdichev would become expendable. Already they were traitors of a sort, defying their new government for personal gain. Glazov and his Moscow contacts had been useful in acquiring the necessary scientific talent—three of the experts, at any rate, with one lost through negligence—but once the Russian brains were all secure inside Iraq, Leonid Glazov would find his bargaining power greatly reduced.

Perhaps to zero.

When that day came, Amal Mashhad would be prepared. He had rehearsed the moment in his mind a hundred times, in several variations. If discretion was required, he'd perform the task himself, and gladly. It would be a simple thing, approaching Glazov in his office, reaching for the compact automatic pistol with its silencer attached. One round between those hungry eyes, and Glazov could be tidily disposed of in the desert, miles from anywhere. A feast for vultures in the land he reckoned to exploit.

And if permission came from Baghdad for a public execution, why, so much the better. It would please

Amal Mashhad no end to watch his enemies as they were bound, blindfolded, led before a military firing squad. He would arrange to give the order personally, standing by to administer the coup de grace as Glazov and Berdichev lay at his feet.

The Russians were a greedy race, barbarians at heart, but they weren't invincible. Afghanistan had taught that lesson to the world, and now the bedrock of their ruling party had been torn asunder from within. The time was ripe for putting Glazov and his cronies in their place, once they had outlived their usefulness to Iraq.

The day was coming. Soon, now. Very soon.

Moscow

JOSEF PETROVSKI CRADLED the receiver of his telephone and heard the scrambler disengage automatically, clearing the line. He sat there for a moment, with his right hand resting on the instrument, as if the contact brought him closer to his man in Al Mawsil.

Petrovski had the utmost faith in Leonid Glazov, or he'd never have trusted Glazov with the job at hand. They had known each other well for years, become as close to friends as wily men could ever be inside the Soviet bureaucracy. As a member of the politburo under Gorbachev, Petrovski had been one of those who saw the risks inherent in *glasnost* and *perestroika,* the weakening of Soviet power and solidarity. He had collaborated with Glazov in the KGB, working overtime to salvage something from the waxing tide of reason, but his efforts ultimately were in vain. Wise enough to avoid being linked with the 1991 coup attempt, Petrovski was still in office, a more-or-less respected member of the establishment, when his beloved Union of Soviet Socialist Republics formally ceased to exist.

So much for the career that had become his life.

Petrovski wouldn't starve, of course. He was a born survivor, with investments under several names in different countries, where the banking laws were lax and privacy revered as if ordained by God himself. A lifelong atheist, Petrovski had no faith in God, but he believed in fate. His fate was inextricably bound up in that of the once and future USSR, a world power momentarily bedeviled by enemies without and traitors within. Dramatic steps were needed to restore that power, and Petrovski was the man to do it... with a little help from his comrades.

Leonid Glazov had been a valuable aide, with his surviving contacts in the Soviet intelligence community. Disgruntled members of the former KGB were anxious to regain their former status in a well-run socialistic state, and Glazov knew which strings to pull, which buttons he had to push to get things done. The sale of scientific minds had been Petrovski's brainstorm, spawned by a suggestion in the Western media, but Glazov was the man who set the wheels in motion, mapping out their stragegy in concrete terms.

Iraq was only one of several nations bidding for the services of Russian scientists no longer valued in the national defense. Khaddafi's Libya was interested, as were the zealots of Iran, and several smaller states in equatorial Africa. Petrovski's final choice wasn't so much financial—though the money helped, of course—as it was based on practical political considerations. In Iraq Saddam Hussein was chafing at his late humiliation by the Western powers, trying to redeem himself before the world. He had an ax to grind and scores to settle, far and wide. The action he eventually took would set the Middle East ablaze and require the full attention of America for months on end. The war would also threaten former Soviet citizens in the new, independent states of Armenia, Azerbaijan and Turkmenistan, producing calls for a defensive reaction from Moscow or Minsk. The threat would automatically create a power vacuum at the top, weak leaders of the Commonwealth incapable of rising to the challenge, and the party would resume its rightful place in charge of Soviet affairs.

From that point on it didn't matter to Petrovski what became of the Iraqis. Let America destroy them in their tents and mosques, for all he cared. Their sacrifice would pave the way for a resumption of the interrupted People's Revolution, rising from the shambles of Yeltsin's experiment with Western-style democracy.

And this time, there would be no hesitation short of victory.

Petrovski rose and crossed his study to the liquor cabinet, selected brandy and poured himself a drink. He wouldn't toast their victory this night, but it was coming. He could feel it in his bones.

Ivan Baranovich was leaving Budapest tomorrow morning under guard. The problem with Vasili Nabakov had nearly ruined everything, but they had caught it just in time. The death in Petrograd was messy, but Petrovski had been left with little choice, all things considered. The alternative was premature exposure, countermeasures by the state—in short, disaster.

Soon, though, it would be too late for anyone on earth to block Petrovski's plan. The moment that Baranovich was safely in Iraq, beginning work on the delivery system needed for the warheads manufactured by Polyarni and Serpukhov, exposure would mean nothing. Petrovski had his own work to do, right in Moscow, preparing the way for a new Soviet revolution to rival that of 1917.

A challenge, certainly, but it wasn't beyond his grasp. He wasn't a minority of one, by any means.

There was a great day coming, thanks to him, and he'd be remembered for his contribution, as were Marx and Engels, Lenin and the rest. His heroes, soon to be the idols of mankind.

CHAPTER SIX

Budapest
Sunday, 0630 hours

Rising early was a habit with Ivan Baranovich. It dated from his days at the university in Volgograd, when he had risen to study in the small hours before dawn, annoying his peers with the extra bit of effort that always earned him top marks. In later life the habit stuck. Baranovich couldn't explain it and he didn't care to try. It was simply a part of him, like his fondness for climbing impossible mountains—or the stub of his ruined right arm.

How long ago it seemed, the climbing accident and all that followed after. The fall itself was nothing but a blur. One moment he was clinging to the granite face; a heartbeat later, he was airborne, conscious of an error in his footing, much too late to take it back and try again. Somehow, the safety line had looped itself around his arm, below the elbow, shredding muscle, ripping tendons free and snapping bone. He could recall the pain in abstract terms, but little else. Necrosis had set in before they packed him down to a physician. Amputation was the only hope.

But he survived.

Baranovich had never been the kind of man to quit when things got rough. He towed the party line, of course—all Russian scientists did that, before the

Change—but he had raised more questions through the years than most. The KGB was known to watch him now and then, on his sporadic trips to Hungary, but since Baranovich had never seriously thought of leaving Russia, he refused to let the scrutiny affect him.

Now, at last, he had no choice.

The Russia he had known was no more. Its government, the very state itself, was swept away, replaced by a society that suddenly de-emphasized his expertise. It might be possible to eke a living from the space program, but there were younger men available to work for lower wages, some of them perhaps his equal or superior in terms of skill. And if the Commonwealth economy continued to decline as it had done the past few months, there would be no work left for anyone in Ivan's field.

What good was outer space, when men couldn't afford to live on earth?

It crossed his mind that communism, granting all its faults as seen through Western eyes, had guaranteed employment for the masses. Never mind that wages might be low, availability of some consumer goods restricted to the point of nonexistence. And if thousands found themselves in boring jobs that they despised, so what? Ask any peasant on the unemployment line if he would rather work ten hours in a wing-nut factory or watch his children starve.

Baranovich was never seriously threatened with starvation in his own life, though. The scientific acumen he demonstrated early on was recognized by his instructors, channeled by the state, until he had become a fine, productive member of the Soviet elite. A rocket man, no less. He had designed or helped design a number of boosters that had carried valiant cosmonauts beyond the stratosphere. In truth most of his rockets had a military application, and he had contributed immeasurably to the carnage in Afghanistan. The victims mangled and dismembered by his rockets never knew Baranovich, of course, nor did he tabulate a running body count. Designs and blueprints, firing tests, wind-tunnel simulations and the like were what he lived for. The rest of it, from in-flight tracking to the final detonation at ground zero, fell to someone else.

It shouldn't be supposed, for all his insulation, that Baranovich was ignorant or misinformed about the use to which his missiles would be put. He simply didn't care. Ivan Baranovich was a perfectionist in terms of rocketry design, performance in the lab and on the test range. Once he verified and double-checked a system's working parts, however, he moved on to something else. A new idea for greater thrust and longer range, perhaps. It didn't matter to Baranovich if his superiors employed his newest tool to plant a colony on Mars or turn New York into a smoking crater. Either way, Ivan Baranovich was confident the rockets he designed would do their job upon demand.

Beginning in a few more days, he'd be building missiles for a different government. No matter. Governments were more or less the same in all the ways that counted. They relied on force to keep their subject populations paying taxes, following the myriad rules and regulations that imposed a kind of order on the chaos of mankind. When strong or greedy men took charge, that force was turned against their neighbors to acquire new territory, raw materials, or transient glory. Weak men at the helm meant economic problems in the short run, long-term danger from adjoining states who smelled their weakness like a pack of hyenas sniffing blood.

Experience had taught Baranovich that weak men seldom had much use for his abilities. They shied away from exploration of the galaxy, intimidated by the prospect of adventure, and they feared the weapons they already owned, much less new models with enhanced destructive capabilities. When weak men came to power, weapons experts knew that hard times were around the corner, closing fast.

So, he'd work for the Iraqis, but he had insisted on another trip to Budapest. Perhaps his last; who could predict such things? Baranovich remembered childhood days, his father stationed in the ancient city for their country's diplomatic service, speaking for the party when the need arose. Some of those memories, he supposed, were more imagination than reality, but to a child of eight or ten it made no difference. His recollections of the city and of Hungary at large were clean and bright, until the final hours of his stay.

Baranovich's father had been summoned home to Moscow when the people's insurrection broke in 1956. Ivan remembered tanks and soldiers in the street, a giant bust of Joseph Stalin lying on the pavement with its craggy features chipped and stained. His last view of the city had been smoke and rooftops as their plane took off, but in his later years, as an adult who saw too much of labs and factories, he sometimes took vacations in the country where he spent the best part of his youth. Remembering.

Like now.

But it was time to go. His escort would be waiting for him in the room next door, or maybe standing in the hall. Mikhail Svobodny was a young man—younger than Baranovich, at any rate—and very serious about his job. Just now, he was assigned to watch Baranovich and keep him "out of trouble," since the upset with Vasili Nabakov in Petrograd. Svobodny could have spared himself the worry, though. Baranovich wasn't about to run away.

Where would he go?

His packing finished, Ivan checked the room one final time for anything he might have missed. He was about to ring the bellboy when he was distracted by the sound of knuckles rapping on his door.

Svobodny. He was early, anxious to be on the move.

Baranovich put on a plastic smile and started for the door.

NIKOLAI TYUMEN HAD BEEN wide awake since half-past three o'clock. It wasn't nervousness, exactly, but a sense of sharp anticipation that prevented him from sleeping later. Even so, his small alarm clock had been set for five a.m. He wasn't taking any chances on the most important mission of his life.

In many ways it was a very different feeling from his five years with the KGB—a whole new ball game, as the curious Americans would say. Tyumen didn't see himself as fighting on the side of freedom versus tyranny, but there was something....

He was lucky, in a way, that his assignment with the KGB had involved foreign counterintelligence. For two years he had manned a set of headphones in a tiny Moscow flat, transcribing tapes of conversations gleaned from bugs inside the British embassy. From there he had been sent to London, working under the Soviet "cultural attaché." In effect that meant he dressed up in disguises, wandered through the streets and parks like any other tourist, meeting spies and double agents to collect reports or rolls of microfilm. Tyumen never knew exactly what he was retrieving, and he didn't care. It was enough to do his job efficiently and thereby serve the state.

And, yes, there had been something of a thrill involved at playing games against the British MI-5 and SIS. There was no danger, really, with the shield of diplomatic immunity to protect him, but failure and exposure would result in his expulsion, being sent home in disgrace. He knew what happened to the failures, how they wound up filing papers in the basement at Dzerzhinsky Square... or worse.

But he had never been found out. Tyumen might be working London yet, if not for the dramatic changes in his homeland that resulted in the abolition of the KGB. New agencies would take its place—already had, in fact—but it would never be the same.

A good thing, too, from what Tyumen heard when he was summoned back to Moscow, revelations leaking to the press in Moscow and abroad. Of course, he had grown up on stories of the dreaded midnight knock, interrogations, secret firing squads and grim "reeducation" camps, but Nikolai had never been involved in such activities. It was a lucky break, all things considered. When the final shake-up came, his record was reviewed for any evidence of impropriety, and he was offered a continuing position with the new regime.

Which brought him back to Budapest this Sunday morning, well before the crack of dawn. He was required to kill a man today, no options having been discovered that would let him carry out his mission in a semblance of security. Inside the Commonwealth itself, Ivan Baranovich and his companion could have been arrested, secretly detained until the job was done, but the Hungarians were in no mood for playing cloak-and-dagger games with Russia at the moment. Nikolai could hardly blame them, but it made his job more difficult and more distasteful.

He had never killed a man before, but when the moment came, Tyumen thought he would be ready. Underneath his coat, he wore a Browning automatic pistol like the one he had given to his contact from the West, no standard Makarov for tracing back to Russia if he wound up getting caught. The pistol had a silencer attached, but he was counting on another weapon for the kill itself.

Inside the deep breast pocket of his overcoat, Tyumen kept an object that appeared to be a simple fountain pen. In fact, if called upon, the "pen" could actually be used for writing, while the ink inside its tiny cartridge lasted. When reversed and primed, however, it became a lethal object, capable of spraying concentrated cyanide for eighteen inches, give or take. Beyond the "pen's" effective range, its lethal charge would dissipate and rapidly disperse. It was a one-shot deal, and if he blew it, Nikolai would have to fall back on the Browning in its shoulder rig.

He had no cyanide dispenser for his gruff companion, but Tyumen wasn't worried. He would let the new "Baranovich" take out the old, aware that Ivan had no reason to be armed or wary of attack. It made him vaguely apprehensive, working with a Westerner—an older, one-armed man at that—but Nikolai had watched the stranger's eyes, seen death reflected there, and knew that he would have no qualms at taking human life.

They met in Tyumen's room at five o'clock, for breakfast, making due with rolls and marmalade, strong Turkish coffee and a block of cheese. They had rehearsed their movements on the night before, and few words passed between them now. When they were finished with their meal and Nikolai had used the toilet, both men took their bags downstairs, checked out and crossed the parking lot through early-morning light to reach Tyumen's vintage Zil sedan. The luggage went in back, and they were on their way.

Five minutes later they were at their destination. Now a fading remnant of its former self, the Grand Hotel Royal had been a palace in its day. Now it ranked in the "budget" or "moderate" class. It stood in the center of Pest's busy commercial district, but the streets were silent on a Sunday morning, with the factories and offices shut down. They parked the car and locked it, circling around the eastern side of the hotel to use an entrance Tyumen had scouted in advance.

The best and most expensive rooms in the hotel were ranged around an inner courtyard, thus affording them some privacy and insulation from the racket of the streets. Tyumen had already bribed the concierge to learn the men they sought were staying in adjacent third-floor rooms. The trick would be to take them both without a serious disturbance that would rouse the other guests and prompt a call to the police.

They rode the elevator up in silence, Tyumen with his deadly fountain pen in hand, his comrade of the moment standing with his one good hand inside his jacket, wrapped around the Browning's grip. The odds against an ambush stepping off the elevator were extreme, but they were in an extraordinary situation as it was, and anything could happen from this point on.

There was no ambush, and the only witness to their passing was a cat that prowled along the third-floor balcony in search of food. Tyumen hesitated, held the elevator door a moment longer than he needed to. The cat stepped in, turned back to face him with an enigmatic murmur, and the car began its slow descent.

They moved along the balcony in lockstep, Tyumen scanning silent doors and windows for a hint that they were being watched. If there were any backup escorts, they appeared to be off duty at the moment.

"Here." His voice was low-pitched, barely a whisper, as he pointed out the first numbered door. "Baranovich."

Tyumen's comrade stopped outside the door while Nikolai moved on. A heartbeat later he stood before the second door, as ready now as he would ever be.

Their knocks were synchronized, three taps on each door to prevent a warning echo. Tyumen was waiting when the sound of muffled footsteps reached his ears. Another moment and he heard the chain released, a man's voice speaking as the door swung open.

Tyumen didn't focus on his adversary's face. His left hand clamped a handkerchief across his nose and mouth, the right extended with the "fountain pen" thrust forward and his thumb clamped tightly on the trigger. Tyumen heard a wheezing sound, perhaps the gas dispenser or his target's dying breath. In any case he saw the slender man fall backward, boneless, dropping like a rag doll to the floor.

He glanced behind him, the handkerchief still covering his nose and mouth. No witnesses. Tyumen dropped the gas gun in his pocket, stepped across the threshold, bent down to grip the dead man's jacket with his right hand and dragged him inside to clear the doorway. Once the door was closed, Tyumen crossed the room and took a pillow from the rumpled bed, returned to fan the air above the prostrate body and disperse the final vestiges of gas. He counted off another thirty seconds in his mind, then dropped his hand and took a cautious breath.

When he was still alive ten seconds later, Tyumen decided that the worst was over. Moving swiftly now, he dragged his victim into the adjoining bathroom, lifted him with hands beneath the flaccid arms and dropped him in the tub. The dead man's skull struck porcelain with a resounding thump, but he didn't complain.

The cleanup crew was waiting for his call. Tyumen used the dead man's telephone and waited for a rough, familiar voice to answer on the second ring.

"Hello?"

"Five minutes. Best of luck."

The line went dead. Tyumen cradled the receiver and left.

BEFORE THE DOOR WAS OPENED, Yakov Katzenelenbogen had his left hand wrapped around t' Browning automatic underneath his coat. He recognized the Russian's face immediately, from the mug shots he had seen at Stony Man. Up close and in the flesh, he lost the sense of strong resemblance that the photographs conveyed.

Or so he told himself, at any rate.

Katz showed the gun and said, "Inside."

The Russian backed away from him, surprised and frightened. Katz stepped in and closed the door behind him, leveling the silenced pistol at his target's chest.

"Ivan Baranovich?"

It was a pointless question, but he felt the need to speak, confirm the man's identity. This way, at least, it wouldn't feel so much like he was murdering himself.

"I am."

"In there." Katz gestured with his stainless-steel appendage toward the open bathroom door. Baranovich obeyed and led the way without complaint. The room was small and steamy from the Russian's morning shower, condensation beaded on the mirror set above the sink.

"Get in the tub," Katz said.

Again the man complied. He didn't raise his hands or offer cash like any hostage in the movies. There was bitter resignation in his eyes.

"Who are you?" Baranovich asked.

"It doesn't matter."

"No." The simple truth.

"It's nothing personal," Katz said, and shot him in the chest. Ivan Baranovich went down without a whimper, twitching briefly in the tub before his limbs relaxed in death. A crimson worm crept slowly toward the open drain.

Katz took the pistol in his stainless-steel claw, bent down and pressed two fingers to the Russian's neck, behind one ear. The flesh was warm, but he could find no pulse.

All done.

His last words to Ivan Baranovich had been a lie. No matter how it happened, death was always personal.

Katz closed the door behind him and found Tyumen waiting for him on the balcony. The Russian looked a little pinched around the mouth, perhaps from scowling. Something in the way of feelings, when he killed, but would that indicate a strength or weakness in the man?

"Let's go."

Tyumen moved off toward the elevator, leaving Katz to follow. Waiting for the car, they checked again for any witnesses and came up empty. If the cleanup crew arrived on time and did their work without mistakes Baranovich and his companion would be gone without a trace.

Phase one. The easy part was over. Once they left the Grand Hotel Royal, it would be open season. Anything could happen, anywhere along the way from Budapest to their intended destination in Iraq.

The elevator car arrived, its door slid open and the cat slipped out between their legs. One predator returning, while another pair departed from their recent kill. Katz wished the feline luck and felt it watching as the elevator door hissed between them.

Stony Man Farm
Sunday, 0100 hours

BARBARA PRICE WAS sipping tepid coffee, watching Aaron Kurtzman at his console. Waiting for the message to arrive. They knew that Striker and the Phoenix Force were in position, ready to begin, but there was nothing anyone could do before Katz made his tag in Budapest.

"They should be done by now," she muttered, glancing at her watch.

"Things happen, Barb. They'll want some distance from the scene before they stop to make a call."

"Okay."

She knew that, damn it, but her nerves were still on edge. It was a different ball game this time, working with the Russians in a move against their own. Toss the Iraqis in for seasoning, and you were looking at a lethal brew. She tried to think of any recent mission where the odds of a potential double cross were greater, but she came up blank.

The computer room was almost silent at this hour of the night—or morning, take your pick. The muted ceiling fixtures made it dark enough to doze if she was feeling sleepy, but the colored lights from several dozen monitors and disk drives were a different story. At the moment they reminded her of shiny rodents' eyes, some winking at her in the semidarkness, others burning steady with a fierce intensity. It felt as if those eyes could stare into her soul and read the doubt she harbored there.

Almost three hours remained before Katz and his Russian escort were required to board the Orient Express, and there was no reason for him to check in with Stony Man the very instant his preliminary work was done.

Another euphemism, Price told herself. "Preliminary work," indeed. If everything had gone according to the plan, two men were dead by now. Three bodies they were sure of, with Vasili Nabakov thrown in. How many more would have to die before the threat of holocaust was neutralized?

She let the question slide. It was an exercise in rank futility, and she wouldn't allow herself to feel misguided sympathy for those who set the juggernaut in motion to begin with. Striker and the men of Phoenix Force would take all necessary measures to defuse the situation and restore some measure of the status quo. If that meant shedding blood along the way, so be it.

Her mind shifted to their satellite communications link, orbiting earth at an altitude of 22,300 miles. She tried to picture Katzenelenbogen's phone call from Budapest, beaming its way through the atmosphere and seeking out the Comsat link, rebounding to a set of waiting ears in the distant Blue Ridge Mountains.

But a watched pot never boiled.

"I'm turning in," she said at last, disgusted, knowing that she wouldn't sleep. At least a shower and a change of scene might help her to relax while she was waiting for the call.

"I'll let you know if we hear anything," Kurtzman said, putting on a sympathetic smile.

"Okay."

She was halfway to the door when the computer whiz's telephone receiver purred, a muted sound like something underwater. He was lifting the receiver now, responding with a monosyllable and waiting, listening. He didn't speak again before the line went dead and he replaced the handset in its plastic cradle.

Price waited, breathless, while he turned his chair around and faced her, really smiling now.

"It's on," he said. "They made the tag."

Instead of the relief she was anticipating, though, she felt the same familiar tightness in her chest. No change.

"All right, I'm out of here."

"Sleep tight."

Fat chance, she thought, and kept it to herself.

CHAPTER SEVEN

Belgrade
Sunday, 0930 hours

"It's almost time."

The sound of Sascha's voice roused Bolan from his private thoughts. He glanced across the hotel breakfast table, found her watching him, a curious expression on her face.

"Still half an hour, if they start on time. Two hours to the border, anyway. Two more to Belgrade, once they get through customs."

"Are you worried?"

Bolan thought about it, running down the mental list of problems that could doom his mission anywhere along the line. Too many wild cards in the deck. He shrugged and asked, "What's the point?"

"These people are your comrades, some of them your friends, perhaps."

"They're all professionals."

"It doesn't make you nervous, working with the Russians?"

"Cautious," he corrected. "Nervous means you haven't done your homework or allowed for unexpected difficulties."

There was no point telling her what any real professional already knew: that preparation for the unforeseen and unexpected only went so far. The men of

Phoenix Force were limited in access to materials, cut off from any real logistical support once they acquired the weapons that would have to see them through the next few days.

How long, exactly? Once again, the answer was unknown. The Orient Express took roughly two days for the run from Budapest to Ankara. From that point, Katz would have to travel overland, six hundred miles or so, to reach the Turkish border with Iraq. Beyond the border crossing it became a deadly guessing game. They didn't know where any of the Russian scientists were stationed at the moment, though a native contact was supposed to fill them in once everyone arrived.

If everyone arrived.

Dividing their already-meager force had been a tactical decision. Katz was on the hot seat, and he needed a clandestine escort as insurance in case things blew up with the Russians. Bolan had detached himself from Phoenix Force to meet their contact out of Tel Aviv. Another form of life insurance, covering all bets against potential leaks from the Israeli end. This way, if Sascha Lentz was being shadowed or had something else in mind besides cooperation with the Stony Man team, it would be Bolan's problem. Gary Manning, Calvin James, and Rafael Encizo would be insulated from the damage, free to carry on their portion of the exercise.

Unless the whole damn thing was some elaborate setup, orchestrated with an eye toward crippling Stony Man once and for all.

It was a paranoid suspicion, granted, but in Bolan's world a healthy dose of paranoia was the next best thing to second sight. Between them, Bolan,

Phoenix Force and Able Team had scuttled Moscow's covert operations time and time again. On more than one occasion, international publicity had left the Kremlin steaming, with fresh eggs smeared on famous faces. Even granting that the recent change in government was totally sincere—a dangerous assumption in the view of certain graybeards in the FBI and CIA—it was conceivable that certain ranking individuals might still desire revenge, a settling of old accounts before the slate was finally wiped clean.

And yet he couldn't see Mossad cooperating with the Russians on a sting against America, when Tel Aviv had so much riding on the line in terms of foreign aid. There was an outside chance that Moscow could have fooled them both—America and Israel—but it was even more improbable that the Mossad and CIA would both be duped by the same disinformation campaign. Back up those odds with the risk to a new Russian regime, if Boris Yeltsin's intelligence apparatus was caught scheming against the West, and Bolan was prepared to take the story at face value...or not.

He hadn't stayed alive this long by allowing himself to be used or manipulated by others. Bolan would put his life on the line for a stranger, if need be, but he didn't leap blindly into no-hope situations, risking life and limb for no appreciable result. There was nothing of the kamikaze in Bolan's makeup, but he didn't turn his back on any challenge out of fear.

"We ought to hit the central station half an hour early, just in case," he suggested.

"Agreed. For all we know, these Russians could be checking on Baranovich at every stop along the line."

"We're busted if they do."

The lady from Mossad responded with a shrug. "At least we will have stopped one rocket scientist from getting through. If we can still make contact with the dissidents in Turkey, it is possible my government could set up a preemptive strike against the nuclear facility."

"You could have done that from the start. What's the holdup?"

"Do you read the papers?" Sascha asked, frowning.

"When I have the time."

"Then you're aware of peace negotiations in the Middle East. Myself, I doubt that anything will come of talking to the Arabs. They are pledged to wipe my homeland off the map and drive my people into the sea. Since 1948 they have pursued that goal with every means at their disposal. When they stop to talk of peace, we understand that they need time to load their guns."

"That's pretty bleak."

"The truth is often bleak. In Israel we have learned to live forever on our guard."

"I guess you're ready for whatever happens, then," he said.

"Count on it."

There was something like defiance in her eyes, as if she were expecting him to challenge her, demand some evidence of her professional abilities. He let it go and pushed his breakfast plate away, the meal half-eaten.

"You've lost your appetite?"

"No problem," Bolan said. "Before we're finished, I suspect I'll have my belly full."

Her smile took Bolan by surprise. "What should we do," she said, "with so much time to kill? Did you have anything in mind?"

"I have a car," he said. "We might as well see Belgrade while we're here... unless you'd rather not, of course."

Before he finished speaking, Sascha Lentz was on her feet.

"How is it you Americans respond? I thought you'd never ask."

Budapest

IF HITTERS WERE WAITING for them at the railroad station, Yakov Katzenelenbogen couldn't spot them in the crowd. An early check-in gave them time to scout the area, watch faces come and go as trains arrived and left the depot, more or less on time. The only persons who remained for any length of time were uniformed employees of the rail lines and a vendor in his early sixties, hawking paperbacks and postcards from a corner stand.

They had no trouble picking out the Orient Express. It was impossible to miss, with ornate scrollwork and the look of luxury familiar from novels, television shows and feature films. Katz would have known the old girl anywhere.

Established in the spring of 1883, the Orient Express had catered to discriminating clientele for half a century before the massive damage wrought by World War Two had threatened closure of the line. The next two decades were devoted to recuperation and repairs, but service was maintained from London through to Instanbul. These days, the line was back in fighting trim, with many of the original coaches refurbished at great expense, providing a touch of old-world charm and grace amid the crush of modern European life.

How many spies had traveled back and forth along this route? Katz asked himself, as he sat drinking coffee with his Russian escort in the station cafeteria. Forget about James Bond, Hercule Poirot and all the other fictional protagonists who sprang from literary minds throughout the years. The Orient Express had always been a living hotbed of intrigue, connecting London, Paris and Vienna with the darker realms of Eastern Europe and the Middle East. At one time, in its heyday, passengers could transfer to the "Taurus Express," rolling on through Aleppo, Haifa, Baghdad, back to Al Mawsil, but those were kinder, gentler times, before the violent birth of Israel and the rise of terrorism in response. It was an ideal meeting place for spies and double agents, saboteurs, assassins and defectors.

Within the next few minutes, he and Tyumen would board the train and settle in to see what happened next. A brief glimpse of McCarter boarding early reassured the gruff Israeli that his back was covered if the set began unraveling ahead of time. Tyumen had performed his tasks efficiently so far, but killing one man by surprise in a hotel wasn't the same as standing fast in battle when the chips were down.

With any luck at all, they would be safe until they left the train in Ankara, but Katz had learned from grim experience that any faith he put in luck was probably misplaced. A soldier made his own luck in the field, for good or ill, by planning in advance and making preparations for the worst scenarios he could anticipate.

"It's time to go," Tyumen said, a hint of tension in his voice.

"All right."

Their luggage had already gone on board. It would be waiting for them in the twin compartments scheduled for Ivan Baranovich and his companion in the first-class section, situated side by side with a connecting door. Katz made his mind up to be doubly cautious on the trip ahead and mold a wedge to block the door from his side while he slept. It would be safer that way, if an adversary moved against Tyumen—or in case Tyumen should himself turn out to be an enemy.

At least he had the Browning tucked inside his belt, its comfortable weight a reassurance as he rose and followed Tyuman outside. Conductors were preparing for departure, issuing their final call for stragglers to board the train. Katz glanced around him, trying to keep it casual as he scanned faces in the crowd. He wouldn't recognize the enemy, of course, but sometimes you could spot the type.

No good.

If they were being watched or followed, it was too late now. The enemy could bide his time and make the next move at his leisure, hoping for a moment when their guard was down.

Not likely.

If he had to stay awake the next two days, Katz vowed that he'd be prepared for anything that happened. It was the only way to stay alive as far as Ankara, and after that...

He shrugged the gloomy thought away.

Tomorrow took care of itself. Sufficient unto this day were the risks and fears he recognized.

Inside the sleeping car, Katz followed Nikolai Tyumen down the corridor toward their compartments. Staring at the Russian's back, he knew that it would be no problem killing Tyumen if the need arose. The young man would be just another enemy if he betrayed their grudging trust.

And dead was dead, no matter where the darkness overtook you.

Even on the Orient Express.

Kecskemet, Hungary

MCCARTER BEAT the lunch crowd with an early visit to the dining car. His growling stomach had demanded sustenance at last, reminding him that he had passed on breakfast in his haste to reach the railroad station ahead of Katz and his companion, watching surreptitiously until he satisfied himself that they hadn't been followed. After that, it was a case of lying low and keeping out of sight until the Orient Express was boarding passengers. It wouldn't do for Katz's escort to observe a stranger loitering around the platform, killing time. A confrontation with the Russian was the last thing that McCarter wanted; even being noticed at the outset of their journey could be fatal to his plans.

He solved the problem by retreating to the men's room, sitting in a toilet stall until his cheeks went numb, then standing for a while before some new arrival forced him down again, to keep appearances intact. It seemed to take forever, but the time eventually passed and they were all on board, the locomotive panting like a wounded dinosaur as it began to gather speed outside the rail yard.

Rolling south from Budapest, they cleared the suburbs, leaving factories behind as they encroached on open farmland. Cattle grazed within an easy stone's throw of the tracks, and there were forests in the middle distance, mountains rising dark and ominous beyond. He was in vampire country now, McCarter thought...or was that in Romania?

No matter.

The night ghouls he was concerned with had no fear of garlic or crosses, but his Skorpion and the P-7 automatic he carried would cut them down to size.

He found a window seat in the dining car, claiming a table for two by himself. The waiter brought a multilingual menu and McCarter ordered roast beef, extra-rare, with baked potato on the side and German beer to wash it down. The first beer came while he was waiting for his food, and he allowed himself another with the meal. The beef was excellent, in keeping with the Orient Express tradition, and McCarter took his time, eating slowly and watching the scenic countryside unfold while his mind reviewed the problem at hand.

He had only the vaguest estimate of numbers when it came to passengers and crew on board the train. A minimum of seventy to start from Budapest, and that would change at every stop as new arrivals came aboard and others disembarked. If he assumed the worst—at least one spy in place besides himself—that still left ample room for others to attach themselves at any point along the way.

Establishing perimeters in such a situation was impossible. One man could never guard a stationary train this size, much less when it was traveling some 1,400 miles with scores of stops along the way. The best that he could hope for was to watch his men, beware of anyone who showed an undue interest in the pair or tried to move against them.

At least he wasn't far from Katz in terms of distance—three doors down, the last compartment in the second first-class sleeping car—but he wouldn't be able to observe the corridor full time without attracting dangerous attention to himself. Instead he'd remain alert and ready to respond at the suggestion of a threat to Katz or his companion. Whatever flowed from that decision, he'd take the consequences and assume responsibility.

Just now, he knew that Katzenelenbogen and the Russian were together in the escort's compartment, presumably discussing strategies for the hours and days ahead. Their very presence on the Orient Express meant they had been successful in the first phase of the mission, taking out Baranovich and his appointed watchdog from the KGB.

Ex-KGB, McCarter caught himself. Times changed, and people too, but it was easier to find new names for governments and institutions than to change the men in charge. When a regime collapsed, somebody had to pick up the pieces and start from scratch. In Germany, on VE Day, the Allies had negotiated terms with certain well-known Nazis to prevent a lapse that would have led to total anarchy. When Howard Hughes was buying up Las Vegas, he permitted mobsters to retain an interest in the gaming clubs he purchased, staying long enough to educate a brand-new team...and skim a few more million on the side.

The more things changed, McCarter was inclined to think, the more they stayed the same.

He had discussed those thoughts with Katz at Stony Man, before they caught the Concorde out of Dulles, and they understood each other perfectly. If there was any sign of Katz's escort trying to subvert the general effort, he'd be eliminated on the spot. It would be difficult to forge ahead without him, granted, but they could only try.

And if the Russian proved himself a loyal companion, then what? Did it mean a new day of cooperation dawning? Washington and Moscow joining hands with London, Paris, Rome, Berlin? To what effect? Could long-term adversaries ever really lay the countless grudges down and start from scratch?

McCarter wasn't sure, and at the moment it wasn't his problem. Finishing the last of his delicious beef and chasing it with beer, he concentrated on the short-term goals. Protecting Katz—and his companion, if the man proved loyal. Allowing them to safely reach the Turkish border with Iraq. Rejoining Bolan and the rest of Phoenix Force in Turkey, for a border crossing of his own.

And after that?

McCarter could have used another beer, but he declined and paid his bill, departed from the dining car as other passengers began to filter in for lunch. All kinds of faces. Friends and lovers, businessmen and pensioners.

The Phoenix Force warrior wished them well and hoped that none of them would have to die on board within the next two days.

NAJRAN ABBAS WAS TIRED of waiting, but it wasn't in his nature to complain. He had been weaned and raised on waiting—for a crust of bread, a cup of tepid water—and his military service in Iran had been the finishing academy in terms of patience. He had managed to survive three years of warfare with Iraq before his special talents caught the eye of an intelligence coordinator and he was removed from uniform to serve his homeland and the holy revolution in another way.

Najran Abbas had learned to kill when he was twelve years old. Already the man of the house since his father had died two years earlier, it was the youth's duty to react when a neighbor raped and brutalized his sister. A report to the police would certainly have been the easy way to go, considering the fact that Najran's enemy was ten years older, larger, stronger, with a background of domestic violence. All the same, it was a debt of honor that could be repaid only in person.

And in blood.

It all came down to waiting for the proper moment. Two months after the assault, when Abbas's target had relaxed, imagining himself secure, he was surprised one night while walking home from work. The fight was brief and brutal, both assailants armed with knives. Abbas spent eight days in the hospital before they turned him out, by which time the police were cognizant of some extenuating circumstances in the case. A burly captain warned the young man not to take the burden of the law upon himself, then shook his hand and left him with a knowing smile.

There was no choice about the army when he turned sixteen. The ayatollah had declared a holy war against Iraq and every man was needed for the cause. Surviving four long years of war had been a miracle, suggesting that God had some greater plan in mind for those he spared. Abbas saw thousands dying all around him, sending some of them to meet their maker with his own two hands.

He became a hunter in those days, sometimes participating in patrols, at other times embarking on his own to strike a special target. On rare occasions he was told to leave the enemy alive and bring back information valued by the state. His closest brush with failure was a case of overzealousness—three victims stabbed to death, instead of one—but his superiors were understanding and forgave him.

Now, the war was over but the enemy remained. Iraq had been responsible for grave atrocities inside Iran. Mass executions, rape and pillage, experiments with chemical agents that killed indiscriminate thousands. No peace treaty could erase that debt of honor, but Abbas would help to pay it off in time.

Now the enemy in Baghdad was preparing yet another weapon of destruction, this one capable of laying waste to nations on a whim. Reports had come from spies inside Iraq, and the abduction of a young Iraqi diplomat in Jordan had confirmed the rumors. Russian scientists were on the auction block, with Baghdad bidding furiously for their brains. Already two had slipped across the border, out of reach, but there was one to go.

It was a plot that must be foiled at any cost. Abbas had been dispatched to Budapest, with orders to pursue his quarry on the Orient Express and choose a perfect moment for the kill. It seemed an easy job, considering the fact that he'd have two days.

Abbas wasn't intimidated by the magnitude of his assignment. It was only fitting, after all that he had done and suffered for the Shiite state, that he'd be rewarded with a challenge equal to his skill. If anything, he feared the job might prove too easy in the final execution, disappointing him with its simplicity.

But he'd see it through, no matter what.

He had his target spotted from advance descriptions, riding in the first-class section of the train. The Russian was a nondescript assassin, but the older man could hardly be mistaken, even in a crowd.

He was the only one-armed man on board the Orient Express.

Abbas couldn't afford to ride first class, but that was no impediment. He could devise a dozen different ways of reaching out to tag his prey.

The execution would be simple.

Najran's challenge would be in making it a work of art.

CHAPTER EIGHT

The Orient Express
Sunday, 1150 hours

The train was running late, of course. A stop in Kecskemet had slowed them down. Katz understood the pace of European railroad travel, and he made allowances. In Italy, before the last world war, Benito Mussolini's greatest claim to fame had been the fact that he made railroads run on time. In 1935, no less than fifty years thereafter, it had been no small achievement.

Never mind.

The train would reach its destination when it got there. Nothing Katz could do would speed things up, and at the moment, he was glad to have the extra time. Alone in his compartment after lunching with Tyumen, Katz was free to kick his shoes off, place his Browning on the lower bunk and watch the countryside unfolding from his window seat.

He had acquired a pair of rubber wedges from the porter to secure the connecting door at night. It saved him the effort of molding moistened tissue paper or whittling wooden blocks, and it would give him something close to peace of mind when he lay down to sleep.

On second thought, Katz made his mind up to use one wedge on the door between compartments and the other on the door that granted access to the outer hallway.

Just in case.

He couldn't shake the feeling that Ivan Baranovich would almost certainly be watched by *someone* on the trip from Budapest to Ankara. It was a feeling in his gut, the kind of thing that Katz would do if he was in the business of transporting human merchandise across the continent. The major problem on his mind, right now, concerned itself with who was likely to be watching, why they were in place, and what they were prepared to do.

If they were dealing with a Russian comrade of Baranovich's escort, then the game was up. Katz might be capable of passing cursory inspection by a stranger, but a watchdog sent from Moscow would already know Baranovich's face—as well as the escort, who had long since been disposed by Tyumen's cleanup team in Budapest. A pair of ringers would begin to sound alarms all up and down the line, but Katz could only guess at when and where the order to remove them would be executed.

On the other hand, it was entirely possible that the Iraqis might have sent a spotting team to track Baranovich. The boys in Baghdad would be angry over losing Nabakov, determined not to let another piece of their investment slip away. The good news, if Brognola was correct, lay in the fact that Katz's double hadn't met with the Iraqis face-to-face. With any luck at all, they'd be working from a general description. If there was a spotting team and they had photographs, how would they take thc news that they were being duped?

Another nagging possibility came back to Katz as he sat watching cultivated fields and scattered trees slip past his window. He was thinking wild cards now, the unknown element that made black operations doubly dangerous. Iraq had enemies to spare, as did the Russians. Katz could name at least a dozen nations that would love to see the plot exposed in banner headlines, preferably with loss of life involved to keep the story going for a while. His own former comrades in Mossad would have the motive and the means, but they were currently cooperating with the Stony Man team...or were they?

There was a time, Katz knew, when Tel Aviv had run a hit team called the Wrath of God. Its members specialized in killing Arab terrorists around the world, avenging this or that atrocity with almost surgical precision, letting baby-killers know that there was no place safe to hide. Officially the team had been disbanded in the latter 1970s, but its successors still had work to do. In February 1992 an airborne task force had removed a leader of the Hezbollah in Lebanon, reacting to a murderous attack on soldiers based in Israel. If it served Israeli interests to expose the latest plot from Baghdad, rather than suppressing it clandestinely, Katz knew his countrymen were capable of striking on a moment's notice, sparing no one in their path.

If it came down to that, he was prepared to carry out his mission as ordained from Stony Man. In any case, when the manure hit the fan, there'd be no time to request a show of ID from his adversaries. Anyone who tried to stop him now, without a recall order from the top, would have to be regarded as an enemy.

The rhythmic sound and motion of the train were lulling him to sleep. Katz blinked the drowsiness away and sat up straighter in his chair. They should be entering Subotica before much longer, pausing for the standard passport check, and Katz would have to let himself be seen, however briefly, by the men of Phoenix Force. His comrades had no method of communication with the train, but they were under orders to observe the Orient Express at certain stops and keep themselves available in the event of any major clash en route to Ankara.

He couldn't picture any group or individual attempting to assault the Orient Express per se, but nothing was beyond the realm of possibility. All things considered, Katz was glad to know his friends were out there, waiting for him, keeping watch.

With nothing else to do, the warrior settled back to wait.

Subotica, Yugoslavia

"WE'RE BARELY GETTING started, and they're late already." Calvin James was visibly disgusted as he checked his watch again and slumped back on the bench, his shoulders pressed against the railroad depot's concrete wall.

"Relax," Gary Manning said, smiling at his friend. "For a European train, she's running right on time."

"That's great. You're saying that we get to drag ass all the way, is that it?"

"Stop and smell the roses, Calvin." There was irony in Rafael Encizo's voice, a thin smile on his face.

"I don't like being this exposed. You might have missed it, but it's not exactly Black History Week around here."

A family of five passed by the bench, the father speaking rapid-fire Slovenian. A couple of the children gaped at James as if they'd never seen a black man in their life. Which, Gary Manning thought, was very probably the case.

"We're tourists," Manning replied when it was safe to speak again, his voice pitched low to make eavesdropping that much harder. "Yugoslavia draws thousands of Americans each year. It's not like you're the man from Mars."

"That's right," Encizo said. "How do you think I feel? I couldn't find an enchilada in this country if my life depended on it."

"I got your enchilada right here."

"Looks more like a taquito to me."

Manning was relieved by their banter, which helped to take his mind off the imaginary problems he had conjured for himself. It was at least a hundred miles by rail from Budapest to the border, two hours on the train if all went well, but Manning had about convinced himself that any hostile moves could just as easily be made along the first leg of the journey as in Yugoslavia or Greece. Why wait, if someone figured out that Katz and his companion were a pair of ringers? Swift elimination could avoid a host of problems down the road.

Forget it. There was nothing he could do about the hundred miles of track in Hungary. McCarter was supposed to have Katz covered on the train, and Stony Man had flashed the word that everything went down according to plan in Budapest. Two hours was a fraction of a heartbeat in the larger scheme of things, but Manning still couldn't suppress a certain apprehension, longing for the question to be answered with a glimpse of Katzenelenbogen in Subotica.

And after that?

More waiting, checking on the Orient Express at major stops along the way, but traveling would occupy their time, relieve a measure of his natural anxiety. If forced to cast a secret ballot, Manning would have said that Katzenelenbogen and McCarter were the strongest members of Phoenix Force, more years of battlefield experience between them, but he couldn't shake the feeling that they needed help.

He checked his watch, unconscious of the gesture until he caught himself and frowned. The train would be there in its own good time. A minimal delay was nothing to incite alarm. He knew about the stop for passengers in Kecskemet, and they'd lose time there, with children acting up and lovers saying long goodbyes.

No problem.

He was more concerned about what happened on the train while it was moving. During the two-day trip, anyone could choose his time and place to make a move along the way. It took only one bullet or a dagger thrust—a simple shove, if Katz was standing on the observation platform—and their plan would instantly disintegrate.

Except that Katz wouldn't allow an enemy to take him by surprise. The oldest member of Phoenix Force hadn't survived this long by throwing caution to the wind. They had discussed the risks for hours on end at Stony Man, and Katz was confident that he could take them all in stride. McCarter would be there to help him, as well as the Russian escort, if he did his job.

Manning hoped he'd catch a glimpse of the Russian in Subotica. It would be helpful to identify the man if things went badly. Track him down and kill him if he sold Katz out.

No mercy existed for a traitor when so much was riding on the line.

On a mission of this type, Manning did his best to ignore the big picture whenever possible. If he began to think in terms of MIRVs, ICBMs and mushrooms sprouting over Tel Aviv or London, he'd lose perspective on the here and now. Each move the Phoenix warriors made was critical, and their attention to minute detail could make or break a mission on the ground. He'd attack each problem as it came, anticipating possibilities, but Manning wouldn't let himself consider failure, the expense in terms of global suffering and death.

It was too much for him to cope with, and defeat could all too easily become a self-fulfilling prophecy. Instead he concentrated on the moment, studying the crowd of passengers and passersby in search of likely adversaries. Was that bulge beneath the old man's overcoat a weapon? Did the young blond woman have a radio transmitter or a pistol in her shoulder bag? Would he be able to detect a Russian shooter in the midst of all these Slavic faces waiting for the train?

He wasn't certain, but the Phoenix warrior knew that he'd do his very best—or die in the attempt.

The Orient Express

NIKOLAI TYUMEN CLOSED the door of his compartment behind him, set the latch and took a breath to let himself relax. For half an hour he had wandered up and down the train, through second class, a pit stop in the dining car, with both eyes for potential enemies. He had a mental list—no names of course, but he'd make do with the faces and prepare himself for any rude surprises that the trip might hold in store.

It was a fact, of course, that anyone on board the train might be his enemy. Tyumen didn't count the one-armed man next door, not really, though a year or even six months earlier they might have been on different sides, committed to destroying each other in the name of national security. Clandestine operations, like politics, made strange bedfellows indeed.

As for the others, he had seven faces fixed in mind for future reference. There had to have been others he had missed, shut up in various first-class compartments, rest rooms and the like, but he'd start with what he had.

Of the seven, five were traveling singly, or appeared to be. He couldn't overlook the possibility of agents working separately toward common goals, the better to preserve their cover in the public eye. Still, he couldn't afford to make assumptions that might throw him off the track.

One couple, then. A man and woman in the dining car for openers. Tyumen placed them in their early thirties. Both wore wedding rings, which meant no more than artificial beards or colored glasses in the spying game. The woman was a trim, athletic blonde; her husband dark and stocky, with a small scar at the angle of his jaw. The woman seemed to stare at the Russian as he passed by their table, while the man avoided looking at him, concentrating on his meal. It could be nothing, or the woman might just be a tease, her husband grown accustomed to her roving eye. And, then again...

The solitary prospects were a mixed bag. Two of them were clearly Arabs, though Tyumen hadn't heard them speaking and he couldn't place their nationality with any confidence. Were they Iraqis, following the merchandise to guarantee its safe arrival? And if so, would they be armed with photographs betraying Tyumen and his Western sidekick as imposters? Were the small dark men discussing ways to kill him, even now?

The Arabs had been riding in different cars, but the coincidence had set alarm bells ringing in Tyumen's mind. The more he thought about it now, it seemed peculiar there weren't more Arabs on the train, with Turkey waiting at the far end of the line, but he supposed they did less traveing in Eastern Europe than Americans or Britons. More reason to suspect them, then, and keep a close eye on their movements if he got the chance.

The other three on Tyumen's suspect list were European males. He could have picked two dozen others just as easily, but there was something in the faces he selected—ruthlessness, perhaps, a quality ingrained in first-rate agents and assassins.

Like himself?

Tyumen thought about it and decided he was getting there.

One of the five had glanced up from a German magazine as Tyumen passed his window seat in second class. It clearly didn't prove he *was* a German, didn't even prove he spoke the language, but at least it was a clue of sorts. East German elements might have a stake in the proceedings, working with their former comrades from the KGB. Germany was united now, the DDR's state security apparatus officially dismantled, but there were still as many diehards in the onetime eastern zone as in the Commonwealth of Independent States. Tyumen wouldn't have put it past the KGB alumni to recruit fresh talent from their German pool.

The other four, all men of unknown nationality, appeared to give no sign of having noticed Tyumen when he passed them in the aisles or eyed them from a cautious distance in the dining car. The lack of reaction could mean they were innocent...or else well trained to cope with hostile scrutiny. On such a job as this, he wouldn't count on meeting skittish amateurs.

Tyumen drew the Browning automatic from its shoulder holster, pulled the magazine and whipped the slide to drop the spare round from its chamber on his bunk. With easy, practiced movements of his hands, he stripped the automatic down to its component parts, examined each in turn and swiftly reassembled them without a second glance. Reloading more by instinct than by conscious thought, he eased the pistol's hammer down and stowed the weapon out of sight.

Whatever happened now, Tyumen was prepared—or hoped he was, at any rate. If there was something he had overlooked, some threat he had neglected to consider, the Russian would know about it soon enough.

When it exploded in his face.

Belgrade

"I DON'T APPROVE of zoos," Sascha Lentz said, when Bolan casually suggested that they make the short walk from their tour of the Kalmegedan Fortress. "All those animals in cages, pacing up and down. I think they should be taken back to where they came from and released."

"Some of them probably were born in zoos."

"Even worse. A creature of the wild that never knows a taste of freedom in its life. How sad and terrible it is."

"And what about endangered species? Some of them would be extinct by now, if not for zoos and breeding parks."

"Because of man," she told him sternly. "We destroy their habitats, appropriate the land, then applaud ourselves when half a dozen pitiful survivors cling to life on barren ground, penned up with metal bars. It makes me think of Indians in the United States."

"Or West Bank Palestinians?"

He felt her bristling beside him, but the gibe was irresistible. Mack Bolan recognized the dark spots in his nation's history and he didn't excuse them, but he had no patience with foreigners who took cheap shots at the United States while glossing over problems of their own.

"It's not the same," she answered with a cold steel edge beneath the cultured velvet of her voice. "In the United States you have vast lands, enough to share for everyone. The Indians befriended you—I know the story of your first Thanksgiving—but you drove them from their homes and clear across the continent. You wouldn't even let them flee in peace."

"That was a bit before my time," Bolan said, "but I know the story had two sides. As for the Palestinians—"

"Subversive traitors," Sascha snapped. "They scheme against us every moment and begrudge us every inch of land. They kill our children in the classroom and assassinate our soldiers while they sleep."

"The British occupation troops said much the same about your Irgun forces in the 1940s."

"They were wrong."

"Of course. And that makes all the difference in the world."

She turned to face him, and the curious expression had returned, eclipsing peevish anger for the moment. "You aren't like other soldiers I have known," she said at last.

"How's that?"

"It's difficult to say. You don't seem to hate the way some others do."

"Is hate required?"

"It's customary."

Bolan shrugged. "I've had my moments. On balance, hating never got me anywhere I couldn't go with basic strategy."

"You don't hate your enemies?"

"I hate the things they stand for," Bolan said. "I think some men deserve to die for what they've done or didn't do. Most times, it's nothing personal."

Not strictly true, he thought as he was speaking. Sascha seemed to read his thoughts and understand.

"But other times?" she asked.

"Of course."

"We understand each other, then."

"I wouldn't go that far."

"You have sustained some mortal loss," she said. "I see it in your eyes. We all have scars."

"Yours don't stand out."

"When I was twelve years old, in the kibbutz near Zefat, on the northern border, Al Fatah attacked the settlement. Eight people died. My parents were among them."

"And you pay the debt back every chance you get."

"Have you not wished for such an opportunity?" she asked.

"Revenge gets old. I started losing track of names and faces, reasons. If you don't have something else, it eats you up inside."

"I have my country," Sascha said. "Today, Iraq would threaten to destroy my home. Tomorrow, it might be Iran or Syria. My enemies are all the same."

"I know the feeling," Bolan answered earnestly, "but watch yourself. If hunting starts to override the reasons why, you know you've got a problem."

"I believe in the security of Israel."

"Fair enough. Let's see what we can do to keep the lid on, shall we?"

"Yes." She hesitated, searching Bolan's eyes, then smiled and said, "I still don't like the zoo."

"I don't much like it, either. Are you hungry?"

"Yes, but you must let me pay this time."

"A liberated Sabra? Are all you native-born Israeli women like this?"

"Indeed. We are all quite liberated, thank you very much. I think it comes from training in the martial arts."

"No sexual harassment in the corps, I guess."

"Not twice."

The warrior checked his wristwatch. "We should have a contact in Subotica by now, if everything's on time. That leaves two hours, give or take."

"I know a restaurant not far from here," she said. "It faces on the river. If we hurry, we can beat the luncheon crowd."

"Suits me."

They walked back to the Porsche 944, and Bolan thought how strange it felt to be discussing lunch in Belgrade, while his comrades were awaiting news of Katz a hundred miles due north. It felt like slacking, hiding out when there was work to do and dangers to be faced, but he knew the plan by heart and he wasn't in a position to revise the script.

That luxury belonged exclusively to Bolan's enemies.

So they would dine, kill time until the Orient Express pulled into Belgrade's Central Station on the Sava riverfront. Manning, James and Encizo knew he was waiting there, and they wouldn't be checking in at Belgrade, rolling on instead to make the next stop on the line. Your basic leapfrog, with a twist.

If any of the players flubbed their moves in this game, it wasn't a simple "out." The losers bought a one-way ticket to the boneyard, while the winners got to play another round.

Assuming there were any winners in the end.

If not, it would be Bolan's job to take as many of the opposition with him as he could. Scorched earth and let the devil take the hindmost, right.

He didn't care much for the odds, but it was still the only game in town.

CHAPTER NINE

Al Mawsil, Iraq
Sunday, 1350 hours

Gregori Berdichev strolled slowly through the garden of his villa, soaking up the kind of sunshine that you never saw in Moscow. It was latitude, he guessed, that made the sunlight in his native city almost brittle, leeched its warmth before it touched the ground or human flesh. Of course it could get hot and muggy in the former Soviet capital, but Berdichev had always felt like he was living in a greenhouse or a pressure cooker. No one but the state-owned athletes and the ranking politicians with their sunlamps ever seemed to have a tan.

In truth the villa wasn't Berdichev's. It had been lent to Glazov for his visits to Iraq, when it wasn't deemed wise to have a Russian visiting the head of state in Baghdad. Later, when the time had come for Glazov and his second in command to leave the Commonwealth behind, they found that there was ample room for two inside those whitewashed stucco walls. The ravages of Operation Desert Storm lay farther south, in Baghdad and beyond, but Al Mawsil was more or less unscathed, except by the loss of young men drafted to die in the "mother of all battles."

What a pathetic joke it had been, Saddam posing for the cameras, shouting defiant phrases from his bunker while the country fell apart, his vaunted army falling back in disarray. He was the last commander in the Middle East to inspire confidence, the latest in a long line of Arab losers, but ironically, that very fact made him ideal for his appointed role in Glazov's master plan.

You couldn't spend five minutes with Saddam before he got around to the Americans. They were controlled by Jews and hated Arabs everywhere, but the Iraqis worst of all. In Washington the President and his advisers schemed nonstop for the destruction of Saddam Hussein, unsettled and intimidated by his strength, charisma, power, courage, nerve. The British were no better, maybe worse. It had been London, after all, that had carved the state of Israel from the sands of Palestine. As for the French, they were a pack of scrawny poodles sniffing in the garbage cans of Pennsylvania Avenue and Downing Street.

Saddam's megalomania hadn't been lost on Berdichev. The Russian knew a madman when he saw one. But Hussein still had enough control to keep his troops in line and manage the affairs of government. Postwar Iraq was suffering from economic woes, starvation and disease, but there was still enough fight left in the Hussein regime to crush political dissent. The Kurds were an example, soon to be extinct within the borders of the country, gassed or shot or driven into Turkey by the thousands. Someday soon, Saddam's approach to government would blow up in his face, but not just yet.

And in the meantime, he was useful to a higher cause.

A speckled lizard darted from the nearby flower bed and paused to glare at Berdichev before it vanished in a flash. It still surprised him, finding wildlife in the middle of a godforsaken desert where it seemed the toughest weed or cactus would collapse and die of loneliness. In fact, if he stood still and listened, Berdichev could hear the hum of insects in the garden, pollinating flowers as they worked from dawn to dusk to earn their keep. The lizard was a hunter, seeking some unwary fly or beetle, and he wouldn't be alone.

The food chain flourished, even here, the strongest hunting, killing to survive. In that way it was much like politics and international affairs. A politician or a state that tried to deal from weakness would inevitably fail. Some larger, stronger predator would come along and grind the feeble adversary into pulp. An easy meal.

Just now, the Commonwealth of Independent States was disoriented, weakened by dramatic changes. Its military strength was still a factor to be reckoned with, but there were grave doubts as to national preparedness, the simple willingness to fight. Most of the officers and men in uniform had been recruited to defend a socialist union of fifteen republics, all of them raised and trained in the doctrines of communism. Now, they marched under the flag of a three-nation merger, and communism was officially dead. A change like that was startling and confusing; worse, it sapped the will to fight by robbing soldiers of a standard they could recognize and understand.

The Commonwealth was safe behind her screen of warheads for the moment, but the pace of arms reduction led by weak-kneed "liberal" politicians was alarming, even dangerous. Once bombs and missiles were destroyed, the factories shut down, there would be nothing to prevent America from picking up production, launching a preemptive strike against her weakened former enemy.

Nothing, perhaps, but a critical diversion in the Middle East.

There was no question of Saddam Hussein collecting MIRVs and missiles to defend himself against some hypothetical attack from nameless enemies. Hussein was an aggressor, every fiber of his being tuned to conquest, plunder and assault. Once he was armed in proper style, the Mideast holocaust would take care of itself.

It was a calculated gamble, touching off a firestorm in Iraq, but any fallout from American reprisals would be swept across the landscape of Iran and Turkey, possibly a taste of radiation for the faithless Georgians and Armenians who had deserted Mother Russia in her time of greatest need. Hussein wouldn't last long, once the Americans and Britons retaliated for his strikes on Israel and selected other targets, but his fate—his worthless people—stood for less than nothing on the scales of history.

But they could still be useful, in their way, by keeping the Americans distracted long enough for Berdichev's superiors to reassert themselves in Minsk and Moscow, reclaiming the power that was theirs by right.

And when the smoke cleared, the Americans would find themselves confronted with a brand-new Russia, sleek and strong.

If Moscow seized the moment, it might be the last thing fascist Washington would ever see.

West of Nineveh, Iraq

SUNDAY WAS A DAY OF REST, and Vladimir Polyarni took advantage of it to the hilt. Although he loved his work and was a globally respected expert in his chosen field, Polyarni still subscribed to the belief that all work and no play make a very dull comrade.

The previous night and that morning, he had been amusing himself with a supple desert fox named Tisa. She was young enough to be his daughter, and her youth excited him, recharged his batteries as nothing else had done for years on end. Six months earlier, Polyarni would have said it was impossible for him to stay awake all night, much less make love on half a dozen separate occasions in as many hours.

At the moment, even with allowances for his fatigue, Polyarni felt like Superman.

He knew that Tisa did it for the money paid for her Iraqi masters, but it hardly mattered. There was something in her attitude, a certain playfulness perhaps, that made Polyarni feel she didn't find him disagreeable or ancient. She enjoyed herself with him, or seemed to, and the physicist wasn't about to question his good fortune on a sleepy Sunday afternoon.

Polyarni was reclining in an easy chair and watching Tisa sleep. The room was warm, and she had kicked the sheets away, allowing him a clear view of her naked buttocks and torso. He could feel himself responding, thought of waking her and put it off a moment longer to appreciate the sight.

There were so many things to think about these days, beginning with the job he had to do for the Iraqis. It wasn't so different from his work in Russia, prior to the collapse, except that with the Soviet regime there was a feeling that the weapons he designed would all be locked away somewhere, in mothballs as it were, and never really used.

Saddam Hussein was something else again.

Polyarni had been introduced to the Iraqi leader briefly, some days after his arrival from Armenia. He didn't trust the demagogue, whose eyes seemed more like chips of flint than living tissue. Even when he smiled, those eyes retained a stony quality, devoid of warmth and all humanity. Such men were dangerous to everything and everyone they touched. If properly equipped, a man like that could set the world on fire.

Destruction on a global scale had always been an abstract concept for Polyarni. He knew all about the thermal, blast, and nuclear effects of warhead detonation on a major population center. He had studied hypothetical fallout patterns and viewed the horrors of Chernobyl firsthand. He was adept at calculating overpressure, megatonnage and radiation yield in milliroentgens. When the end came, if it came, Polyarni would anticipate and recognize each phase of his destruction.

But he never really thought, somehow, that it could touch him personally. He wouldn't be staying in Iraq forever. When his work was done, perhaps a year from now, he'd be moving on. Baranovich and Serpukhov were free to stay or leave as they desired, but Vladimir Polyarni would be rich enough by then to start a new life in the West. Despite his training as a child of socialism, he was looking forward to a period of decadence.

Saddam Hussein wouldn't be able to erase all that, no matter what he did with his new arsenal. Polyarni understood the Arabs well enough. They hated Jews and longed for their destruction. Tel Aviv would doubtless be the first selected target for Hussein. Perhaps a few shots at Iran, Kuwait or Saudi Arabia. At some point the Americans and British would retaliate, perhaps with some assistance from the Commonwealth of Independent States. In the end Saddam and his regime of animals would be reduced to smoking ash.

But Vladimir Polyarni would be safe and far away by then, perhaps in Amsterdam or Paris, maybe even Rio de Janeiro.

Yes, the more he thought about it now, the tropics sounded nice. It would be warm year-round, and no one would be looking for him there. Polyarni might learn Spanish, get himself a tan. Go native, if he felt the urge.

But at the moment, he was feeling very different urges.

Tisa giggled as he climbed in bed beside her, turning over on her back. She smiled coquettishly.

"I wondered how long you could wait."

PIOTR SERPUKHOV DECIDED he'd have to pass on vodka for a while. His head was pounding, there was acid churning in his stomach, and it felt like something very old had crept inside his mouth to die. Disgusted with himself, he washed four aspirin down with bottled water, nearly brought them up again, and swallowed hard to keep the tablets down.

Yasmina hadn't spent the night, apparently. He couldn't blame her, when the alcohol reduced his amorous performance to the minimum and launched him into pointless stories of his youth, most often told in Russian while she sat and listened, trying not to yawn.

It was pathetic, but he couldn't help himself. The vodka helped him think... or was it helping him forget?

Serpukhov's stomach was growling, but the thought of food at the moment made him feel vaguely nauseous. Instead he thought about another drink, and that was even worse.

Deprived of options, Serpukhov turned on the bedroom television set and flipped around the dial. They were connected to a dish antenna at the compound, granting him a wide selection from American feature films to Japanese news broadcasts, but nothing appealed to him at the moment. Finally he walked back to the living room and sat on the couch directly opposite a set of sliding doors that faced the courtyard. It seemed bright enough outside to blind a man.

He wished Ivan Baranovich would hurry and join them at the compound. When he got there, maybe they could speed up their production of the weapons for Saddam Hussein and thus fulfill their contract. At the moment Serpukhov was anxious to be gone, and never mind Yasmina's many charms.

He wasn't troubled by morality or ethics, never had been. Now that there was no more People's Revolution to defend, he manufactured warheads for the highest bidder. That was life, and Serpukhov pronounced no judgment on himself for trying to survive in style. The problem, never voiced to anyone, was a pervasive sense of dread that followed him around each day and perched upon his shoulder like a raven, croaking doom.

He hadn't stopped to think before he made the deal with Glazov and agreed to work for the Iraqis. They were offering a fortune and he couldn't turn it down. But now, Piotr Serpukhov had ample time to mull the risks involved. He thought about the damage done by the Americans in Operation Desert Storm and how their "smart bombs" targeted Iraqi missile sites, reactors, factories. He knew of the Israeli strike in 1981 and had no reason to suspect that Tel Aviv would be averse to launching further raids, if they discovered what was happening a few miles west of Nineveh.

A child of communism, Serpukhov didn't associate the name with any biblical connections, but he understood the region's role in history—crossroads for the old nomadic tribes, contested by crusaders and their Muslim adversaries in the Middle Ages, recently a hotbed of revolt and terrorism with selected targets all around the world. Piotr Serpukhov didn't feel privileged to be there; rather, there were times when he felt caught up in a conflict he had no ability—or real desire—to understand. An architect of death, he had no interest in the men who pushed the buttons, or the thousands, millions, they intended to destroy.

The problem was that now, someone he never even met could be intent on killing *him*, Piotr Serpukhov, because he was employed by the Iraqi government. The Jews weren't alone in wishing to eliminate Saddam Hussein or, alternately, to deprive him of the weapons that would give him power to expand his borders, whip his neighbors into line. If they couldn't attack Hussein himself—and some had tried, without success—what better way to frustrate his design than killing off the experts he employed to build his arsenal?

Serpukhov lighted a Turkish cigarette and drew the smoke deep into his lungs, willing the nicotine to help him relax. His fears weren't entirely groundless, but security was tight around the compound and he had no reason to suspect that anybody knew what they were doing. Still, there was the matter of Vasili Nabakov, whom they were told wouldn't be joining them as planned. An auto accident, as Berdichev explained. So sad.

And why should Serpukhov suspect that Berdichev was lying, hiding something? There were countless fatal highway accidents around the world each day, the death toll mounting into tens of thousands. It would be suspicious if a project such as this did *not* experience a setback now and then.

Still...

In his mind he pictured Nabakov reneging on his bargain, fleeing with the cash advance. Where would he hide from Glazov and the others? Would he spill the story as a form of self-defense, expecting the Israelis or Americans to take him in? If he was truly dead, but it wasn't an accident, did that make Serpukhov, Polyarni and Baranovich expendable?

He wouldn't dwell upon that possibility, at least until his stomach calmed itself enough to take more vodka. Maybe he should try the indoor swimming pool, just float and soak awhile to let himself unwind. He wished that he could reach out for Yasmina, hold her tight and let her occupy his mind, but calling on her now would be a sign of weakness. Later, possibly, when he had bathed, shaved and brushed his teeth.

Tomorrow was another day, and by next weekend he expected to complete preliminary drawings for a MIRV deployment system in the range of thirteen megatons. It wasn't large, as payloads went, but there was no point doing any more until they had Baranovich on-site to help with the delivery. The warheads were irrevelent without a way to get them in the air.

He felt a little better when he focused on his job, dismissing private fears and interpersonal relationships. The Jews hadn't arrived to kill him yet, Yasmina was a whore who mostly did as she was told and Serpukhov was being paid a very handsome salary to do what he did best.

All things considered, he decided he had no grounds for complaint.

Al Mawsil

AMAL MASHHAD WATCHED Glazov moving through the garden like a tourist, soaking up the sun. Since his arrival in Iraq, the Russian had begun to lose the pallor that identified an outsider on sight. He wasn't yet a full-fledged desert dweller, never would be, but he still seemed to appreciate the change.

He should enjoy it while he could. If the Russian thought that he was in control of what went on at Al Mawsil, he would be well-advised to think again.

Mashhad had lost a nephew and at least a dozen friends in the assault the Americans called Desert Storm. He went to sleep each night and woke each morning with a hunger for revenge, determined that it would be satisfied at any cost. His major feud wasn't with the Israelis now, although he still believed that there would be no strife and bloodshed in the Middle East without them. Every act of violence that had shaped Mashhad's existence could, in fact, be traced to 1948 and the creation of the Zionist preserve, some eighteen years before Amal Mashhad was born.

And now, at last, he had an opportunity to change the status quo. Not overnight, perhaps, but it was coming. With Saddam Hussein to guide their nation and the Russian scientists to arm them, the Iraqis soon would strike a blow for freedom, in defense of the uprooted Palestinians and every Arab who was sick of standing by and watching while his holy birthright was debased.

Mashhad was vague on how the Palestinians in Israel would be saved before the missiles flew, but sacrifice was part of every war. In the jihad, ordained by God, Muslim warriors had the satisfaction of believing that a death in battle meant direct ascension to the halls of paradise. If several thousand Palestinians were accidentally incinerated on the Day, at least their sacred memories would be revered throughout all time to come.

Mashhad was pleased with the solution to his mental problem. As he often thought in terms of sacrifice, the answer brought him peace of mind and put a smile on his face. His eyes returned to Glazov for a moment, and he saw the Russian disappear around a corner of the villa, following the garden out of sight.

Not long.

The missile builder was en route to Al Mawsil that very moment, though his foolish fear of airplanes would delay arrival for another day or two. It hardly mattered, if his talents were as great as advertised. He was supposed to know the various designs by heart, but the construction of the rockets would require some time. There were components to be found or fabricated, fuel to be refined, all manner of details to be worked out by the technicians in their laboratory. They would work as hard as necessary at their tasks.

Amal Mashhad would see to that.

The Russians were a condescending breed, regarding other races with the same contempt colonial oppressors always saved for those they dominated. It made no difference when they were cast as mere employees of the state. Their monthly salaries were high enough to feed a hundred peasant villages for months on end. The going rate encouraged them to view themselves as indispensable—and so they were, for now—but that would soon be changed.

Mashhad could hardly wait.

He knew that patience was a virtue, but experience had taught him that the slow man off the mark was often crushed to death before he could complete the first lap of his race. The winner made his own odds, broke the rules when necessary, but he kept faith with his people and himself.

Mashhad would be winner yet. He was fated to succeed and strike a blow against the enemies who would destroy his people, given half a chance. When Muslim scholars wrote their histories of the engagement yet to come, his name would be remembered and revered.

It was the best a man could hope for in uncertain times.

Glazov reappeared, retracing his steps through the garden as he walked back toward his quarters. Safe behind the tinted glass of his office window, Mashhad raised one hand like a pistol, drew a bead along his index finger, flexed his thumb to simulate the hammer dropping on a firing pin.

It would be just that easy, when the time came.

Meanwhile, he had more important work to do.

CHAPTER TEN

Subotica, Yugoslavia
Sunday, 1240 hours

Calvin James was waiting when the Orient Express pulled into the station forty minutes behind schedule. He had divided up the platform with his comrades, staking out a section sixty feet in length and settling back to wait, making himself an established part of the scenery. After close to an hour of waiting, his initial self-consciousness had faded to a minor form of background irritation, gnawing restlessly around the edges of his mind.

He wasn't much on trains, but James had to grant the Orient Express was handsome. Nothing like the El that used to rumble past his family's housing project in Chicago, filthy from the diesel smoke, graffiti-scarred, with pensive faces trapped behind the smudgy panes of glass. You always knew exactly where the El was going, carrying its human cargo off to work and home again.

The Orient Express, meanwhile, possessed a more exotic air, almost a touch of mystery.

Too many late-night movies on TV, the Phoenix Force warrior told himself. He stood up from the bench without appearing anxious, stretched both arms above his head to get the circulation going, just like any other stiff who'd spent an hour sitting on his butt.

The mighty train slid past him, braking to a halt, the locomotive heaving noxious clouds.

James had the first-class section covered, Gary Manning next in line with part of coach, and Rafael Encizo bringing up the rear. Exit formalities had been dealt with on the Hungarian side of the border, in Szeged, but now the passengers had to repeat the procedure for Yugoslavian authorities, displaying their passports, submitting to baggage checks if a customs official smelled trouble. James watched a line of uniforms emerging from the depot and wished he was invisible.

The contact would be played by ear, depending on the circumstances. If he had a chance to disembark before the Orient Express pulled out again, Katz was supposed to show himself. Alternatively he'd find a way to flash some signal to his comrades from the train...or not. They would be watching for McCarter, too, perhaps a confirmation from the backup man if Katzenelenbogen was detained.

It was a waiting game at this point, and a guessing game if Katz couldn't elude his escort and the immigration people long enough to show his face. The Phoenix Force warriors couldn't go on board to search the train, that much was certain, but they were expected to report their findings back to Stony Man without delay.

So James had to get it done. He moved along the platform, working backward from the locomotive to the first-class sleepers, idly checking out the windows on compartments where the drapes hadn't been drawn. A child stared back at him from one, nose pressed against the glass, all wide-eyed at the vision of a black man strolling past the window. Two compartments down, a woman showed her face for just a moment, looking flushed as if from strenuous exertion. Sex? Perhaps a quickie to commemorate the border crossing?

James frowned. He was imputting motives to a total stranger now, instead of tending to the job at hand. The second sleeping car in line was coming up, more curtains open here than on the first one. It occurred to James that he was missing fully half of the compartments, all those on the port side of the train, but there was nothing he could do without attracting dangerous attention to himself.

If Katzenelenbogen and McCarter were aboard the Orient Express, it would be their task to reveal themselves.

He cursed the distances involved, the lag time in communication back and forth to Stony Man, to Bolan farther south. The Comsat link helped relay data from the Farm, but in the absence of an adequate transmitter, they were forced to place their check-in calls from public telephones to prearranged receiving numbers maintained by the CIA. At that point messages were taped and "squirted" through the atmosphere to ricochet and wind up back on Earth, specifically on Aaron Kurtzman's console; if any deviation from the plan was called for, Stony Man would beam its orders back the same way, in reverse.

In practice, that meant someone from Phoenix Force had to check in periodically, with intervals depending on their access to a telephone. Where they were going, south through Yugoslavia and east through Greece to Turkey and beyond, James didn't count on finding public booths at every intersection.

They'd have to search and scrounge to stay in touch at all.

James was projecting gloomy thoughts when suddenly, ahead of him, he caught a glimpse of Katz's profile through a window in the second sleeping car. If the Israeli saw James passing by, he gave no sign. That could mean he had company—perhaps his Russian escort, or an immigration officer—or it could simply be an oversight. Confined to his compartment for the passport check, he simply left the curtains open, trusting one of his teammates to pass and make the tag.

Like now.

James picked up his pace, keeping both eyes open for McCarter as he moved along the platform, knowing it would be an almost hopeless long shot to connect with both team members on a second pass. He had enough for now, a confirmation Katz had caught the train and they were still in business.

The Phoenix warrior spotted Gary Manning in the crowd and changed his course to intercept the tall Canadian. A nod in passing, and he knew without observing it that Manning would be falling into step behind him, breaking off the search and moving toward the far end of the platform where Encizo stood his watch.

They had their man—or one of them, at least—and it was time to find a telephone. James noted the acceleration of his pulse and made the rush work for him, driving him along.

The game was shifting to another phase, but they'd still be playing for the standard stakes of life and death.

Belgrade

THE CONTACT NUMBER was a local call, but when a female voice came on the line it had the hollow, tinny sound of distance to it, like a patch designed to circumvent a trace. For all Mack Bolan knew, he could have been conversing with an operator in Vienna or Berlin, Milan or Paris.

"Striker," he announced without preliminaries. "Checking in for confirmation of a visual."

"The sighting is confirmed. Arrival time was forty minutes overdue."

His nameless, faceless contact on the other end wasn't excited by the news. The odds were that she had no real idea of what they were discussing. Need-to-know was still the rule of thumb.

"I copy that," he said. "No message in reply."

"No message."

Bolan waited for the dial tone, then he cradled the receiver, checked the coin slot on the public telephone and walked back to the bench where Sascha Lentz was waiting for him, watching over Bolan's Porsche.

"The train was late," he told her, "but we've got a confirmation from Subotica. They're on the way."

"So far, so good."

There was no pleasure in her tone and no concern. In fact, her voice reminded Bolan of his distant contact on the telephone. A trained professional, she wouldn't let her feelings interfere with the performance of her duties in the field. Besides, Bolan reminded himself, Katz and the Russian were total strangers to Sascha Lentz. She had no interest in the men as individuals, beyond the impact of their personal performance on the mission. Even though, her first concern would be for Israel's interest.

The Orient Express was running forty minutes late already, and he doubted whether it had even left the station at Subotica by now. He frowned and sat down on the bench to Sascha's left.

"We've got at least two hours, I'm afraid. It could be more."

She took the news in stride, a gentle shrug. "I don't have anyplace to go."

He estimated twenty minutes to the Belgrade Central Station, give or take another ten for Sunday traffic. That still left at least an hour and a half before they could expect the train.

"Ideas?"

"We should be early at the station," she remarked, as if invested with the power of reading Bolan's thoughts. "To check it out."

"Agreed. If we get hungry, they should have a cafeteria or something in the depot."

He had parked near the Botanic Garden on 29 Novembra, christened for the date in 1945 when a constituent assembly proclaimed Yugoslavia a federated republic, with Josip Broz—a.k.a. Marshal Tito—as the ruling head of state. The Porsche 944 responded instantly to Bolan's touch and they were on their way, crossing Dzordza Vasingtona, westbound toward the heart of Belgrade with its National Theater, Natural History Museum and the imposing Albanija Building. Bolan turned south on the Terazije Marsala Tita, veering off two blocks later to pick up Sarajevska Balkanska. From there, it was a short jog to Belgrade's public transportation center, where the bus depot and central railroad station stood a hundred yards apart. Foot traffic was moderate to heavy, but most residents of Belgrade still couldn't afford automobiles, and Bolan had no trouble finding a slot for the Porsche. He parked and locked the car, Sascha falling into step beside him as they crossed the asphalt parking lot.

At the proper depot, Bolan checked the posted schedule for the Orient Express, ignoring times and concentrating on the assigned track number. He got his bearings with a rapid visual scan, chose his direction and nodded for Sascha to follow him along the platform.

Both of them were on alert, examining each passerby for any sign that might betray an enemy. Did this one stare too long or glance away too quickly, indicating guilt? Was that one carrying a camera for his holiday along the Adriatic coast, or had he been assigned to capture certain faces on film? Had the umbrella flourished by the tall young man in front of them been fitted with a listening device? Was there an infant in the pram now rolling toward them on the platform, or perhaps a lifeless doll concealing automatic weapons?

Bolan took the job in stride, detecting no apparent adversaries, nothing that would set alarm bells jangling in his brain. That didn't prove they were secure, by any means, but he had done his best until the moment when an enemy revealed himself.

An ambush in the Belgrade station would imply a certain desperation from the other side, but he wasn't prepared to rule it out. The fact that Katz and his companion were aboard the Orient Express didn't mean they were free and clear. Their cover was a fragile thing, at best, and it could fall apart at any moment, anywhere along the way.

Which meant that Bolan had to remain alert, considering all manner of unlikely possibilities. It was a situation he knew well enough from long experience.

In fact, it almost made him feel at home.

The Orient Express

MCCARTER WAS RELIEVED to have the border crossing well behind him, with the train in motion once again. His papers had been good enough for immigration at Szeged and in Subotica, the toughest crossings he'd face until he rejoined Phoenix Force and tried to penetrate Iraq.

With any luck they'd be rolling into Belgrade in another ninety minutes, give or take. From there, it was 275 miles to the Greek frontier, with time out for scheduled stops in Nis, Skopje, and the next border station at Gevgelija. Perhaps eight hours if they made good time, with the crossing well after dark.

He hadn't glimpsed the other men of Phoenix Force when they were at the station, but he trusted Katz to make the subtle touch, however fleeting. By now, the message would have been relayed to Bolan down in Belgrade—but who else was listening in?

McCarter didn't like the fact that other agencies were sharing portions of the game with Stony Man. It made for heightened leak potential, multiplying the inherent risks for all concerned. If anything went wrong...

Instead of dwelling on the thought, he checked his Skorpion again, making sure that it was ready for emergencies. He still hoped they'd manage to avoid a firefight on the train, but he'd be prepared for anything.

As a beginning, he had bribed the porter in his sleeping car to get a copy of the first-class passenger list. There was no such roster for coach, where tickets often sold without advance reservations and the customs men at border crossings moved along the narrow aisles, matching passports to faces.

Scanning down the list, he skipped the names Baranovich, Kirovski and McGill—the latter matching up to his own passport. That left twenty-nine compartments occupied, fifteen of them by couples, plus one family of three. He scratched the family to start, deciding it was too bizarre for anyone to send an eight-year-old along as cover on a killing mission, moving on from there to pick up with the solitary riders first.

Thirteen names. A baker's dozen. Would it prove unlucky for McCarter and his friends this time around? He could tell nothing from the names alone. Eight of them sounded vaguely Slavic, two were Greek, one French, one German, and the last one British or American. For all McCarter knew, the whole thirteen could be a list of pseudonyms for spies and smugglers, fugitives, adulterers, dishonest businessmen. Mistrust was an occupational hazard in McCarter's profession, where names and faces were seldom what they seemed.

Would he have time to check the thirteen travelers before some of them disembarked—or made a move on Katzenelenbogen and the Russian? It was doubtful, but he felt obliged to try.

As for the couples...

All of them were married, if you went by surnames from the list, but that alone defied all demographic odds. Assuming some had lied, intent on keeping up appearances, they might have other secrets tucked away behind drawn curtains. In the old days it had been SOP for Soviet agents to operate in the guise of married couples, young or old. Some of them actually were married, encouaged to cohabitate as a means of preserving state secrets, while others were barely introduced before setting off on their latest assignment. Either way, the domestic cover was effective, diverting suspicion from "average" couples while their suspicious targets were busy looking for dark men in trench coats and snap-brim hats. The Russian teams were—had been—efficient killers, often with the female specially trained to make the final tag.

McCarter wished he could have bugged the various compartments, listened in on private conversations, but he didn't have the time or the equipment needed for the job. No matter, since the language barrier would still have stopped him cold.

The plain fact was that even when he scratched the family of three, he still had twenty-eight compartments and forty-three suspects to cover in first-class alone. By the time he got to coach, the odds were clearly hopeless and he gave up in disgust.

The best that he could do was shadow Katz discreetly, keep his hardware close at hand, and be prepared to jump on anyone or anything that seemed remotely out of place. It left the field wide open for mistakes, but he was strapped for fresh ideas. At least, McCarter thought, the train itself should limit options for a hit on Katzenelenbogen. Barring air strikes or derailment, shooters hoping to escape when they were finished with their work would have to synchronize their movements with a scheduled stop.

But if there was a hitter, and he didn't care about his own survival in the aftermath of an attack...

McCarter frowned and let his right hand come to rest on top of Skorpion.

So much for peace of mind.

Novi Sad, Yugoslavia

IT WAS Rafael Encizo's turn to drive. He held the Citroën sedan at sixty-five along the southbound highway, wishing he could read the road signs as they flickered past him and receded in his rearview mirror. At least the highways were labeled with Arabic numerals, and Gary Manning had done a fair job of navigating from a map so far, but Encizo disliked operating in an area where no one on the team could speak or read the local dialects.

It would be touch and go past Belgrade, when they got to Nis. A wrong turn there and they could wind up in Bulgaria, instead of rolling south toward Greece. Encizo trusted his sense of direction, but he couldn't suppress a vague anxiety as they continued on their way.

Above all else, he hated losing sight of Katzenelenbogen and the Orient Express. The long wait in Subotica had climaxed in a fleeting glimpse of Katz's profile through a window on the train, and they were off to leapfrog Belgrade, shooting for the next stop down the line.

For what?

If someone meant to take the gruff Israeli and his escort down, it stood to reason that their adversary would be waiting on the train itself. There were at least a dozen ways to do the job, once Katz was spotted as a ringer, and they wouldn't have to run the risk of striking at a train in motion, acting like some kind of Slavic Jesse James. A blade or silenced bullet in the corridor or dining car, and you could ditch the weapon in a heartbeat, even jump to freedom if you didn't feel like sitting tight and bluffing out the hand.

The more he thought about it, Encizo suspected they were wasting precious time. It would be smarter all around if they made haste through Greece and Turkey, linked up with their contact for the crossing to Iraq, and ironed out any weak points in the penetration plan before it blew up in their faces. Still, they had their orders, and Brognola had his reasons for arranging things as he had done.

Their course followed the eastern river basin of the Velika Morava, mountains looming on the western flank. The farmers in the area grew corn and grain, tobacco, sugar beets. Smaller villages were spotted here and there between the major towns, with isolated cottages visible from time to time, their chimneys trailing smoke. Encizo spotted tiny figures in the midst of rolling fields, some of them herding sheep or cattle over grazing land. It all seemed alien, a world away from the sordid, violent mission on which they were embarked.

"How far to Nis?" Calvin James asked. He shifted in the Citroën's back seat to make room for his legs.

"About 140 miles southeast of Belgrade," Manning told him, double-checking with the road map lying folded on his knee. "The rate we're going, say three hours plus a little if we don't get lost or stop for anything."

"Like food, you mean?"

"No problem. We're ahead of schedule as it is."

"I don't like dragging out the game this way," James said. "It makes me feel like we're a bunch of sitting ducks."

Encizo knew exactly how he felt, but they were in it now, committed to the plan. "We don't have any choice."

"Besides," Manning interjected, "these ducks can shoot back."

"If they don't pick us off on the wing," James groused.

"We're in the clear, so far. If anyone's expecting heat, it should be Katz."

"You hope we're clear," the onetime Navy Seal replied. "First thing I learned in basic training, just because you don't see hostiles, doesn't mean they're not around."

"You worry too much," Manning said. "Which is nothing but a premature down payment on disaster."

"Geez, now we're stuck with a philosopher."

"You'd rather spend the next two days holed up in some hotel along the Turkish border, waiting for the jump-off to Iraq?"

James thought about it for a moment, his reflected image scowling back at Rafael Encizo from the rear view. "What I wish," he said at last, "was that we had these monkeys spotted somewhere nice and private. We slip in and do our thing, then shag ass home again before Saddam and half his freaking army know we're in the neighborhood."

"Too bad nobody asked us, eh?"

"You got that right."

"Well, since we're here..."

Manning left his comment unfinished, no point in completing the statement. Every member of Phoenix

Force knew where they stood in terms of duty and responsibility.

"We see it through," Calvin James said.

"I guess that's right," Manning agreed.

Encizo felt a slow smile tugging at the corners of his mouth.

"That's right," he said to no one in particular. "I guess that's right."

CHAPTER ELEVEN

Belgrade
Sunday, 1450 hours

A speaker mounted on the wall directly above Bolan's head hissed static for perhaps three seconds, then a scratchy voice began announcing the arrival of the Orient Express in half a dozen major languages. He caught the name first time around, and he was on his feet with Sascha at his side before the bored announcer took a stab at broken English with a heavy Slavic accent. Moving swiftly down the platform, he heard Sascha jogging to keep up.

"What are we looking for?"

"A high sign, almost anything," he said. "Some kind of visual to let us know the game's still on."

It had occurred to Bolan that he didn't have the vaguest physical description of the Russian who was paired with Katz on board the train. The man could easily have passed him on the street, unrecognized, but there was little he could do about it now. At that, the Executioner decided he was better off than Sascha, who was flying blind without a clue what any of the players looked like.

On one hand, that could be an edge of sorts, if she had any kind of double cross in mind. Conversely there was no way she could help him in the hours and days ahead if Bolan kept her in the dark. She'd be less than half an ally then, perhaps an active hindrance.

By the time they reached the train locomotive he had his mind made up. If and when Katz showed himself, Bolan would point him out to Sascha for a visual ID. That way, if anything went wrong and Bolan was eliminated from the game, she'd be able to continue on her own.

But he wouldn't point out McCarter. Not just yet.

A wary player always keeps his hole card to himself.

Without the rigor of a customs check in Belgrade, it was simpler to off-load passengers and board another batch with destinations ranging to the south and west. It still took time, however, and the passengers continuing from Belgrade were at liberty to leave the train and shop or simply stretch their legs, provided that they kept their tickets close at hand.

Three minutes into Bolan's vigil he picked out McCarter, moving briskly toward the depot's magazine stand, glancing left and right along the way. Their eyes met briefly, locked for something like a heartbeat, then McCarter went about his business, bought an English-language paper and began a slow walk back in the direction of the train.

Two minutes later, Yakov Katzenelenbogen stepped down from the second sleeping car, a younger man behind him, sticking close. It had to be the Russian, playing out his role as escort and protector for the benefit of any prying eyes.

"I've got him," Bolan said to Sascha.

"Where."

"At one o'clock. Gray hair, the artificial hand."

"Ah, yes. The younger man beside him?"

"Has to be the Russian," he replied.

Sascha frowned. "Next time, I must bring a camera."

Katz spotted him a moment later, light blue eyes acknowledging a friend and comrade, moving on without enough delay to make a curious observer ask himself what Katz was staring at. The Russian whispered something to him, leaning close, and Katz responded with a shrug. They moved in lockstep toward the station's gift shop, ducking inside and out of sight.

"Let's wait until they're back on board before we leave."

"Of course."

They both knew that the greatest risk of interference would be during scheduled stops. A sunny day like this, with passengers, well-wishers and attendants on the platform, anyone could brush past Katzenelenbogen in the crowd and jab him with a poisoned needle, slip a blade between his ribs. The Russians and their allies had perfected such techniques, so there was some small comfort in the thought of Katz relying on a former agent of the KGB to watch his back. That way, at least, one fox might spot another coming and react before the golden goose became fast food.

How much of Bolan's apprehension was uncalled for? He couldn't have said with any certainty. For all he knew they might be wasting time and effort, watching out for nonexistent enemies along the route of travel when they could have put that time to better use in other ways. But on the other hand...

He saw a slender, dark-skinned man of Arab descent slip through the crowd and hurry toward the gift shop. Bolan fell in step behind him, leaving Sascha on her own to stay or follow. He had closed the gap between them to arm's length when Katz and his companion suddenly emerged. Katz saw the Arab coming, Bolan close behind, and braced himself, his left hand disappearing underneath his jacket. The Executioner's palm was itching for the feel of the Beretta, but he kept it holstered for the moment, picking up his pace and almost stepping on the Arab's heels.

The dark man brushed past Katz without a second glance and disappeared inside the gift shop. Bolan had no option but to follow him, continuing the flow of motion, killing time as he perused a rack of postcards. Sascha stayed outside, her back turned toward the shop as she watched Katz and his companion stroll back to their sleeping car and climb aboard.

Outside, she greeted Bolan with a sympathetic smile. "A false alarm," she said. "It could have been the real thing just as easily, you know."

Behind him, the Arab emerged with several magazines, a paper bag containing candy bars, and started back toward second class. No danger there... or had it simply been a dry run, checking out the target's personal defenses? Did the point man have a spotter hidden somewhere in the crowd, observing Bolan's move to intercept?

If so, too bad.

He didn't have the luxury of standing back and waiting for the final instant to decide if Katz was being jeopardized. All things considered, his response had been appropriate and he'd do the same again.

"We might as well take off," he said, frustration bitter on his tongue.

Another 275 miles to the border, give or take. Six hours minimum before he would be seeing Katz again.

A lifetime, right.

But first, he had to get in touch with Stony Man.

Stony Man Farm
Sunday, 0815 hours

AARON KURTZMAN was working on the remnants of his breakfast when Carmen Delahunt appeared in the staff dining room. Ex-FBI, a natural redhead with the temper to match, the divorced mother of three had been manning computers for the Bureau at Quantico when Hal Brognola lured her away with offers of improved benefits and a personal challenge she couldn't resist. These days, she comprised one-third of Kurtzman's staff in the Stony Man computer complex, sharing duties with colleagues Huntington Wethers and Akiro Tokaido.

At the moment Carmen was on duty with Akiro in the Farm's basement nerve center, and Kurtzman knew it would take something special to bring her upstairs in the middle of her shift. The only question was, would it be special good... or bad.

She made her way past half a dozen members of the grounds crew, chowing down, and walked directly to the table where Kurtzman sat by himself, mopping up some egg yolk with a bit of whole-wheat toast. She sat down uninvited, facing him across the table with a level gaze that had been known to make some fellows lose their train of thought.

"What's up?" Kurtzman asked, thankful that the apprehension didn't come through in his tone.

"We got a call relayed from Striker," Carmen told him. "Visuals confirmed on Katzenelenbogen and McCarter out of Belgrade, more or less on schedule."

Kurtzman shoved his plate away, relief deflating an uncomfortable tightness in his chest. "That's good to know."

"I thought you'd like it." Carmen's smile wasn't predictable, but it was always radiant. "So, have another cup of coffee. I'll be getting back."

"I'm floating as it is," Kurtzman said, wheeling back to clear the table with his chair. "I'll keep you company."

"Suits me."

One of his chairs was motorized, but Kurtzman used the manual whenever possible. It kept his upper body fit and spared him from feeling like the stereotypical "handicapped" person. With a beer or two inside him, Kurtzman had been known to challenge members of the staff at large to arm wrestling, best two of three, and he rarely came out second best.

When he reflected on the shooting that had robbed him of his legs—not often now—it seemed to Kurtzman like a simple twist of fate, no more, no less. He didn't agonize about injustice or the fickle will of God. Life was a crap shoot.

The stairs were too much for his wheelchair, so they passed through the computer room to reach the elevator. Huntington Wethers was running programs on his free time, fingers flying over a keyboard with lightning speed. The black professor, late of Berkeley, glanced up from his work and smiled a silent greeting as they passed.

The elevator took them down one level to the basement War Room, where Akiro Tokaido was holding the fort, chewing bubble gum with intense concentration, the earphones of a compact CD player clamped to his skull. The echoes of Metallica were audible from twenty feet away, and Kurtzman wondered what it must have sounded like inside Akiro's head, but the hellacious music never seemed to break the young man's concentration. Rather, the "distraction" somehow managed to enhance his work, as if the raw energy of screaming voices and guitars combined with Akiro's innate genius, pushing the unique mind toward critical mass.

Tokaido saw them coming, raised a hand in greeting to his boss and went back to the program he was running. Kurtzman didn't have to check to know the younger man was keeping track of several fronts at once. Their forces were divided, physically at risk, and there was built-in lag time to the system of communication borrowed from the CIA. Unfortunately there was no alternative, as even Stony Man didn't possess the requisite technology to keep her agents constantly in touch, regardless of their situations or locations on the globe.

So they made due with what they had, and it was never good enough in Kurtzman's mind. He worried every moment that the team was out of touch, although he seldom let it show. Displays of sentiment were worse than useless in strategic situations; there was nothing to be gained from muttered oaths and wringing hands, but dabbling in emotion could distract a handler when his agents in the field required his full attention. Better he should fret in silence, concentrating on his job, than watch his best friends die because his mind was elsewhere when it should have been at work.

Around the War Room, giant wall screens were connected to the satellite surveillance system shared by various components of the American intelligence community. At the flick of a switch Kurtzman could tune in Ukrainian wheat fields, the reeking slums of Calcutta, or the busy coca trails in Peru. Advanced technology permitted him to scan the license plates outside the Russian embassy in Paris, maybe count heads at Khaddafi's birthday party in Tripoli. Each passing month brought new advancements in the field, but he could see and know only so much.

And in the last analysis, it still came down to soldiers on the ground, bold men who took the information gleaned from spies, bugs and satellites, devised a working strategy to solve specific problems, and went on to risk their lives in situations where the odds on their success were slim to none.

This time, at least, the Stony Man team had allies in the field, albeit grudging ones. Relations had been strained with Israel during recent months, and no one yet knew what to make of Russia or the brand-new Commonwealth of Independent States. Kurtzman personally thought the recent change in Russia had been too widespread and fundamental to be any kind of trick or double cross, but there were other analysts—some of them highly placed—who still saw any overture from Moscow as a baited trap.

Kurtzman wheeled himself into the U-shaped control console, stroked a half-dozen keys, and a detailed map of Eastern Europe filled one of the screens. Another keystroke, and the focus zoomed in, cropping the map to an area between latitude 35 degrees and 45 degrees north, and longitude 20 degrees and 30 degrees east.

Here lay the battlefield where Striker and Phoenix Force would spend most of their time in the next two days. South of Belgrade, the rail lines and major highways ran through Nis and Skopje in Yugoslavia, crossing the Greek frontier and continuing eastward through Sérrai, Dráma, Xánthi, Komotiní. In Turkey their first major stop would be Instanbul, guarding the Bosporus, before the long run through Izmit, Adapazari, Bilecik and Eskisehir, into Ankara.

And then?

He didn't bother shifting focus on the map. Once Katzenelenbogen and his escort left the train, their route of travel would be anybody's guess. With an Iraqi escort there could be no checking in along the way. It would be just like dropping off the map until, God willing, they showed up again along the border, bound for a location yet unknown where Katz's Russian "colleagues" were constructing warheads for Saddam Hussein.

Two days—less now, that they were underway from Belgrade. On the one hand, Kurtzman longed for swift solutions, anything to bring his good friends safely home. But on the other, when he thought about the distances involved and all they had to do, he wondered whether two days was enough.

"They'll make it." Carmen Delahunt was standing at his elbow, studying the giant wall screen.

"Maybe."

"Maybe, hell. I wouldn't want to be the other team right now."

He thought about that for a moment, and finally said, "Let's see what we can do to help. I want a double check on Langley's contact in Iraq. Let's tap the Company's computer on the QT, if we can."

"No sweat."

"I want to know what this guy has for breakfast, where he has his laundry done, you name it. If he likes the girls—or boys—I want a rundown."

"Getting personal?"

"Damn right. If this thing blows up, I don't want anybody coming back with how we could have saved it if we'd only done a little more."

"You know we can't get any guarantees."

"Agreed, but there's the flip side, too."

"How's that?"

The Bear looked grim as he replied. "If there's a setup in the works, we'll have to go for payback. I want to be ready in case we have to reach out and touch someone."

"Good thinking. Shall I run Hal's Langley contact, just in case?"

"It couldn't hurt."

But he was wrong on that score, Kurtzman thought. If they were being set up for a sellout, anywhere along the line, he meant to see that someone hurt like hell.

Arlington, Virginia

HAL BROGNOLA HAD considered going in to work that Sunday morning, but he didn't want to call attention to himself by deviating from his set routine. Instead he got up early, cheated out of sleep by anxious thoughts, and fixed himself a frozen waffle in the toaster oven. Helen was away that weekend, visiting her sister in Vermont, which meant the big Fed had the house all to himself.

The call came through ten minutes after it was logged at Stony Man, a hundred miles away. No details, but they had a visual on Katzenelenbogen and McCarter at their second major stop, in Belgrade.

They were on their way.

Brognola felt a churning in his stomach, unrelated to the frozen waffle. It had been some time since he had run an operation in the field, and he could still remember butting heads with Bolan in the early days of Bolan's "hopeless" one-man war against the syndicate. A firefight in Las Vegas had come dangerously close to being Hal Brognola's last hurrah—or Bolan's—but the two of them had pulled it out somehow.

Now here they were, a world away from each other, but the war went on. The more things changed, the more they stayed the same.

Brognola's den was situated in the southeast corner of the house, its window offering a view of grass that sloped away to trees in back. Beyond the trees, a winding tributary of the grand Potomac, where the *Monitor* and *Merrimack* had dueled within an easy cannon shot of Washington.

The old days, right.

Nowadays, your enemies could spy on you from outer space or plant computer viruses in software that would send ballistic missiles looping miles away from their programmed targets. Warships didn't need to navigate the Chesapeake when they could lie two hundred miles offshore, submerged, and drop cruise missiles on the White House steps.

The war went on, but it was everywhere. Some days, Brognola felt that he had seen and done enough, that it was time to pull the pin and let some youthful eager beaver take the helm. Before he had a chance to let the feeling settle in, though, there was always something to distract him. Some new crisis that demanded personal attention, something he'd rather do himself, in lieu of trusting it to less experienced hands.

A file lay open on the desk in front of him, and Brognola made every effort to concentrate. Sometime Saturday night, Able Team had slipped across the border from San Diego into Baja California and they were still out of touch, suggesting a problem that might be severe. They'd been assigned to break a ring of scavengers that had been running wets and drugs across the border, killing anyone who tried to stop them and a few who stumbled on the route by accident. Such deaths were almost routine in southern California, and it had taken the machine-gun slaughter of thirteen illegal aliens—stripped of their meager belongings and left to rot in the desert—before anyone started to take the problem seriously.

Now, three of Brognola's men had dropped off the face of the map in enemy territory, and it didn't get any worse than that.

Unless he looked eastward.

When he thought about it that way, every field operative he had was in mortal jeopardy at the moment, all of them effectively beyond his reach. If something went drastically wrong between Belgrade and Ankara, there was precious little Brognola could do to relieve the situation.

At least his men were out of Hungary, thank God. Authorities in Yugoslavia were no less strict, but Langley had been flirting with the government for years, and there might still be some faint hope of working out a deal. The best place for a showdown, if it had to come, would be in Greece. The Greek police were poorly trained and organized, habitually overworked and understaffed. The Turks, in contrast, had been waging war on terrorists and narco-smugglers for years, acquiring valuable experience in hunting desperate men.

As for Iraq, the big Fed didn't even want to think about it, but he had no choice. The satellite surveillance photos showed him half a dozen sites well north of Baghdad where a nuclear facility could be established, tests conducted as the need arose. Of course, when it came down to detonating warheads there would be no way to cover up the evidence. But Brognola was troubled by a thought that had begun to haunt him, cropping up at all odd hours of the day and night.

Suppose they didn't need to test the warheads? Everybody knew that many of the tests conducted in Nevada's underground facility were pointless, going over old, familiar ground with warheads tested time and time again. You started out with a dozen bombs, identical in their construction and component parts. You detonated one to find out if it worked, and then it was gone. That left eleven, but the only one you're *sure* about had been reduced to pulsing molecules.

It was a costly, endless cycle, never mind environmental trauma, but suppose the Russians and Iraqis didn't waste their time on tests? Polyarni and Serpukhov knew their jobs inside out, no reason to suspect they'd construct a dud when they had each built several thousand weapons in the past two decades. If Saddam Hussein was ready for a leap of faith, he could unleash a shitstorm on the world without the warning of a test launch that would give his precious site away. For all they knew the bastards could be working underground.

Brognola felt a headache coming on. He closed the Able file, rocked backward in his swivel chair, knuckling his temples until the pain receded slightly and settled into a slow, steady throb at the base of his skull. No problem, he could knock it back with coffee and Excedrin anytime he wanted to.

He thought briefly that he was getting too old for this, but closed his mind to the suggestion of retirement, giving up the ship. His people needed him right now.

More to the point, he needed them.

CHAPTER TWELVE

The Orient Express
Sunday, 2250 hours

The border crossing into Greece was a formality without the detailed scrutiny applied to every passenger in Hungary and Yugoslavia. It was well after dark when they crossed the frontier, rolling south to Thessaloníki, then doubling back for the loop past Sérrai. Yakov Katzenelenbogen let himself relax a bit with Yugoslavia behind them, knowing that the Soviets had never had a strong influence on the Greeks since the traumatic civil war in 1948.

They weren't safe, by any means, but for the next two hundred miles Katz was, perhaps, a trifle more secure than he had been while traveling through nations of the former Warsaw Pact.

It was a shame, Katz thought, that darkness would obscure his passage through the marvelous Greek countryside. Sunrise would find them somewhere west of Istanbul, the best part of eleven hours from his final destination on the Orient Express. From Ankara the rest of it remained a vague trek overland to reach the Turkish border with Iraq.

Long years had passed since Katz was last in Greece, on a vacation, resting up from injuries sustained on a covert assignment in Tunisia. He had come to love the people, with their easygoing view of life, their classic flexibility when it came down to rules and regulations. Smuggling was a way of life in Greece, especially in the islands, but the men and women involved were cut from a nineteenth-century mold, more adventuresome than strictly criminal, akin to early buccaneers. There had been lazy evenings, fueled with ouzo, when the gruff Israeli told a somewhat altered version of his life to new acquaintances and heard their stories in return. He sometimes thought he might retire to Greece one day... if he survived that long.

Now, here he was again, just passing through, dark purposes concealed by outer darkness as the countryside was masked in shadow. It was better so, he thought, his frown reflected in the windowpane. This way, the country he had come to love wouldn't be tarnished by the memories of Katzenelenbogen's present job, whatever it entailed.

He hadn't spoken to his Russian escort since they parted in the dining car after supper. The walls between compartments weren't thick, but built-in noises of the moving train allowed for privacy on a par with the average American motel room. Lying on his bunk, doors firmly wedged, his left hand resting on the Browning automatic, Katz reviewed his day and searched for anything he might have missed, some bit of information that could give him an advantage at the other end.

It had been close in Belgrade, with Bolan moving toward him through the crowd as Katz emerged from the station's gift shop, the slender Arab sandwiched in between them, heading on a hard collision course. A false alarm, as it turned out, but Katz's stomach had been churning as he got back on the train. Tyumen had remarked upon the incident in passing, but he made no mention of the tall American or anybody else.

How much, in fact, had Tyumen seen? It would be foolish to mistake his silence for blindness. He had to have seen Bolan, another face in the crowd, but if he linked the stranger with Katzenelenbogen, the Russian was content to hold his tongue. At supper there had been no reference to the Belgrade stop, but Tyumen had seemed even more alert than usual, checking out their fellow diners, flicking glances back and forth at anyone who passed along the center aisle.

Katz had to assume the worst and keep his guard up. If Tyumen had a mental fix on Bolan, it would simply mean a need for greater caution when they next crossed paths. The Russian would be neatly filed away in Bolan's mental mug file by now, preserved for the duration as a hedge against mistakes.

There had been something else, as well—or someone else, to be exact. A woman, young and pretty, following in Bolan's tracks as he prepared to take the Arab down. Coincidence, perhaps, but Katz knew that the Executioner was supposed to meet with an Israeli agent. Tel Aviv's contribution to the international team effort. Would the Mossad send a woman out to do this kind of work?

He knew the answer going in: of course they would. Outnumbered and surrounded, with their backs against the sea, the Israelis had pioneered sexual integration of the military and intelligence services in 1948. Women fought on the front lines in Israel's wars, both overt and clandestine. Any dated notion of the "weaker sex" had long been washed away by blood in Gaza, on the Golan Heights, along the nation's borders where an endless war of hit-and-run had dragged on, more or less unbroken, for the better part of half a century.

When every living body counts for self-defense, discrimination on the grounds of sex was more than simply out-of-date. It could be tantamount to suicide.

Katz switched off the overhead light, returning to the window and watching the dark ridge of mountains roll past. He imagined bright sunshine on vineyards and olive trees, children playing on the rocky hillsides, naked men and women sunning at the beach.

Another time, perhaps.

This night, he had a long dark journey to complete, and he was less than halfway there.

When he had seen enough of darkness, Katzenelenbogen lay back on his bunk and closed his eyes.

Xánthi, Greece

DINING LATE was fashionable in Greece, and the stylish restaurant selected by Bolan would be serving patrons until one a.m. He didn't plan to take that long, but he was hungry from the drive and hadn't felt like making due with substandard room-service fare at the hotel. Sascha Lentz, seated opposite Bolan and wearing a simple, low-cut dress, seemed none the worse for wear from hours on the road.

They had made decent time from Belgrade, but their plans didn't extend to driving through the night. The Orient Express was well behind them now, and they'd be in hot pursuit again before the train pulled out of Istanbul. Meanwhile, the interests of their mission weren't served by terminal fatigue.

"You've been to Greece before?" Sascha asked, sipping a domestic wine.

"In passing." There seemed to be no point in spilling out his whole life story, when he couldn't even trust the lady with his name.

"I visited the islands once, two years ago. It is my first time on the mainland."

"Join Mossad and see the world?"

"I've seen my share. And you?"

He shrugged. "The dark side, mostly."

"Is there any other side?"

"I'd like to think so."

"In my homeland we are taught to understand that every day may be our last. It is twenty years now since the last declared war with our neighbors, but the killing never stops. You read about some of the larger incidents in Western papers, but the rest are lost. Along the borders, in the kibbutzim, a week does not go by without some act of violence directed at my people."

"Last I heard, you didn't take it lying down."

"Why should we? If the Holocaust has taught us nothing else, it must reveal the lethal folly of appeasement and collaboration with our enemies."

"You'll get no argument from me on that score," Bolan said.

"And yet, your government would rather we kept quiet, sitting on our hands while terrorists invade our homes."

"You know as well as I do," Bolan answered, "that reality and politics are sometimes worlds apart."

"Which brings us back to here and now. Is this reality?"

"I haven't quite made up my mind."

"You were prepared to kill that man today in Belgrade."

"If I had to, yes."

"Does it come easily?"

"I do my job," he said, "whatever it entails."

"Then we are not so different, you and I. We come from pain and dedicate ourselves to the protection of our countries. May I ask you something?"

"You can always ask. I might not answer."

Her voice dropped to a whisper. "Are you really from the CIA?"

"Let's say we have a common interest in the outcome of our present difficulty."

"So. I knew it. You are not the type."

"What type is that?" he asked.

"The cloak-and-dagger, Cold War type. I know a soldier when I see one."

"Is that good or bad?"

The lady frowned and took another sip of wine.

"I'll let you know."

The Orient Express

NAJRAN ABBAS HAD MADE his mind up to eliminate the Russian pigs that night. Tehran had told him to apply his own initiative, and so he would. There was no point in waiting to report or calling for assistance when one man could do the job alone. Abbas hadn't been chosen for his fluency in languages or expertise in European history. He was a killer, and he knew exactly what he had to do.

The first thing he required would be a porter's uniform. There might be spares on board, but he couldn't expect to find them in the time required. Abbas was anxious to be finished with his work before they reached the Turkish border. He'd leave the train at Alexandroúpolis, before the frontier crossing, and make his own way back to Iran in good time.

As for the Russians who had made it safely to Iraq, Najran Abbas hoped he'd be dispatched to kill them soon. A clean sweep for the Holy Revolution and his motherland if he succeeded. If he failed, a place in paradise was guaranteed.

It was a no-lose situation, either way.

The young man left his overnight bag wedged beneath his seat, rose silently and moved along the aisle in the direction of first class. The dining car was closed to customers, but you could still pass through in transit to another car. He reached the first-class carriage farthest from the locomotive, caught a glimpse of the conductor moving toward him from the other end and slipped inside the nearest lavatory. Standing in the darkness there, he left the door ajar, his keen eyes covering the narrow wedge of corridor that he could see. He made no move to draw the pistol or the dagger that he wore beneath his coat.

It was a relatively simple move. As the conductor passed his hiding place, Najran Abbas slipped out behind him, locked one arm around his victim's throat and put his weight behind a vicious twist from left to right. The crack of separating vertebrae was clearly audible, the stranger going limp, deadweight in Najran's arms.

He dragged the corpse into the lavatory, locked the door this time and set about collecting his disguise. Unfortunately there had been no time to choose a perfect fit. The slacks were loose around his waist and short in the leg, but he compensated by wearing them low on his hips. He kept his own white shirt and slip-on shoes, relieving the conductor of his black knit tie. The jacket, once again, was half a size too large, but he preferred the loose fit for a fast draw with his pistol or in case he had to fight.

Surprisingly the dead man's cap fit Najran perfectly. He checked his image in the bathroom mirror, left the jacket open for quick access to his weapons. If a passenger should glimpse him with his uniform in disarray, it would be logical to think that he was finishing his shift. And if someone had the nerve to stop and question him, it would turn out to be a terminal mistake.

One matter left, before he went about his business. The conductor was a problem, taking up a public rest room where his corpse might be discovered anytime by anyone. Najran Abbas was counting on a simple execution and a peaceful ride to the next scheduled stop, where he'd disembark and vanish. Let the two dead Russians be discovered at the Turkish border crossing, or perhaps in Istanbul. It made no difference, just so long as he wasn't aboard the train.

Emerging from the lavatory, he glanced left and right along the corridor. He brought the dead man out, one lifeless arm across his shoulders so Najran appeared to be supporting someone who was drunk or feeling ill, perhaps a first-class passenger who needed help returning to his own compartment for the night.

But they were moving toward the observation platform now, between the dining car and sleeper. Once inside the noisy air lock, Abbas checked his flanks again before he opened the door. A sudden rush of wind assaulted him, almost removed his stolen cap, but the assassin raised a hand to hold it fast.

No time to waste. He lifted the conductor like a sack of grain and dragged him to the open doorway, balanced on one hip. A twist and hurl, jujitsu fashion, sent his victim sprawling through the door and into rushing darkness. One foot struck the doorjamb with a heavy thud before it disappeared, but the conductor was beyond all pain by now.

When he had closed and latched the door, Abbas took time to straighten his rumpled uniform and check the silenced pistol in its shoulder rig.

All ready.

He was smiling as he left the observation platform, moving easily along the corridor past various compartments where a dozen strangers were contending with their dreams.

Komotiní, Greece

"WE NEED TO MAKE a pit stop," Gary Manning told his two companions, glancing at the Citroën's fuel gauge.

"I could use a pit myself," James said.

"It's late to look for a hotel," Encizo noted, shifting his position in the cramped back seat.

"Don't need a room," James answered. "Anyplace at all to stretch and catch some Zs would suit me fine."

The more he thought about it, Manning realized that he could also use some rest. "I'll see what I can do."

They found a filling station on the western edge of town. The owner was about to close up for the night, but hospitality and simple greed persuaded him to fill the Citroën's tank and check the oil. He also told them of a campground five miles down the road, where Western tourists often parked their cars and spent the night without harrassment from police or thieves.

This night, they had the campground almost to themselves. A single compact car stood dark and silent on the far side of the gravel parking lot, and Manning nosed in the Citroën as far away from the other vehicle as possible. The Phoenix warriors stretched their legs, shoes crunching on the gravel underfoot, and James went off to scout the nearby hillside, returning moments later with a bright smile on his face.

"I found my bivouac," he said. "Soft grass, fair cover, gravel on the slope to tip me off if anyone comes calling. You two want to split the car up, be my guest."

"Hey, thanks a million." Encizo made a sour face. "Why don't we all sleep on the hill?"

"You snore, amigo. Anyway, this spot I found is just my size."

"Take some insurance with you," Manning cautioned, "just in case."

"You read my mind." James opened the Citroën's trunk and removed a squat Beretta submachine gun, tucking it inside a blanket. "Me and little snubby ought to sleep just fine. I'll see you boys at sunup."

"Don't be late," Encizo said. "We might forget and leave without you."

"What, and miss my smiling face?"

When he was gone, Encizo drew a coin from his pocket, spun it high into the air and caught it in his palm. "Heads takes the back seat, 'kay?"

"Suits me."

Encizo showed the coin, a frowning profile stamped in bronze.

"Don't let that gearshift cramp your style, amigo."

Manning released his breath in a long, weary sigh. "You're all heart."

"So I'm told."

The Orient Express

IN RETROSPECT, McCarter thought it was a fluke he saw the man at all, much less in time to head him off. Emerging from his own compartment in frustration, foiled at sleeping by an overactive mind, he spotted the conductor coming from a distance, paused, and did a rapid double take.

McCarter didn't recognize the man—no reason why he should—but it wasn't the same conductor he had met on two occasions, climaxed by McCarter's payoff for the first-class passenger list. Still, any train this size must have a number of conductors working different shifts and stations. It wasn't the simple notion of an unfamiliar face that set McCarter off, so much as the appearance of the man.

For starters he was clearly not a European. Arab from the look of him, or possibly a dark-skinned South American. His jacket didn't seem to fit, and it was open in the front, a breech of etiquette that would have earned the man at least a reprimand from his superiors. Most curious of all, he held a dark blue bundle in his left hand that appeared to be a rolled-up jacket with a matching pair of slacks.

It was no way to treat a suit, unless the owner had more pressing matters on his mind than fashion.

The short conductor met his gaze with eyes that skittered out and back, like nervous insects, breaking contact after half a second. There was something furtive in the gesture as he brought his right hand up to pull the gaping jacket shut.

Concealing what?

McCarter's mind was racing as he stepped aside to let the dark man pass. He had a choice to make, and precious little time for calculating odds and averages. The man was headed straight for the compartments occuped by Katz and his companion. If McCarter tipped his hand with the conductor and it turned out his suspicions were erroneous, his cover would be well and truly shot to hell. But if he didn't act...

His mind made up, McCarter turned abruptly, came up on the dark man's blind side, palming the H&K P-7 automatic in one fluid movement. His left hand gripped the conductor's shoulder from behind, the muzzle of his weapon boring in behind the man's right ear.

"Don't make a sound. We're going back to my compartment, right?"

The dark man stiffened, recognized the cold steel pressed against his flesh and opted not to struggle. Nodding, he offered no resistance as McCarter steered him back along the corridor in the direction he had come from, standing frozen in his tracks while the Briton unlocked the door and pushed it open.

"In."

The conductor did as he was told, arms hanging limp at his sides, his left hand still clutching the bundle of clothes. McCarter shut the door and latched it with his free hand, keeping his prisoner covered all the while.

"Now turn around," he said. "Let's find out who you are."

The dark man turned to face him, cold eyes concentrating on the gun. His face betrayed no anxiety or fear. He seemed almost accustomed to the fact of weapons being pointed at his chest.

"Your clothes?" McCarter nodded toward the bundle in his captive's hand.

The stranger nodded, still not speaking.

"Let it drop."

A soft plop sounded as the rumpled slacks and jacket hit the floor.

"You need to find yourself another tailor, mate. That uniform's a rotten fit."

The man shrugged, made no reply.

"Let's see what's underneath the jacket, shall we?"

Grudgingly McCarter's hostage started to remove the jacket, right arm first, the thin strap of a shoulder holster visible as one arm wriggled free.

"That's far eno—"

Too late. The dark man hit a crouch and whipped his jacket off the other arm, shiny buttons glinting as he flung it in McCarter's face. The Briton chopped his pistol down and sideways, whipping the coat aside, and saw his adversary groping for the weapon slung beneath his arm.

The Phoenix Force warrior launched himself through space, straight-arming the dark man with an open palm that mashed his lips and nose. Off balance, they went down together, the assassin wriggling free and kicking backward toward McCarter's face. The former SAS commando took it on the shoulder, rolled away and came up tugging at the jacket, which had wrapped itself around his gun hand.

Dammit!

The dark man was reaching for his pistol again, a snarl etched on his face. McCarter let his own P-7 go, still tangled in the uniform jacket, and threw himself at the assassin with both hands outstretched. His target tried to sidestep, but McCarter caught him with a forearm to the jaw and knocked him backward, sprawling on the bunk. A wild kick grazed McCarter's hip and staggered him, but he recovered swiftly, boring in.

The gunman had his pistol out, its muzzle fitted with a compact silencer. McCarter chopped the gun aside and heard its dull report, the bullet drilling through his mattress and away. His knee made grinding contact with the shooter's groin, and then he had the gun arm pinned beneath him, both hands locked around his adversary's throat.

The knife came out of nowhere, flashing toward his face. McCarter parried with an elbow, gripped the slender wrist and held it off with one hand, fingers clenching tighter on the other as his enemy turned red, then purple, running out of oxygen. It took the best part of a minute and a half to strangle him, and even when his body had relaxed in death, McCarter kept his hold for sixty seconds more.

Insurance.

Afterward, he had the task of cleaning up. His adversary was a small man, and the window served him nicely as an exit hatch. He worked the body out by stages, carefully avoiding contact with the trousers where his adversary's bowels had loosened in the final instant of his life. The jacket, gun and dagger followed, lost in darkness, and McCarter left the window open to air out the compartment, dispersing gun smoke and other smells. There was nothing he could do about the mattress, short of stalling any porter who arrived to make the bed.

One down, and he had very nearly blown it, first by missing his opponent, then by hesitating for a micro-second when he should have dropped the bastard in his tracks.

How many other enemies were on board the train?

McCarter grimaced at the thought and said a silent prayer of thanks for his insomnia.

There would be time enough to sleep if he survived the next two days.

CHAPTER THIRTEEN

Ipsala, Turkey
Monday, 0630 hours

Once beyond the border checkpoint, Bolan let the Porsche unwind, taking advantage of the Bosch K-Jetronic fuel injection system that could bring the sports car from a standing start to sixty miles per hour in 8.4 seconds. The Porsche's top speed had been clocked at 145 miles per hour, but Bolan settled for a comfortable eighty-five, trusting his skill plus the independent front and rear suspension systems to keep him on the road. Sascha seemed to enjoy the ride, cranking her window down and letting the wind blow her hair out in tawny streamers behind her.

They had turned in shortly after midnight, up again at five o'clock for a breakfast of black coffee, rolls and preserves. It was a short drive from Alexandroúpolis to the border, where their passports were scrutinized by a sleepy-looking customs officer. He asked them several questions, ascertained that they were both on holiday with nothing to declare, and let them pass without examining the vehicle.

The Orient Express would be ahead of them by now, en route to Istanbul, but Bolan had no doubt that he could overtake the train before it crossed the Bosporus. From there Katz had the last leg of his journey into Ankara, with Phoenix Force presumably on hand to cover him while Bolan made a beeline for the border and a scheduled meeting with their contact from Iraq.

Eight hundred miles and then some, once they cleared the sprawling mass of Istanbul. Another long day on the road before they finally settled down to business.

"It seems too easy, so far." Sascha's voice was quiet, introspective.

"Does it?"

She was half-turned in her seat to face him now, one leg drawn up and tucked beneath her. "They were ready with Vasili Nabakov in Petrograd," she said. "It makes no sense that they would leave Baranovich unsupervised."

"He had a watchdog with him, you'll remember. That's the point of putting in a two-man team."

"I don't mean that. One pair of eyes is not enough with so much cash and international embarrassment at stake. If the Mossad was handling this project, we would have at least two backup agents covering Baranovich around the clock until he was delivered in Iraq."

"You think we're blown?"

She frowned. "Let's say I'm happy that my orders don't require me to change places with your friend."

"Who said he was a friend?"

"You didn't have to. Back in Belgrade I saw more than just concern for a successful mission."

"So, they're training psychics now in Tel Aviv."

"I don't need ESP," she told him. "Everyone has feelings. Almost everyone."

They drove in silence for a time, Bolan keeping an eye out for highway patrols as he held the Porsche up to speed. He had covered another five or six miles when Sascha spoke again.

"You trust the contact who will take us to Iraq?"

"I've never met the man."

"Then your superiors must trust him."

"To a point, at least."

"I think he might not be so helpful if he knew I represented the Mossad."

"We'll let it be our little secret," Bolan said.

"And when we cross the border, then what?"

Bolan shrugged. "We take it one step at a time. Locate the target, check it out, go on from there."

"You understand the way my people feel about Saddam Hussein?"

"I have a fair idea."

"Right now, he is the worst of those who plot against us. There are others, certainly, but they take turns. Today Khaddafi is a 'moderate,' and the Iranians are more concerned with their domestic problems than jihad. Tomorrow we might have to deal with Syria's Assad. The names and faces change, but they are all the same at heart."

"I know the feeling," Bolan told her.

"Then you will understand if I am not content to simply find our target, even 'check it out.' Destruction of Iraq's atomic weapon program is a top priority for Israel."

"And for the United States," he said. "We might not have an army sitting on the border, but we're not about to let Saddam start World War Three if we can help it. I was sent to take all necessary steps to neutralize the threat."

"We understand each other, then."

"I thought we worked that out in Belgrade," Bolan replied.

"I don't want any failure to communicate. This mission is of critical importance to my country. Anyone who tries to interfere with disposition of the matter will be treated as an enemy."

"I hope your disposition doesn't call for suicide."

"I'm not afraid to die," she told him, but her face had lost a bit of color.

"That doesn't make it mandatory," Bolan said. "Where I come from, we like to live and fight another day, if possible."

"If possible," she echoed, turning back to face the highway straight ahead. "And if it's not?"

"We do our best," the Executioner replied, "and raise some hell before we go."

The Orient Express

NIKOLAI TYUMEN was awakened early by the sound of voices in the corridor outside. He rose and took the Browning automatic pistol with him, moving barefoot toward the door. A cautious man, he listened for a moment with his ear against the door before he threw the latch and inched it open, peering through the crack.

Two men in blue conductors' uniforms were arguing, the younger, taller man gesticulating as he spoke, punctuating his answers with shrugs and frowns. They didn't seem to notice Tyumen, but he kept them covered from behind the door and eavesdropped on their conversation for another moment.

"He must be here," the older man snapped. "Where could he go?"

The young man shrugged again and spread his hands. "An accident, perhaps."

"What kind of accident?"

Tyumen cleared his throat to silence them. "Excuse me. What has happened?"

This would be the moment, if they meant to rush him, and his finger tightened on the Browning's trigger. Any hostile move from either one of them and he would open fire directly through the door.

"Excuse, sir. It is nothing to concern the passengers."

"Someone is missing from the train?" Tyumen asked.

The older man was blushing now. "It seems that one of our conductors has decided not to work today. When he is found, the unemployment will become a permanent condition, I assure you."

"Ah. Good luck."

When neither of them made a move in his direction, Tyumen closed the door and locked it after him. He kept the pistol cocked and easily within his reach as he began to dress, mind turning over what he had been told.

Employees failing to report for work were commonplace, almost routine in any job. It would be more unusual, he thought, on board a train where there was no escape from duty, nowhere for a slacker to conceal himself. The man couldn't step out to have a drink or see his mistress, pack his car and drive away on some unscheduled holiday. It stood to reason that his comrades would have checked the lost man's quarters, checked the train from end to end in case he might have fallen ill or suffered injury. If he was gone, it meant that he had left the train somehow, but surely the conductors still on duty would have noted and reported a departing colleague.

In other circumstances Tyumen would have instantly dismissed the problem from his mind. It made no difference to him if a train conductor lost his job for taking off without official leave. In terms of service one man more or less would hardly cause a ripple on the Orient Express.

This time around, however, the Russian was forced to look at each and every odd event through different eyes. There might be dozens—even hundreds—of convenient explanations for a conductor's disappearance on the train, but all that he could think of was his mission and the strange coincidence.

If it could even be described as a coincidence.

He'd assume the worst, then. Let his paranoia run amok and see where it could take him with a theory to explain the facts. If the conductor disappeared, the action must be either voluntary or against his will. Deliberate flight could point to a variety of motives, one of which might indicate a watcher paid to shadow Tyumen and his charge. Conversely, if the missing man had been abducted, even killed, he might have witnessed something he wasn't supposed to see.

The preparations for an ambush on the train, perhaps?

Tyumen knew he should have asked what time the man disappeared, but it would seem too curious for him to barge outside and ask the question now. Besides, it sounded like the two conductors had retreated from his car, their voices trailing off to nothing shortly after he had closed his door.

It might be possible to ask around the dining car, perhaps some other member of the staff. The timing mattered only insofar as it related to a possible assault upon Tyumen or the man posing as Ivan Baranovich. If the conductor had been missing for a period of hours, killed by an assassin to prevent his sounding an alarm, the stalker should have made his move by now. The longer he delayed, the more risk he incurred—as now—from an alert among the other members of the staff.

But if the man had gone missing in the past half hour, say, then Tyumen should still be on alert, prepared for anything.

No problem there. He had been watching since the day before he met his Western contact, back in Budapest. He wouldn't let himself relax until the job was well behind them and his smallish flat in Moscow welcomed his return.

Tyumen finished with his tie, slipped on his jacket and tucked the Browning out of sight beneath his arm. The dining car would just be opening for breakfast, and danger always gave the Russian operative an appetite. He'd invite his colleague to join him, go on by himself if "Baranovich" preferred to remain in his compartment.

In either case he'd remain on maximum alert.

It was the only way to stay alive.

Istanbul, Turkey

IN ONE RESPECT Istanbul's main railway station was literally the end of the line. Bounded by the Sea of Marmara on the south and the Bosporus on the east, it was a terminus in every sense of the word, requiring passengers to board a ferry and cross to the east bank before they could continue their journey by rail. There was a bridge four miles north for pedestrians and motorists, but this would be the place for Mike Belasko to catch another glimpse of his friend, before the ferry sailed.

In Sascha Lentz's view it was the perfect place for touching base with her control.

Belasko had his cutout numbers for the CIA, and she had hers for the Mossad. In Istanbul she used a pay phone at the railroad station, dialed the number of a small apartment in Topkapi and her call was automatically relayed to Tel Aviv. She didn't recognize the voice that answered her, but she could picture the facility, its bank of telephones, with three or four young men and women dressed in casual attire, recording coded messages as calls came in from all around the world.

With nothing major to report she didn't linger on the line. Identified by reference to a password, she announced that they were still on schedule, ready for their second contact with the transit team. No difficulties yet, and no word of a final destination in Iraq. The message, couched in language that a simple tourist might employ while speaking to a friend or relative back home, took something less than sixty seconds of her time. As Sascha cradled the receiver, she could only wonder how her various superiors would feel with no news coming in.

At least, she thought, they were securely tucked away in Tel Aviv. The mission wouldn't truly cast its shadow over anyone at home unless she failed and the Hussein regime was able to complete its deadly work. In that case, Sascha calculated, she'd already be dead, a failure to her people and her native land.

But not just yet.

She picked out Belasko, a tall man with his back turned, standing in the shadow of the railway station, checking out the platform. They had beat the Orient Express to Istanbul, but it was due at any moment now, crowds gathering to board or greet arriving passengers. She scanned the faces, profiles, backs of heads, as if she could detect an enemy on sight, perhaps pick out a man or woman whom she recognized.

They had a bulging file on Arab terrorists in Tel Aviv, complete with photographs and dossiers that cataloged events from childhood to their latest escapade. Each working agent was required to memorize those faces, hold them fast against the day when one might accidentally present itself in person and alerts could be dispatched, a hit team fielded to retaliate for still-unpunished crimes.

It was a rule of thumb in Israel that the military and Mossad would never rest until a terrorist responsible for crimes against the state was found and made to pay for his atrocity. Sometimes the hunt went on for years or decades, as with Adolf Eichmann, but the searchers wouldn't rest until conclusive proof of death was finally in hand. Mossad had debts outstanding from the Munich massacre of 1972, and there were those who still insisted Dr. Mengele had managed to survive, despite four separate skulls identified by aging friends and relatives.

With the Iraqi missiles, though, she understood that there could be no "next time." If Saddam Hussein achieved his goal of building an arsenal, there'd be no one left in Israel to pursue him with the vengeance of the just. From Metulfa in the north to Elath in the south, from Rafah to Jerusalem, there'd be nothing but a wasteland where the sand had melted into glass and every sign of human habitation was erased.

A holocaust beyond the wildest dreams of Hitler's *Wehrmacht* if she failed.

And so, she couldn't fail.

She made her slow way through the crowd to stand beside Belasko, feeling somehow safer in his shadow. It wasn't his size or strength, per se—if necessary, Sascha reckoned she could match him in a hand-to-hand engagement—but the air of confidence that he exuded in his every word and deed.

Not over confidence, the cocky attitude one sees in soldiers who haven't been blooded, but a simple understanding of his own abilities as proved on the firing line. This man knew who he was, what he could do when called upon in crisis situations. He had proved himself and felt no need to keep on doing so for others.

She wished there was a way to really know this man, his story, understand the pain and violence that had brought him to this point. Whatever else he might be, "Belasko" was clearly not the stereotypical xenophobe so often found in the clandestine services. He didn't even seem to hate his enemies, specifically, so much as he despised their actions and the impact of those actions on the innocent.

Sascha caught herself before she lapsed into amateur psychoanalysis. She didn't know this stranger well enough to probe his mind and issue broad pronouncements on his motives. If their mission went as planned, she'd be in his company for two or three more days at most. No time to learn a stranger's darkest secrets, even if she tried.

A haunting whistle sounded from the west, somewhere beyond her line of sight, and speakers mounted on the wall behind her answered by announcing the arrival of the Orient Express. Belasko started moving casually along the platform, Sascha on his heels.

The amateur analysis would have to wait.

Right now, she had a job to do.

Komotiní, Greece

JAHROM SHIRAZ WAS naturally uncomfortable, dealing with the Greek police. It jeopardized his cover, possibly his life, but there was no alternative. He had to find out what had happened to Najran Abbas and pass the news along before their mission fell apart.

Shiraz wasn't prepared to take the blame alone if anything went wrong. He was a soldier, trained to follow orders, and he had no part in plotting strategy. His various superiors in Tehran would certainly demand full credit if the plan went off on schedule. He intended to make sure they also shouldered full responsibility for failure, if it came to that.

And it was getting there, he realized, more rapidly than he would ever have conceived.

Abbas had been among the best available, a smooth assassin, doggedly committed to jihad, the holy war against all infidels. It should have been no problem for the man to kill two strangers on a train and make his getaway unseen.

But he had failed somehow, and now Shiraz was sitting in the tiny, claustrophobic office occupied by the police in Komotiní, waiting to explain how he had known Abbas and what the two of them had planned to do in Greece.

The plan had been a simple one. Abbas would drop his targets sometime after nightfall, while the Orient Express was still in Greece. He'd escape and make his way to Komotiní, where Shiraz would meet him with a rented car and they would drive across the border like a pair of tourists, back through Turkey to Iran.

No sweat.

Except Shiraz was running late that morning, stalled by engine trouble with the hired car. He asked about his friend at the hotel where they had planned to meet, but Abbas was nowhere to be found, and he had settled down to wait. Ten minutes later the police arrived with questions and demands that he accompany them to their headquarters several blocks away.

Two bodies had been found along the railway line from Xánthi, west of Komotiní. One had been identified as an employee of the Orient Express, specifically a Yugoslavian conductor. The other was an Arab, but he carried no ID, although he wore an empty shoulder holster and a pair of pants that didn't seem to fit. Was there a chance that he might be the missing friend Jahrom Shiraz was looking for?

Shiraz had viewed the body in a local undertaker's parlor, stripped of clothing, with a rough sheet drawn up to the chin. An officer had jerked the sheet aside in a dramatic gesture to impress Shiraz, revealing cuts and bruises everywhere, presumably sustained when Abbas left the train. The dead man had a broken neck, but there was also signs of strangulation on his throat. The police considered the possibility that he was murdered on the train and thrown off after he was dead, but they had nothing to go on.

Could Jahrom Shiraz add anything at all?

The young Iranian sought refuge in a hasty screen of lies. He didn't recognize the dead man, but he grieved for any victim of a violent crime. His friend was somewhat older, taller, an entirely different person. He was thumbing rides from Athens, having started two days earlier, but who could say what might have slowed him down? He was a rambler, rather irresponsible, and prone to striking off in new directions on a whim. The two deaths were a tragedy, of course, but they meant nothing to Shiraz. Of course, he didn't own a gun and wouldn't think of bringing weapons into Greece against the law.

The officers had listened, frowning at him as he spoke, and ordered him to wait while they discussed the case. There was no evidence of any crime for them to hold him on, and he knew that they'd have to let him go in time.

The question was, would it be soon enough?

His quarry was escaping even as he sat there, probably in Istanbul by now. He had to warn the backup team in time for them to intercept the target. If the Russian made it to Iraq...

He took a deep breath, held it for a moment, concentrating on his pulse and willing it to moderate. He felt a headache starting in the space behind his eyes and tried to focus on a neutral image, open desert in his homeland, with a dry wind sketching abstract patterns in the sand. He wouldn't be arrested, though they might detain him for a few more hours, hoping he'd crack and spill some nugget they could use against him in a court of law.

Shiraz could feel himself unwinding as he thought about his adversaries, proud but ignorant. Provincial constables were large fish in a tiny pond, but they possessed no extraordinary powers. If they tried to hold Shiraz beyond another hour, he'd make a scene, demand to speak with someone from the embassy in Athens. Harmless tourists were supposed to be immune from inquisitions. Targeting an Arab on the basis of his race or nationality bespoke discrimination of the rankest sort. The press would be involved, along with diplomats and lawyers. The police would be embarrassed while their neighbors stood and watched the show unfold.

He felt much better now. If nothing else, Shiraz was certain that he could persuade the officers to let him use their telephone. One call would be enough, and if they traced it afterward, at least he'd have done his best.

The target would belong to the someone else, but ego had no part in this. Whoever brought the Russian down, his action served the interest of Iran. By implication, they were doing God's sacred will.

Shiraz was satisfied to play his humble part.

CHAPTER FOURTEEN

Izmit, Turkey
Monday, 1015 hours

Technically Yakov Katzenelenbogen was no longer aboard the Orient Express. He'd be traveling by rail as far as Ankara in a sleeping compartment owned by the same railroad line, but the names changed beyond Instanbul, upon crossing the Bosporus, and much of the old line's romance seemed to vanish at the same time.

He had caught a glimpse of Bolan at the station, shadowed by the same young woman last seen in Belgrade. It was a fleeting glimpse, but at least their presence told him things were still on schedule, running more or less as planned. A full day had passed since he climbed aboard the Orient Express in Budapest, and Katz was still alive.

It was, he thought, a modest victory of sorts.

The ferry crossing was a pleasant change of pace. He rode the upper deck with Nikolai Tyumen, enjoying the salt breeze in his face after twenty-four hours of diesel fuel and stale cigar smoke. It was just a breather, but he took the opportunity to stretch his legs and scan the crowd of passengers for any hostile or familiar faces.

There was no one but McCarter, looking somber as he stood against the rail, hunched forward, with the sun warm in his face. He glanced at Katzenelenbogen and his frown grew darker, more intense. Katz saw a message there, but with Tyumen watching he couldn't approach his Phoenix Force teammate and discover what it was.

Some trouble on the train, perhaps, though Katz was unaware of any problems up to now. Whatever it might be, McCarter was alive and ready to proceed without aborting the mission. For the moment Katzenelenbogen let his mind go blank and concentrated on the water, glinting bright with sunshine as the ferry made its crossing.

Once across, they had three hundred miles to go before they reached the Turkish capital at Ankara. Seven hours at least, with scheduled stops in Adapazari and Eskisehir. Beyond Istanbul the railroads dropped any pretense of running on schedule, and Katz knew they'd be lucky to reach Ankara by sundown.

No matter.

He was in for the duration, if the trip took seven hours or seventy. In Ankara, it would become a whole new ball game, meeting up with their Iraqi guide and praying that he hadn't seen a photo of Ivan Baranovich ahead of time. From Ankara, if they survived that first encounter, came the long trek overland to reach Iraq.

There was a sudden, sour taste in Katzenelenbogen's mouth. No matter what he tried or how his luck was running, the Iraqi crossing was his point of no return. Inside Iraq there'd be individuals who knew Ivan Baranovich on sight, and Katzenelenbogen's hours would be numbered. Once across that line, survival would depend upon his own abilities, Tyumen's courage and the timing of the rest of Phoenix Force. Any single failure was enough to get him killed.

Katz wished that he could touch base with McCarter, find out what was troubling him. The worst part of the mission, so far, was the severance of communications with the other members of his team. Katz had the point, in a manner of speaking, but he was still flying blind. If he stumbled into danger, there was no one from the team to help him or make note of his predicament except McCarter. On the other hand, if Striker or the others should uncover information vital to the job, transmission of the message would require that someone blow his cover.

Either way, it left him with a sense of being virtually on his own. Tyumen could be helpful in a pinch, but there was still a deficit of trust between them, a resistance Katz wasn't sure he could overcome, no matter how long they were thrown together by the job. A year earlier, Tyumen could have been his mortal enemy, and there was simply no forgetting that.

Katz checked his watch. At least an hour and a half remained until lunch, and breakfast was a fading memory. He concentrated on the Turkish countryside, aware that he was technically in Asia now. The rules were different east of the Aegean and south of the Caucasus. Life was cheap around the world, these days, but Asia slashed the rates to bargain-basement levels. The farther east he traveled, even with the proximity of Israel, Katz knew he was putting distance between himself and the Western concept of civilization.

If he had been a decade younger, if the stakes weren't so high, Katz would have been tempted to pull the plug, disembark at their next scheduled stop and let Tyumen continue the suicide run on his own. As it was, he felt the not-so-subtle hand of duty prodding him along toward some inevitable resolution. Duty didn't care if he survived or not, as long as he performed. And if it cost his life to see the mission through...

Katz shrugged the notion off. He had encountered risks before, and he was still around. If this job proved to be the last, it made no difference.

And when the Phoenix Force warrior's time ran out, he wouldn't go alone.

Adapazari, Turkey

WAITING FOR THE FERRY to depart had cost some time, but Bolan made it up once they were in the Porsche. Across the bridge, with Sascha navigating, he put Istanbul behind them with a minimum of wasted time and hit the open road. There was no sign of anyone pursuing them along the highway, and he made good time, veering wide around peasant carts or bicycles, braking once for a flock of sheep that clogged both lanes.

A quarter of an hour from the city, Sascha asked him, "Do you have another man on board the train?"

He felt a tingling as the small hairs stiffened on his nape. "What makes you ask?"

"There was a European in the crowd and later on the ferry, paying close attention to your friend."

"What did he look like?"

"Six feet, around 190 pounds, green eyes, blondish brown hair. He wore a nylon jacket with a turtleneck and denim pants, suede loafers."

Her description fit McCarter to a tee, and Bolan let himself relax a bit. "No problem. He's another friend."

"Do you have others I should know about, in case I have to pick my targets in a hurry?"

Bolan thought about it for a moment, then finally told her, "No one on the train."

"But following?"

He took a chance on trusting her. "A three-man team. They're probably ahead of us by now. And you?"

She frowned and shook her head. "I had a contact back in Belgrade. There is no one else."

It had the ring of truth, but Bolan had a hard time believing the Mossad would entrust such a critical mission to one operative. He wondered if there might be others watching, agents Sascha didn't even know about. But if she didn't know, there seemed to be no point in asking.

How much more should he reveal? The warrior took a leap of faith.

"You won't have any trouble spotting my backup," he told her. "One's black, one's Hispanic and the third is a six-foot Canadian."

She laughed at that. "The famous melting pot in action, is it?"

"More or less. It works, sometimes."

The lady shifted gears. "What will we do in Ankara?"

"Hang out and keep our eyes open," he replied. "Cover the meet with the Iraqis, if we can."

"They do not know your friend?"

"That's what I'm told. If I've been misinformed, we'll know it right away."

The prospect of a firefight in the Turkish capital set Bolan's teeth on edge. He wouldn't hesitate to act if necessary, but a blowup meant the end of everything, no matter who came out on top. With the police involved and the Iraqis warned of treachery, a border crossing would be tantamount to suicide.

And hopeless gestures weren't Bolan's style.

"It is a long way to the border yet," Sascha said.

"We're getting there."

"Before this mission was assigned," she said, "my supervisor asked for volunteers. He warned us that whoever took this job might not return."

"There's always that."

"Of course, but this was different. He seemed... almost certain."

"And you volunteered regardless?"

"Certainly. We all did. Fourteen agents in the section."

"How'd you get the booby prize? Short [illegible]aw?"

"It was my turn in the rotation. On a normal job I would have been assigned in any case."

"What happens if we blow it?" Bolan asked.

"You mean from Tel Aviv?" She shook her head again. "We're not advised of strategy, except where necessary in performance of a given task. I would anticipate a firm response."

"Which could mean war."

"The war will come in any case if we allow Saddam Hussein to build his warheads. If nothing else, an early strike may minimize the loss of life in Israel."

"What about Iraq?"

"I have no private quarrel with the Iraqi people," she replied, "though most of them would gladly see me dead. They have allowed a vicious madman to control their lives, as once the Germans did. He must be stopped at any cost, before he spreads more suffering and death."

"If we pull this off," Bolan said, "it still won't break Hussein."

"Who knows for sure? It will delay him, at the very least, and he has enemies at home. Perhaps if he is beaten and embarrassed one more time, it will encourage them to act."

"And if it doesn't?"

"There are other ways."

He couldn't fault her logic. It had been his own since he returned from Vietnam to find his family in ruins, striking off along the vengeance trail that gradually changed to something else, a long crusade in which personal anger had little or no place. He wondered if Sascha had reached that point yet, or if she would ever have the chance.

"Do you have family in the United States?" she asked, catching him off guard.

"A brother," Bolan answered. "No one else."

"I've often thought that loved ones are a weakness," she remarked. "They make you vulnerable."

"They can also make you strong."

She studied Bolan's profile for a moment and finally said, "I wish that we had met in different circumstances."

"These are all we have," he answered.

"Yes."

He goosed the Porsche to ninety miles an hour, concentrating on the highway as it carried them away.

Eskisehir, Turkey

"GETTING THERE," Calvin James said, his big hands easy on the Citroën's steering wheel.

"It's still 150 miles," Gary Manning reminded him. "At this rate, I estimate another hour and a half."

"Just don't get stopped for speeding," the Canadian replied. "Somebody might decide to check the car."

"Bad luck for them," Rafael Encizo said, grinning. "I just might have to take their guns away and tie them up someplace."

"And guard them for the next twelve hours while you're at it?"

"Never mind the cops," James said. "I haven't seen a squad car in the past three hours, and the ones I did see couldn't catch this wagon if I let them have a handicap."

"I thought your name was Calvin James, not Jesse."

"Hey, you never know. Might be a honky in the woodpile if you check it out."

"I'll pass."

"You don't know what you're missing, bro'."

"I've got a fair imagination, thanks."

Encizo had lost interest in their banter, thinking forward to the set in Ankara. "I wish we had a layout on the station."

"No sweat," James said. "We beat the train by ninety minutes, give or take, and we've got time to nose around. Nail down the track they're coming in on, and we can spread out any way we need to for the set."

"We'll have McCarter back by that time," Manning added. "Striker too, with any luck."

"All kinds of shit could still go wrong," Encizo reminded them.

James watched him from the rearview mirror, frowning now. "That's why we get those big five-figure checks, amigo. Making sure that nothing *does* go wrong."

"Five figures?" Manning asked him, going with the flow.

"Thing is, a couple of them always show up on the wrong side of the decimal."

"That must be why I can't retire," Encizo said.

"You can't retire because you love it, bro'. What other job you ever hope to find where you can cruise around all day, soak up the sun and see the world like this?"

"You've got a point."

"Damn straight."

"I didn't plan to mention it," Manning said, "but if you could grow a little extra hair on top, it wouldn't show."

"Oh, perfect. Everybody's a comedian these days. You're keeping me in stitches, white boy."

"Anything to help the cause."

In front of them an ancient flatbed truck was rumbling down the middle of the road. James swung around it on the left-hand shoulder, spitting gravel from the Cirtoën's back tires, and left the farmer in a drifting pall of dust.

"So much for Old MacDonald."

"Where'd you learn to drive?" Manning asked.

"On the South Side of Chicago," James replied. "In my neighborhood, we started out with hubcaps, worked our way up to the driver's seat."

"I'm glad we cleared that up. It gives me greater confidence."

James tried the radio, came up with different sets of strident voices, one faint station where the Beatles' greatest hits were being sung in Turkish, and he switched it off.

"No R&B, I don't believe it."

"You're a long way from Chicago," Manning told him, staring out his window as the hilly countryside rolled past.

"You got that right."

Encizo swiveled sideways in his seat to give his legs more room so that he could watch the road behind them. Just in case. He knew that any tail from Istanbul would certainly have shown itself by now, but you could never be too cautious on a job where every move was fraught with peril and your life was riding on the line.

Beside him, loosely covered by a blanket on the floor, the two Czech Vz.58 assault rifles were loaded and ready for action. James had the short Beretta submachine gun tucked beneath his seat, and each man wore a P-220 automatic in a shoulder sling or on his belt. If they were intercepted by an enemy right now, at least Encizo knew they had a fighting chance.

It would be different in the railroad station, once they got to Ankara. Allowing for the hour, dusk or later by the time they reached their destination, they could get away with jackets to conceal their pistols. James could probably devise a way of packing the Beretta SMG, but they'd have to leave both rifles in the car. That limited their striking power at the outset, and Encizo was concerned that they might find themselves outgunned.

Or, maybe not.

He had no reason to believe there was an ambush waiting at the depot. More than likely, Katz would meet his contact, kill some time in small talk, finally hit the road.

If it went sour, though, Encizo was prepared to do whatever was required. Turkey was new ground for the Cuban commando, but he knew the deadly game by heart. The rules varied slightly from place to place, names and faces changing among the opposition, but it all came out the same when you were done. The winners walked away and left the losers where they fell.

Encizo knew his teammates well enough to trust them with his life. In fact, he had already done precisely that.

The bets were down, and he'd play the hand as it was dealt.

It was the kind of game where jokers turned up every second card or so, and all of them were wild.

CHAPTER FIFTEEN

Ankara, Turkey
Monday, 1930 hours

Ankara was the end of the line. Katz had his suitcase packed an hour before they reached the depot, joining Nikolai Tyumen in the Russian's compartment for small talk and last-minute adjustments to strategy. There was a minimal amount of preparation to be done, and they fell back on idle conversation just to pass the time.

For all his prior complaints, Katz found himself regretting that they had to leave the train. At least in his compartment he was able to defend himself, predict the angle of attack an enemy would have to use for the approach. Once they were on the road, by car or otherwise, the danger might lie anywhere.

And so, what else was new?

From the Israeli army to Mossad and on to Phoenix Force, Katz was accustomed to living on the edge. It was the only kind of life he really cared for, with a chance to make a difference now and then. It wasn't a crusade with Katzenelenbogen, but it made him feel alive.

And he was living now.

The engineer sounded his whistle, and they could feel the train braking now, slowing into the station. Katz rose and used his prosthesis to lift the suitcase, leaving his left hand free for tickets, passport—and the Browning automatic, if it came to that. His recognition signal was a wilted flower in the buttonhole of his lapel.

The railroad station smelled of grease and diesel fuel, compressed humanity and frying food, the general pollution of the Turkish capital. Except for dress and dialect, he might as easily have been arriving in Cairo or Damascus, even Karachi. Everything around him had the smell and clutter of the East, at once seductive and repugnant. Images of Beirut and Calcutta flashed through Katzenelenbogen's mind before he caught himself and focused on the present.

Any lapse in concentration for the next few moments could be fatal. He had to keep his wits about him if he wanted to survive.

Katz moved along the platform with Tyumen at his elbow. They had no spare luggage to collect, and so escaped the milling crowd around the baggage car. No sign of Bolan or the others, but he knew they'd be hanging back, observing from a cautious distance to avoid disrupting Katz's meet with the Iraqis.

If the bastards showed.

There was a fallback option, in case something went wrong and either side was delayed. If they couldn't make contact at the depot, Tyumen had been furnished with the address of a small hotel where they'd take a room and wait. No matter what went wrong, their contacts would devise a way to get in touch before the night was out.

In all, the plan didn't inspire tremendous confidence, but it was all they had. At least, Katz thought, their contacts would be motivated by the fear of disappointing their supreme commander. Those who failed Saddam Hussein on major projects had the life expectancy of mayflies in the barren desert.

They were moving slowly toward the cabstand when a short, dark stranger in a rumpled suit stepped out in front of them. His smile flicked on and off as he addressed Katz in a raspy voice.

"Ivan Baranovich?"

Katz nodded, watching the Iraqi glance down at his metal claw. It seemed to do the trick.

"I am Ali Birjand. You will accompany me."

It didn't come out sounding like a question. They fell into step behind him, past the line of waiting taxis, toward the crowded parking lot. Katz noted that the vast majority of cars in evidence were scarred and battered but meticulously clean, as if the Turks took pride in polishing their vehicles to use them as offensive weapons on the streets and highways.

Katz scanned the lot in search of lookouts, snipers, anyone at all. From all appearances they were alone with the Iraqi.

"My car."

The aging Volvo had a rental sticker in one corner of the windshield, and its doors and fenders sported fewer dents and dings than the surrounding cars. Dumb luck, or else the rental agency made a half-hearted effort to preserve appearances. Birjand opened the trunk, waiting for Katz and Tyumen to stow their bags before he unlocked a back door and waved them inside.

The interior smelled like tobacco and sweat. No air-conditioning, of course. The vinyl seat covers were stretched and molded to fit the buttocks of previous passengers. Katz wriggled around to make himself comfortable, avoiding a spring that jabbed painfully into his coccyx. He reached inside his jacket, readjusting the pistol before Birjand slid into the driver's seat and turned his key in the ignition.

They were on their way, for good or ill.

And there could be no turning back.

FROM ALL APPEARANCES the meet had gone like clockwork. Bolan was watching as the Iraqi accosted Katz and his Russian escort, calculating range and angles for a long shot with his side arm if the meeting suddenly went sour. Realistically he knew that there was little he could do from fifty yards away, but he'd have to try.

He had a fix on Gary Manning in the crowd, but none of the others were visible. James and Encizo would take special care in the mostly Turkish crowd, and he didn't worry about missing McCarter. The ex-SAS officer was a master at passing unobserved, even in situations where a European would normally stand out like the proverbial sore thumb.

Sascha, for her part, was on position thirty yards away, triangulating their scrutiny of Katz and the others. That way, if Bolan lost track of his men for a moment, the odds were good that Sascha could keep them in view.

The car was a dark blue Volvo four-door. Bolan watched Katz and the Russian drop their luggage in the trunk, then climb into the back seat while their contact held the door. He made an unconvincing chauffeur, but at least he seemed to be alone. There was no sign of any backup gunners lurking on the sidelines, shadowing his moves.

It felt wrong to the Executioner, but he couldn't rule out the possibility that the Iraqis sought to minimize their risks by letting one man handle pickup and delivery. The fewer men they had on-site, the less their chances of discovery, but it would also leave the pointman painfully exposed in case of any problems at the meeting.

Bolan watched the Volvo cautiously retreating from its slot, the driver shifting gears and rolling toward the exit where he was required to pay a toll. That done, he waited for the automatic barrier to rise and pulled out into spotty traffic, lost to sight before he reached the nearest intersection with a major street.

From this point the track came down to Phoenix Force. Bolan didn't wait to see which car picked up the Volvo, trailing far enough behind to keep from tipping off the driver while they kept his vehicle in sight. It would be touch and go, a chancy operation, knowing that continual surveillance on the road would give their game away.

And much could happen in the periods when they were out of touch.

As for the Executioner and Sascha Lentz, they had a date in Cizre, near the border of Iraq, to meet a man whom neither one of them had ever seen before. Their contact was supposed to have a fix on the facility where Russian scientists were building ultralethal weapons for Saddam Hussein, but they wouldn't be sure of that until they reached the desert site.

But if the lead was false, they'd have wasted all this time and, very possibly, their lives.

Bolan retraced his steps through the milling crowd, met Sascha, and set off for the Porsche with determined strides. He followed the Volvo's presumed course through downtown Ankara and out of the city, picking up the southbound highway that followed the

Kizil Irmak River as far as Nevsehir before striking off to the east. Five hundred miles as the vulture flies, plus another hundred, easily, for winding mountain roads and detours into towns or villages. Perhaps nine hours in the Porsche 944 with stops for fuel and other needs.

Beside him, Sascha had her handbag open, lifting out a compact semiauto pistol. Bolan recognized the Walther P-5, a compact descendant of the venerable P-38 so prized by soldiers of all nations in the European theater of World War Two. Modern refinements placed an emphasis on ease of operation and built-in safety features, making the P-5 one of Western Europe's most respected and widely used autoloading pistols.

It was also Sascha's first display of hardware since their Belgrade meeting, and while Bolan had assumed that she was armed, the pistol made him stiffen for an instant, until he verified that she was merely double-checking the load and firing mechanism for her own peace of mind. When she was done, the weapon disappeared inside her bag, and Sascha faced the highway with a thoughtful frown.

"Expecting trouble?" Bolan asked.

She half turned in her seat, still frowning. "What if the Iraqis know about the switch?"

"We've covered all the angles I can think of," Bolan answered. "Nothing we can do but keep our fingers crossed and run it by the numbers."

"Numbers?"

"By the plan," he told her. "One step at a time."

"You trust that method?"

"Ask me in a day or two, and I'll let you know."

"I hope I have the chance."

"Me too."

He concentrated on the highway after that, holding the Porsche around seventy-five miles per hour and passing slower vehicles at speed. The farmers in their horse-drawn wagons didn't seem to mind, but several Turkish motorists let their horns do the talking, bleats of peevish protest lost in Bolan's wake.

It was a race of sorts, from Ankara to Cizre, never certain of the route that Katz would take or how his contact put the Volvo through its paces. It was critical, from Bolan's point of view, to synchronize arrivals with the men of Phoenix Force and make a timely border crossing. Once across the line, he knew that Katzenelenbogen's hours would be numbered, with exposure, interrogation and death waiting at the end of the line. The only way to save him was to get there promptly, wrap the mission up and expedite withdrawal in a timely fashion.

Hopefully without a loss of friendly life.

Bad odds, the warrior realized, but they were all he had to work with at the moment. A familiar situation in his everlasting war against the savages.

"Do you believe in God?" Sascha asked, taking Bolan by surprise.

He blinked. "I have some trouble with the Bible stories, but I don't reject the concept."

"Never mind," she said. "I'll say a prayer for both of us."

Somehow, it struck him as appropriate, this comely agent of Mossad who prayed and kept a Walther P-5 automatic in her purse.

"It couldn't hurt," the Executioner replied.

MCCARTER NEARLY MISSED his rendezvous with Phoenix Force, or so it seemed. He had been watching Katzenelenbogen at the railroad station, standing in the doorway of the depot men's room when their contact suddenly appeared from nowhere, buttonholing Katz and his companion on the sidewalk. Words were passed, inaudible from where McCarter stood, then all three moved off in the direction of the parking lot. He was about to follow when a strong hand gripped his left arm just above the elbow, holding him in place.

McCarter stiffened, glanced down at the firm, restraining hand. Dark fingers wrapped around his biceps, barely trying.

"Manning's got them covered," James advised him. "Come with me."

"He might need help," McCarter said.

"There's Striker and his number two."

Reluctantly McCarter let himself be led away from the depot, losing sight of Katz and the Russian in seconds. It felt wrong somehow, after dogging his tracks across four countries and killing a man to bring him this far. McCarter had a sense of shirking his responsibility, regardless of the fact that he had known about this shift since Friday afternoon.

"Where are we?"

"Over this way," James replied, leading him toward a separate, smaller parking lot where Encizo waited at the wheel of a four-door Citroën sedan. Encizo smiled and shook McCarter's hand before the former SAS commando stowed his bag and climbed in back.

"Let's move it," James said when they were settled in their places. "Gary's waiting."

Encizo brought the Citroën to life and wheeled out of the lot, following a two-lane driveway north to reach the main parking lot. A metered gate trapped cars inside once they had crossed the point of no return, but Manning waited outside, sliding into the back seat beside McCarter when the Cuban braked to a halt.

"They're on the southbound highway," Manning said. "I'd estimate a ninety-second lead."

"No problem."

And no hurry, either, since their goal wasn't to overtake the other car and thereby give themselves away, but merely parallel their tracks if possible. It was a good thing, too, McCarter thought, as traffic flowing from the airport slowed them down in spite of Rafael's best efforts. Turkish drivers were fearless when it came to bashing fenders, but a goodly number of them also loved to talk and sightsee while they drove, delighting in the bleats of protest issuing from horns behind them as they took their own sweet time. Five minutes from the airport, and McCarter estimated that the Volvo was no doubt miles ahead.

"We'll make it up," James said, "once we get out of town."

"No problems on the train?" Manning asked.

"Well, I wouldn't go that far."

He briefed them on his confrontation with the nameless gunman, his companions listening with rapt attention while he ran it down. When he was finished, James released a long, slow whistle.

"Did you make this guy for an Iraqi?"

Once again McCarter thought about it, running down the meager clues, and shook his head. "I couldn't tell you. No ID. I'm sure he was an Arab, but beyond that, your guess is as good as mine."

"Which means they could have bowled Katz out before he got to Ankara," Manning said, tight-lipped as he spoke.

"You think they would have tried to dust him at the station?" Encizo asked.

"Why," James countered, "when they have a chance to take him for a one-way ride?"

McCarter felt the old, familiar churning in his gut. "I didn't say the shooter *was* Iraqi, only that I couldn't tell for sure."

"What other options have we got?" James asked.

"Someone who doesn't like the thoughts of Baghdad holding nukes," Manning said. "The Iranians, let's say, or possibly an Arab contact agent working on commission."

"Who picks up the tab?"

"You name it. In the past few years Hussein has stirred up everybody in the Middle East. Except for Syria, they all sent troops against him during Desert Storm. The hard part would be finding anyone outside Iraq who thinks he *should* be armed with MIRVs."

"Terrific. Now we're taking on the world," James groused.

"Not quite," McCarter said. "The Russians and Israelis are supposed to be on our side, right?"

"Supposed to be," Encizo snorted. "Boil this down, we've got enough stray personal agendas for a couple extra wars."

"I heard that, brother." Even in his gloomy mode, James sounded more or less relaxed. "This bucket got a few more miles per hour underneath the hood, or what?"

"I'm working on it."

"Fair enough. I know we're not supposed to dog him, but I'd feel a whole lot better if we caught another glimpse of Katz, you follow? Just make sure he's on the road, instead of lying in a ditch somewhere."

McCarter nodded and focused on the thinning crush of traffic up ahead. They'd be clear of downtown in a few more moments, rolling south through residential suburbs toward the open highway, hoping that they didn't miss a turnoff where their quarry might have been diverted to a literal dead end.

"If something happens..." McCarter said, speaking almost to himself, but he stopped short, refusing to express his fear.

"You got that right," James agreed. "If something happens to the man, we go ahead and do our job the best we can. Whoever's left from that comes back and kicks some major ass."

That settled in their minds, the Phoenix Force warriors concentrated on the highway, each man searching for the Volvo sedan that held the final member of their team.

Nevsehir, Turkey

NIGHT DRIVING SPARED THEM certain difficulties, Sascha thought, which could have slowed their progress during daylight hours. Nightfall had removed the vast majority of horse- or ox-drawn carts as farmers holed up with their families for supper, curtains drawn against the night. Most Turkish motorists were also daylight creatures, in the hinterlands at least, and there was room to let the Porsche unwind along the rolling highway south of Ankara.

They stopped to dine in Nevsehir, at a small café with candles on the table, oil lamps on the wall. The menu was a mystery, but they got lucky with a waitress who could manage broken English—"shattered" would have been a better term—and ordered double portions of a native goulash, beef and vegetables baked inside a fresh loaf of bread. It was delicious, and Bolan went along with her suggestion that they share a bottle of wine, though Sascha noted that her companion barely touched his glass.

"Will we be stopping for the night?" she asked.

Bolan shook his head. "No time. We don't know if the others will be laying off or driving through, but I can't take the chance."

"All right," she said. "I'll drive from here into Malatya if you like." That made 250 miles on unfamiliar roads, in darkness, but she had no fear of getting lost.

The American's easy shrug took Sascha by surprise. "Suits me," he said.

"You don't object?"

"To what, a woman driving?"

"Well..."

"That seems to be your hang-up more than mine."

"Outside of Israel," she replied, "I have become accustomed to a different attitude. Some nations openly discriminate against their females. Others promise not to do so and forget their words in every way that counts."

"You should have been a feminist crusader."

Sascha smiled despite herself. "Perhaps I am."

"I guess that means you're doubling, then."

She shook her head. "Israel comes first."

"Before your sisters?"

Sascha felt the smile begin to slip, and in another heartbeat it was gone. "Our enemies make no distinction in their targets based on sex or age," she said. "Without security there can be no equality, no rights at all."

She felt him watching her, the color rising in her cheeks. What was it that provoked her so about this tall American?

"You might have guessed," she said, "I don't believe in turning the other cheek."

"It crossed my mind."

"But on the other hand, I almost never shoot my friends."

"Almost?"

Her smile was back now, turning mischievous. "The odd exception," she informed him. "Birthday parties, formal teas."

"Of course. All the major occasions."

It felt good to laugh, some of the tension unwinding inside her, escaping with the sound of her voice. Sascha recalled an American magazine, its title lost to mind, that compared laughter to medicine in one of its regular columns. The editors were right, she thought. It helped to put your cares away, however briefly.

"So," Bolan ventured, "does that mean we're friends?"

"Perhaps," she said, refusing to be serious so quickly. "Do you have a birthday coming up?"

"Just missed it, I'm afraid."

"Some other holiday, in that case," she replied.

"I'll make a note."

The moment passed, Sascha turning back to her goulash while her companion did the same. It could be perilous to work with friends, she realized, much less with lovers. On a mission such as this, where death was always waiting in the wings, it made more sense to keep your distance, learn to trust your partner on the firing line without creating some emotional attachment that could harm you later, if he—

Died.

She focused on the word as she had done in other killing situations, understanding that the outcome could go either way. Her own life was at risk, not just Belasko's or their decoys traveling with the Iraqi.

If the mission soured on them, Sascha told herself, there would be death enough to go around.

CHAPTER SIXTEEN

East of Kayseri, Turkey
Monday, 2315 hours

Their contact drove like a bat out of hell, flashing his headlights and leaning on the horn if anyone or anything appeared in front of him, threatening to slow him down. At such times he'd mutter to himself in peevish tones, the words inaudible or indecipherable from where Katz sat. When things were calmer and he had the highway to himself, he kept his mouth shut, driving with the concentration typical of novices, though he apparently possessed substantial skill.

It was a blessing, Katz decided, to be spared from small talk, much less a deliberate interrogation on the road. There might be questions later, when they stopped to eat or rest, but Katz imagined he could hold his own with vague opinions and even vaguer technology. He had abandoned Mother Russia when he saw her growing weak—that, and for the money offered by Saddam Hussein, of course. The missiles he designed were too complex for simple explanations to Iraqi laymen. Basically the heat and energy came out one end, which made the rocket take off in an opposite direction and continue on its way until the engines starved for fuel.

He had expected greater difficulty back in Ankara. More men, for one thing, though he couldn't rule out backup agents in the depot crowd. Perhaps a photograph that would betray him on the spot, but if his escort had a clue that he was moving bogus goods, he hid it well enough to rate an Oscar. At the very least, Katz had expected someone to prepare their guide with loaded questions, something to confirm their bona fides, but he seemed satisfied with a glancing at their passports once they put the sprawl of Ankara behind them and were on their way.

Too easy?

Katz had learned that he should never look a gift horse in the mouth. Not every step of every mission was a mortal challenge. Enemies got careless sometimes, as did friends, allowing confidence to generate a sense of false security. It was entirely possible that the Iraqis thought they had it made. Two Russians in the bag, a third one on his way, and they had used up all their bad luck on the Nabakov affair, in Petrograd.

So much for wishful thinking.

The Iraqi driver was a small man, but he seemed to have a wiry strength about him and he kept himself alert. Back at the railroad station, Katz had spied the outline of a bulky weapon underneath his coat, perhaps a compact submachine gun in a shoulder sling. It made good sense, of course, that the Iraqi would be armed in case of an emergency. Still, Katz hadn't been able to escape the thought that he and Tyumen might be marked for death once they were safely out of town.

Three hours and some two hundred miles later, he was no longer worried on that score—but the worst was still ahead. Proceeding at their present rate of speed, with stops for petrol, they had five or six more hours on the road. Allow for preparations at the border, even if they didn't sleep this night, and he couldn't imagine a successful crossing prior to dawn on Tuesday.

After that...

Katz made his mind a blank. Until dawn on Tuesday.

He'd live at least that long.

A pair of headlights showed up in the rearview mirror, slowly gaining on the Volvo from behind. Their driver noticed, but it didn't seem to worry him. He didn't own the road, no matter how he acted when he felt an urge to pass some slower car or motorbike along the way.

Katz wouldn't bet on the Iraqi speaking Russian, though he couldn't absolutely rule it out. He took a chance, addressing Tyumen in the agent's native language. "I expected more security precautions than a simple passport check," he said. "It seems too easy."

"Count your blessings. Maybe they are careless where this midget comes from."

"And if not?"

"Then we will find out soon enough," Tyumen said. "It does no good for us to worry in advance."

He was correct, of course. Preparedness and raw anxiety were vastly different things. They had prepared themselves in Budapest before they caught the Orient Express, and they had come this far without a hitch. There would be trouble later on, but that was built into the plan and reinforcements would be standing by.

Please, God.

It was an almost carefree feeling, in a way, to know that the inevitable march of circumstances would soon dictate his actions. Once he met the enemy and battle was joined, his soldier's instinct could take over, allowing Katz to seize the initiative and run with it.

Above all else, he was tired of waiting for the other shoe to drop. There came a point where anything was better than uncertainty, postponement and delay.

Soon now, he told himself. It won't be long.

He made an effort to relax and focus on the darkness rushing past his window, pinpoint lights suggesting dwellings set back from the road.

The Phoenix Force warrior was as ready now as he would ever be, but it was not his time.

Soon now, his mind repeated.

Soon.

BUSHEHR AHVAZ WAS TIRED of waiting. His legs were stiff from sitting in the car too long, a loaded AK-47 rifle braced between his knees, but he was still more comfortable than the others. Lying in the roadside ditch or crouching in the copse of trees across the highway, they'd be a feast for ants, mosquitoes, biting flies. At least inside the car he had a chance to roll the windows up and swelter if he chose to, an alternative to being drained of blood a few drops at a time.

Just now, he had the window halfway down in a concession to the muggy night and the complaints of his companions. Kerman, at the wheel, was overweight and sweated fiercely in the heat, his body odor strong enough to make Ahvaz rethink his hatred of the swarming flies. In back Qatif was silent now. He also had his window down and never mind the insects. It was cooler that way, but his chief concern would be an unobstructed field of fire. The Uzi submachine gun on his lap was cocked and locked, with extra magazines beside him on the seat.

The message from Jahrom Shiraz, in Greece, had taken everybody by surprise. It was expected that the Russians would be dealt with by Najran Abbas on board the Orient Express. Instead Abbas was living on an undertaker's slab in some Greek village far from home, Shiraz was being questioned as a suspect and Bushehr Ahvaz would have to do the job himself.

It was an honor, if you thought about it that way. Picking up the pieces where a more experienced, more trusted member of the team had failed. Not only failed, but lost his life. Ahvaz would surely be promoted when he pulled it off. A decorated hero of the Holy Revolution, he'd instantly command respect. More challenging assignments would be earmarked for his disposition, or, perhaps he'd be drafted to instruct the future freedom fighters of Iran.

In truth the latter option carried more appeal than working field assignments, risking life and limb to rub out strangers in a foreign land. At thirty-three Ahvaz was still a young man, but the losses suffered by his unit served as a reminder of his own mortality. It was a great relief, of course, to know that God saved a special place in paradise for warriors. Still, if he was asked to choose, Ahvaz would certainly have opted for a longer stay on earth, a chance to spend more money, share himself with members of the female sex.

There was a chance his quarry might have holed up somewhere for the night, but it would make no difference in the end. Ahvaz and his selected triggermen would wait for days if necessary, sending Kerman to the nearest village for supplies. The odds were in their favor, though. Their targets would be making for Iraq with all deliberate speed, intent on finding safety there and starting work on weapons that would make Saddam Hussein the ruling strongman of the Middle East. It was a thought too terrible to contemplate, on top of the atrocities Hussein's barbarians had already committed in Iran.

No more.

It ended here.

Ahvaz knew little of the Russians who were already at work inside Iraq, but he was told that this one made the difference. Something in the area of rockets and delivery systems, subjects well beyond Ahvaz in their complexity. He didn't have to understand the Russian's special knowledge to destroy him, though. The famous infidel would bleed and die like any other man.

A mile or more downrange, approaching from the west, Ahvaz made out the spark of headlights. One car, traveling at speed, its driver bent on going somewhere fast.

Ahvaz had no description of the car, and only vague descriptions of the man he was supposed to kill. For all he knew there might be five or six men in the vehicle. It might not even *be* the car he wanted...but he couldn't take that chance.

If there was a mistake, Ahvaz would have his soldiers drive or push the car away and hide it while he waited for the next one...and the next. He wouldn't leave his post until the Russian rocket scientist was dead, no longer a menace to Tehran.

"Get ready!"

Kerman twisted the ignition key and brought the car to life, shifting from neutral into first gear. Ahvaz cranked his window all the way down and lifted his

Kalashnikov, resting its barrel on the padded windowsill. Behind him, he heard Qatif humming softly to himself as he released the safety on his Uzi SMG. Ahvaz did likewise, slipping his index finger inside the AK-47's trigger guard.

"Go!"

The sedan lurched forward, lights off, its rear wheels raising plumes of dust and gravel, out across the two-lane blacktop, skidding to a halt and blocking off the road. The headlights of their target vehicle were set on high beams, almost blinding as they took Ahvaz directly in the eyes, but he could solve that problem instantly.

Without another word the would-be hero of the Holy Revolution opened fire.

FROM HIS PLACE in the rear of the speeding Volvo, Nikolai Tyumen saw a dark shape lunge across the highway, stopping short to block their path. A heartbeat later, headlights showed him a black Peugot parked broadside in the middle of the road, with guns protruding from the windows.

"Down!"

Before the warning left Tyumen's lips, his one-armed comrade was already sliding to the floor, his left hand wrapped around the Browning automatic. Tyumen ducked and felt the Volvo start to swerve as bullets raked the car, some punching through the windshield, others striking doors and fenders with a rapid-fire metallic plunking sound.

Tyumen couldn't see their driver from his hunched position in the rear, had no way of determining if the Iraqi was alive or dead until he heard the dark man cursing in his native language, grappling with the steering wheel. They left the pavement, bounced across a shallow drainage ditch and came to rest with the front bumper of the Volvo buried in a dirt embankment on the south side of the highway.

It was time to move, Tyumen bailing out on his side, with the Volvo screening him from snipers in the other car. "Baranovich" was close behind him, going down on all fours in the weeds as he emerged. Birjand slid out a moment later, joining them in the huddle while bullets rocked the Volvo, taking out one headlight, flattening two tires.

And there were other guns now, winking at them from the darkness. One or two in front, from where the car had been concealed; at least three more behind them, with the snipers closing in to cut off any prospect of retreat. Tyumen sighted on the nearest muzzle-flash and squeezed off two quick shots to keep the gunner down, if nothing else.

Birjand was momentarily surprised to see his passengers with guns, but then he seemed relieved that he wouldn't be forced to carry on the fight alone. He drew a compact automatic weapon from beneath his coat—Tyumen recognized the Polish PM-63—and snapped down the folding foregrip. Chambered for the 9 mm x 18 Makarov cartridge, the 13-inch machine pistol emitted a loud, ripping sound as it joined the battle, spraying rounds at the Peugot.

The plug gunners were drawing closer now, and Tyumen could see that there were four of them, not three. The darkness spoiled their aim, and he was thankful that the Volvo's headlights had been smashed on impact with the bank. The car was useless now in any case, with two flat tires, except where it provided cover from the gunners at his back.

Tyumen shifted his position slightly, following the nearest hostile gunner with his pistol, both hands wrapped around the Browning autoloader in a target shooter's grip. He took a breath, released some of it through his nose and held the rest, a trick to keep his weapon steady as his trigger finger took up slack.

His third shot found its target and pitched the sniper over on his back in knee-high weeds, some kind of automatic rifle blasting at the heavens as he fell. A final tremor in the weeds, and Tyumen's target came to rest.

By that time the Russian was shifting to his left, surrounded by the sounds of mortal combat, looking for another mark. His lack of cover on the west side made him vulnerable, but he trusted speed and cunning.

It was too late when he recognized his grave mistake.

The hostile snipers were prepared to sight on muzzle-flashes, too. The first round struck Tyumen on his right side, just above the hip, and slammed him back against the Volvo's door. The automatic in his fist exploded aimlessly, a reflex action, as a second slug ripped through his abdomen below the sternum. He had braced himself for pain, but there was only pressure and a sudden numbness, spreading outward from the center of his body, paralyzing arms and legs.

He felt himself slip sideways, going over in a slump, but there was no way he could stop himself. Another moment he felt the gravel rough against his cheek, but still no pain to speak of. Tyumen's single dominant sensation was a feeling of despair and impotence that made him rage against his flaccid limbs.

The sounds of combat seemed more distant now, already fading, and he let the darkness carry him away.

KATZ HEARD THE BULLETS strike Tyumen, saw him fall on the periphery of vision, but he couldn't help the Russian now. He had his hands full with the enemy, and so far only one of them had been disabled. Even he might be alive, but for the moment he was down and out.

From where he huddled in the Volvo's shadow, Katzenelenbogen marked the muzzle-flash that dropped Tyumen, sighting down the Browning automatic's slide and pumping three quick rounds into the night. He was rewarded by a grunt of startled pain, already dodging to his right and flattening himself beside the car as two surviving gunners opened up. Their bullets drilled the door where Katz had been a moment earlier, but the response hadn't been swift enough.

He spied their silhouettes, some twenty feet apart, and took the nearest shooter first. The rounds hit dead-center on the hulking man-shape, and he watched the rifleman collapse.

The final gunner burst from cover in the roadside ditch, a submachine gun blasting as he ran, but haste makes waste in marksmanship, as in the other walks of life. His bullets had the range, but they were easily two feet above his target, burning in where Katzenelenbogen's thighs and pelvis would have been if he was standing upright.

In a game of life and death the gunner could expect no second chance.

Katz gave him two shots on the run, a third round for the clincher as his target faltered, dropped to one knee, letting out a strangled cry that might have been surprise or agony.

Ali Birjand was holding down their opposition on the north side, but he needed help. Katz hunched his way around Tyumen's prostrate form, picked up the Russian's fallen automatic with his metal claw and held it in reserve.

Across the moonlit tarmac, he could see one gunner stretched out on his face, unmoving. Three more guns were flashing from behind the black Peugot, a fourth away to Katzenelenbogen's right, concealed in shrubbery beside the road. He pegged a shot at that one, heard his bullet strike the pavement and adjusted for another round.

The gunner scooted backward, shouting out what sounded like a curse in Farsi. For the first time Katzenelenbogen had a fix on who their adversaries were and why they would desire to see him dead. Iran had every bit as much to lose as Israel, if Saddam Hussein went nuclear. He could appreciate their motives, but the fact remained that they would have to die before he could proceed and do his job.

Birjand unleashed another burst that ripped the Peugot's right rear tire to shreds. A rush of air escaping made it sound as if the car had broken wind. Three guns responded with staccato bursts as Birjand dropped back out of sight, reloading his machine pistol, bracing himself for the next round.

Beside the road, Katz saw the fourth man rising from his cover, moving like a shadow on the run. He tried to take advantage of the wild fire from his comrades, but the twenty yards of open pavement offered no protection once he cleared the ditch, his AK-47 spitting short bursts from the hip.

Katz used his last four rounds to stop the gunner in his tracks, switched pistols, ready with Tyumen's Browning if he needed more, but it was finished. Two dead on the pavement now, with three behind the car, and they'd have to root the last three out of cover soon, if they were going to survive.

Katz thought the sounds of battle had to be carrying for miles. He pictured Turkish peasants huddled in a farmhouse somewhere, wide awake and staring at the shadows as they listened. Would there be a telephone? Would anybody care enough to ring up the police? If so, what kind of a response time could he count on in the middle of the night?

Better to finish it now, while there was time, before they had to deal with uniforms. The gunmen first, then they could think about evacuation from the scene.

He caught Birjand's attention, communicating with hand signs, running through it twice before the gunman flashed a smile and nodded comprehension. Katz held up four fingers, counting down, his muscles coiled and ready when the Iraqi popped up from cover and unleashed a scathing burst toward the Peugot.

Katz rolled out to his right and fired beneath the Volvo's bumper, angling for the Peugot's gas tank. Two rounds, three, and then he saw a spark catch light, flames spreading hungrily beneath the damaged car. It took another moment for the enemy to recognize their danger, one man breaking off in each direction while the middle gunner chose to stand his ground and fire a parting burst.

It cost him dearly as the Peugot's fuel tank detonated, spewing gasoline for yards in all directions, lighting up the battlefield. Katz heard the gunner's dying scream and saw a figure thrashing in the midst of the inferno, but his focus was reserved for others, tracking those who still constituted a viable threat.

He found one shooter breaking for the open desert on his right, the weapon in his hands forgotten as he raced for cover. Katzenelenbogen led his target with Tyumen's Browning, used two rounds to bring him down and one more just to keep him there.

Birjand mopped up the final gunman, spotting him by firelight, emptying his submachine-gun's magazine to make the dead man dance. Another moment and the only sound between them was the hungry crackle of the flames devouring upholstery and rubber, spreading to the roadside weeds.

Katz scooted back to check Tyumen's pulse, found none and let it go. He spent another moment on his knees, reloading both automatics and tucking one in his waistband before he palmed the other, rising to help Birjand police the scene. One of the Iranians was still alive but fading fast. They left him to sit on his own, concerned about their need for transportation now, with two cars totaled on the road.

A rapid head count told Katz there should be another vehicle close at hand. They found it hidden by some trees that they had passed on their approach, keys still in the ignition, extra magazines and weapons lying on the floor in back. They ditched the guns, retrieved their own belongings from the Volvo and proceeded on their way, Birjand still driving, swerving off the pavement to avoid the Peugot and its passengers.

In front of them the highway seemed to stretch forever, only darkness waiting at the other end.

CHAPTER SEVENTEEN

East of Kayseri, Turkey
Tuesday, 0015 hours

Driving with his window down, Mack Bolan smelled the battleground before he saw it in the Porsche's headlights. There was the stench of cordite, gasoline and smoke, burned rubber, roasting flesh. It added up to mayhem on the highway and he made an instant choice, decelerating on the final curve with one hand on the steering wheel, the other tucked inside his jacket, clutching the Beretta in its shoulder sling.

"Dear God!"

Sascha Lentz's shock didn't distract him. Bolan saw the scattered bodies, one car nosed into the bank and pocked with bullet scars, another smoking in the middle of the two-lane road. The flames had mostly died away, but there was still upholstery and carpeting to be devoured inch by crackling inch.

"I need to check this out," he said. "You take the wheel. If anything goes wrong—"

"I'm coming with you," Sascha told him.

"No. If it's a trap, we'll need to get the word back. That means someone has to stay alive. We don't have time to argue now."

He left the Porsche without another word, the sleek Beretta in his fist, and Sascha climbed across the center console, settling in the driver's seat. She left the headlights on, and Bolan circled wide to take advantage of the darkness, coming at the battleground obliquely, on the north side of the road.

It had been bad, he knew that much. The bullet-riddled Volvo might have been a different car, of course, but Bolan didn't like the odds and he was no believer in coincidence. At least, from all appearances, its occupants hadn't gone down without a fight.

The first dead man he found was lying in a clump of weeds some thirty feet from the car, sprawled on his back, eyes open, dark blood drying on his shirt. The weapon near his right hand was AK-47, and the ground around his corpse was bright with scattered cartridge cases.

Bolan passed him by, drew level with a gunman lying facedown on the pavement. Nearby, another body lay spread-eagle on the highway's center stripe, blood pooled beneath it, humming like nocturnal insects. On the far side of the road, illuminated by the Porsche's headlights, he could see a pair of shoes protruding from another clump of weeds, the feet and legs unmoving.

Closer to the Volvo, he found a fifth man huddled in the shadow of the car. His life had drained away through several bullet holes, his dark suit saturated with the spill of blood. The face was slack and pallid, but familiar. Bolan recognized the Russian agent who had been assigned to shepherd Katz on board the Orient Express.

Stone dead.

He checked inside the Volvo and found it empty, no apparent bloodstains on the carpet or upholstery. The other car, a smoking hulk by now, was thirty feet away, another lifeless body lying sprawled between the vehicles.

Bolan approached the burned-out Peugot with caution, smelling the fate of one unlucky passenger from a distance. The others had broken to right and left, running for cover—perhaps when the car caught fire—but neither one of them had made it.

Nine men dead, and that left two that he was sure of. Katz and the Iraqi contact still weren't accounted for. A search of the surrounding countryside could take all night and well into the morning, time that Bolan couldn't spare.

He was retreating toward the Porsche when he noted tire tracks on the sandy shoulder of the highway, swerving wide around the wreck of the Peugot. A simple passerby would almost certainly have stopped and doubled back to summon the authorities, which told him that third car had survived the firefight and continued eastward.

Katz and the Iraqi?

If they were still alive, they might be hostages, but Bolan wasn't betting on it. From the carnage visible around him, the attackers had contrived an ambush and it blew up in their faces. Bolan's gut told him Katz was still out there, moving toward his destination, more or less on schedule.

But without his Russian escort.

What kind of complications for their mission would the loss entail? For Katz it meant there'd be no one on the scene to watch his back if things went wrong, but mortal danger wouldn't frighten him away. The Phoenix Force warrior had too much experience, determination and raw courage to cut and run in a crunch.

Which meant he needed allies all the more.

He checked one of the bodies for ID, found nothing, and dismissed a wider search as so much wasted time. Sascha saw him coming, scooted over to the shotgun seat again and let him take the wheel.

"One down," he told her, "two still running."

Sascha tucked the P-5 automatic back inside her handbag, buckling her seat belt as he put the Porsche in gear and steered around the Peugot's wreckage.

"Someone doesn't want your friend to make it," she remarked.

And someone, Bolan thought, might try again before Katz reached his destination in Iraq.

Pinarbasi, Turkey

THE LIBERATED CAR was a Mercedes, six years old but fairly well maintained by Turkish standards. Once they cleared the wreckage of the battlefield, Ali Birjand had driven like a pro, flat-out, with one eye on the rearview mirror just in case they had a tail. The rest of his attention, as with Katz, was focused on the road ahead, alert to any warnings of a secondary ambush waiting in the wings.

Now they seemed to be alone, the momentary threat behind them. Katzenelenbogen wouldn't let himself relax entirely, and he kept one of the Browning automatics in his lap, the other riding heavy in the waistband of his slacks.

A dozen miles beyond the ambush site, Birjand remarked, "You fight well, for a scientist."

Katz tried to read the driver's tone, relief at being still alive, with maggots of suspicion nibbling around the edges. It would be ironic, he decided, if the very act of self-defense should get him killed.

"In Russia I had military training," he replied. "It was a long time back, of course, but some things I remember."

"And the pistol?"

"My companion thought there might be trouble. He insisted that I travel armed."

"A wise precaution. Sadly he didn't possess your skill."

"I'd call it luck."

"As you prefer."

They drove in silence after that, miles ticking off on the odometer, Katz half expecting the Iraqi to produce his SMG and open fire at any moment. The attack had forced him to reveal his hand—or part of it, at any rate—but he couldn't turn back the clock. The mission would be scrubbed if he was forced to kill Birjand before they reached their destination, but Katz didn't plan to sacrifice himself without result.

He thought of Nikolai Tyumen lying dead beneath the velvet sky and wondered what the man had seen in his final seconds of life. Did he consider it a worthwhile cause before the darkness swallowed him? Was any death worthwhile, from the perspective of the man about to die?

If not Tyumen, it could easily have been Katz lying on the pavement, cool and stiff by now. At that, the Russian's death created brand-new problems down the road. Birjand was already suspicious of his martial skills, and Katz couldn't be sure his hasty explanation would have done the trick. Ahead of him lay other meetings, obstacles for which his escort had been more or less prepared. They had discussed the different hurdles while en route from Budapest, but even knowledge was a hazard now. The enemy wouldn't expect Baranovich to function properly without his handler. Katz could overdo it if he wasn't careful—might have done too much already, in the firefight, as it was—and thus outsmart himself.

For now, Birjand would be the man to watch. If Katz was forced to kill him, he'd have to scrub the mission outright. The Iraqi's death could be explained—another ambush by the nameless enemy—but there was no way that Baranovich would make his way across the Turkish hinterland and find the secret rendezvous alone.

Nor, for that matter, could he.

Somewhat reluctantly Katz tucked the Browning out of sight beneath his jacket. It was a concession to reality, but hardly one that put his mind at ease. For all intents and purposes, he was beyond the point of no return. Worse yet, if anything went wrong for Katz, his comrades would still forge ahead, unaware of his setback. It could turn into a massacre, and all in vain.

But he had time. By Katzenelenbogen's calculations, they were still at least 350 miles from any border crossing to Iraq. The others—some of them, at least—would be behind him, bringing up the rear. When they discovered what had happened, it would put them on guard. If nothing else, his friends would know that someone had decided it was time to raise the stakes.

And in the meantime...

Turning toward Ali Birjand, Katz cleared his throat. "Those men back there," he said. "Who were they?"

"Possibly Iranians." The driver shrugged. "Iraq has many enemies today, but we will triumph over all." His tone of confidence was absolute.

"About my comrade..."

Birjand fanned the air with one hand in a gesture of dismissal. "There is nothing you can do to help him now."

"I was not briefed in any detail on the border crossing, or what follows after."

"Never mind. Your only obligation is to go where you are told and do your job."

"Perhaps, if I had some idea where that would be..."

"In time," the driver said. "All things in time."

The odds were long against Birjand possessing any knowledge of their final destination, and he let the matter drop. He had already pushed it far enough to make Birjand suspicious; any further questions would only place his mission and his life in greater jeopardy.

It was enough for now.

Katz settled back and closed his eyes, pretending to relax. His left hand stayed within a few short inches of the Browning automatic. Just in case.

East of Kayseri, Turkey

GARY MANNING WATCHED his comrades walking back in darkness toward the Cirtoën—one on each side of the road, one moving down the center stripe—with weapons in their hands. The SIG-Sauer automatic in his lap was cocked, the safety off, his index finger curled around the trigger. If required to list his feelings at that moment, Manning would have rated dread above all else.

Encizo slid into the seat beside him, James and McCarter climbing in the back. "All dead," the Cuban said. "Eight Arabs and the Russian Katz was running with."

"That's it?"

"No sign of Katz or his Iraqi wheelman," James declared with evident relief. "There was another car, though. Drove around the wreck up there and kept on heading east."

"Well, dammit!"

"Anyway," James said, "the odds are he's alive."

"Alive and kicking, from the looks of things," the Cuban added.

Manning put the Citroën in gear and maneuvered around the corpses lying in his path, following the same route Katz had taken when he—or his captors—circumnavigated the burned-out Peugot. When they were clear and rolling eastward again at seventy-five miles per hour, he let his mind focus on the still-unanswered question.

"You said Arabs."

"Right." Encizo's mouth was frozen in a scowl. "No ID on the ones I checked."

"Same here," James said.

"Iraqis?" Manning asked.

Encizo thought about it for a moment, finally shook his head. "No way. They would have had their own man at the wheel. No point in driving Katz out here to dust him, and I can't see the Iraqis taking out his escort, leaving Katz alive."

"So, who?"

"The same blokes from the train," McCarter suggested. "They missed him once and had to try again."

"Which means they've missed him twice," Encizo said.

"You hope." McCarter didn't sound convinced.

"I'm betting on it," the Cuban replied. "For one thing Katz's contact isn't lying back there on the road. To me that means they're still together. Still on course."

"I should have grilled that bastard on the train," McCarter said.

"And how were you supposed to pull that off?" James asked. "From what I understand, he wasn't the cooperative type."

"I could have found a way."

"And then what? Scrub the mission, maybe? I don't think so. Even if you found a way to tip Katz off that he had people on his ass, it wouldn't tell him when and where the opposition had an ambush planned."

A moment later, Gary Manning spoke into the brooding silence. "Right. The good news is, if Katz was dead we would have found him back there at the ambush site. Agreed?"

"Okay."

"I'm with you so far."

"Now, the bad news. He'll be going in alone, without his escort."

"Do you think it matters?" Encizo was drumming fingers on the dashboard as he asked the question.

Manning shrugged. "It might, if there's some kind of recognition signal. Either way, it's one less gun on his side when the shit hits the fan."

"We'll have to be there for him," McCarter said, staring into the darkness.

"There's one more thing."

"Which is?"

"A melee like we saw back there," Manning replied, "could produce a change in plans. His guide might go to ground or try an airlift, damn near anything at all. We might be going in ahead of Katz or much too late."

"It isn't like we have a lot of choice," Encizo said.

They were agreed on that, and Manning got another six or seven miles per hour from the Citroën as they sped toward the coming sunrise. Would the new day bring disaster or a slender hope? He thought of Katz, effectively beyond their reach for now, and wondered whether he'd ever see the gruff Israeli's face again.

If not, so be it. Friends were no more bulletproof than enemies, a lesson driven home for Gary Manning over years of hard experience. The trick was making sure more enemies than friends went down in any given combat situation.

At the moment Manning reckoned they were still ahead. The Russian paired with Katz had been an unknown quantity, perhaps a friend, but they'd never know for sure. Against his loss, eight hostiles dead in Turkey, plus another liquidated by McCarter on the Orient Express. That made it nine to one for Manning's team, so far, but they were still a long way from their goal. The odds could change with deadly speed, no warning whatsoever, catching players with their guard down if they let themselves relax.

No fear of that.

His nerves were strung out like piano wires, a deadly situation in itself. Anxiety would work in favor of his enemies from this point on, distracting Manning from the homely details that were vital to his craft. The first time he slipped up could be his last.

And he couldn't help Katzenelenbogen from a grave.

"One thing we'd better do," said Calvin James, "is find a telephone."

He was correct, of course. The had to report the ambush back to Stony Man without delay, in case it meant a change of orders. Which presented Manning with another problem—were there any public telephones available at one a.m. in rural Turkey? Would they have to drive for miles and hours to connect with Stony Man?

He focused on the brilliant tunnel of his headlight beams and stood on the accelerator. In a pinch, the next best thing to being there was making tracks.

Stony Man Farm

BARBARA PRICE WAS encoding a message from Able Team, marked Priority for Hal Brognola's eyes, when Carmen Delahunt came into the computer room. At first Price hardly noticed the stately redhead, focused on her work to the exclusion of all else.

She had some good news for Brognola this time, after their concern with Able dropping out of sight in Baja. Lyons, Schwarz and Blancanales were alive, if not precisely well, and they had wrapped their mission save for mopping up a few loose ends. Schwarz had a bullet in his leg, but Lyons deemed it "nothing serious," and they were wrapping up the job before they headed home for R & R. It would require some time to sort out the results, but late reports from Cabo San Lazaro indicated a substantial loss of life and property among their adversaries. A corrupt police department was compelled to grant that drugs were "almost certainly" involved, and five or six surviving suspects where in custody.

The lucky ones.

"Can I disturb you for a minute?"

Price glanced up from her terminal, blinked twice and slumped back in her swivel chair. "Please do."

"We just picked up a relay call from Phoenix, out of Turkey. They'll be roughly halfway to the border now, place called Malatya."

"And?"

"They ran into some trouble on the road. Or Katz did, I should say." The former FBI computer analyst held the mission controller's gaze with solemn eyes. "Some kind of ambush by a well-armed hit team. Katz apparently got through it with his guide, but someone nailed the Russian."

"Damn."

Price felt her stomach tighten as the mental images flashed through her mind. A darkened highway. Muzzle-flashes and the jarring sound of automatic weapons. Bodies sprawled in awkward, boneless postures on the tarmac, waiting for a hearse to come and carry them away. A reek of gun smoke mingled with the pungent smell of death.

"That's all we have right now," Carmen said. "Phoenix is proceeding with the track, and we've had nothing back from Striker since the visual in Ankara."

"Okay, I'll pass it on."

The older woman frowned. "Are you all right?"

"What makes you ask?"

"You look a little green around the gills."

"I'm fine."

"Whatever."

The coded access door hissed open, closed, leaving Barbara Price alone. The report from Phoenix Force had momentarily erased her thoughts of Able Team, sweet relief giving way to a new apprehension and dread.

Sometimes she felt helpless, useless, sitting in her little fortress while the frontline troops engaged their adversaries half a world away. There were moments when she felt like an outsider, watching through a one-way mirror while the Stony Man warriors risked their lives in mortal combat. Worse, there were the times—like now—when she caught glimpses of a hazard in the making and she had no way of warning those at risk.

The men of Phoenix Force were on their guard by now, but what of Bolan? He was used to living on alert, but was he conscious of the momentary danger close at hand? If not, was there a way for her to reach him and prevent his being caught in a trap?

When he checked in—if he checked in—the message would be relayed by his nameless contact from the CIA, but there was no set schedule for a call. It might be hours yet before he saw the need to telephone, and in the meantime...

Price concentrated on the field report from Able Team and finished it inside two minutes flat. Then she spent another five encoding Carmen Delahunt's report on Phoenix Force and Katzenelenbogen's brush with death. It was the good-news, bad-news syndrome, and the bad news always seemed to dominate.

One day, she thought, it would be nice to win a battle free and clear, no downside written into the equation. Just one time, to pick up all the marbles and retire without a sense of loss.

Good luck.

The present mission was a perfect case in point. They were cooperating with a former enemy—the Russian government—but dissolution of the old USSR hadn't imposed some magic, beatific peace upon the world. Instead they had new enemies to cope with, savages who preyed upon their victims in the same old way, through terrorism, violence and coercion.

War without end, amen.

As Stony Man's mission controller, Barbara Price found herself at the heart of the action, and yet once removed. It was the curious dichotomy, in fact, that prompted much of her frustration and dissatisfaction at the moment.

But there was work to do, and she couldn't afford to put if off. Brognola had to be informed of late events in Turkey and in Baja, California. One would cheer him up, the other set his teeth on edge, but they were flip sides of a single coin.

The currency of danger.

CHAPTER EIGHTEEN

Al Mawsil, Iraq
Tuesday, 0145 hours

At first Leonid Glazov mistook the rapping for part of his dream. In that fantasy world, he was riding a young Arab dancer, bringing her to climax with his worldly expertise, the power of his rhythmic thrusting movements drove the headboard into jarring contact with the wall. Except he realized, there was no headboard on his bed. No woman lying underneath him. No...

His eyes snapped open and the digital alarm clock on his nightstand told Glazov the time. He found the lamp and switched it on, muttering a curse as he swung his legs out of bed and reached for his robe. Glazov belted it loosely around his waist, covering the remnants of his fading erection as he stepped into slippers and shuffled from the bedroom of his small apartment, toward the outer door.

A summons at this hour could only mean bad news, a notion verified when Glazov opened up the door and saw Amal Mashhad. The slim Iraqi, always somber, wore a dark scowl on his face.

"What is it?"

"There has been an incident in Turkey."

Glazov turned away and left Mashhad to close the door behind him. Moving to the nearby couch, the

Russian sat down and crossed his legs. The fleeting vision of his dream and its results were banished from his mind.

"What sort of incident?" he asked.

Mashhad picked out a chair and settled into it, facing Glazov across a low coffee table. "We have contacts with the various authorities in Turkey. They report an ambush on the highway, between Kayseri and Malatya. Nine men dead, two vehicles destroyed."

"Baranovich?"

"From all appearances he managed to escape. No trace of him was found by the police. My agent also got away. Unfortunately..."

"What?"

"One of the dead men had a Russian passport. It would seem your rocket scientist has lost his escort."

Glazov frowned. He didn't know the dead man, but a Russian killed on Turkish soil was bound to raise some questions at a time when they could ill afford embarrassment. He'd be forced to warn Petrovski, let the politician do his best to cover the unfortunate mistake.

"Nine killed, you said. The other eight?"

"Iranians." Mashhad pronounced the word like an obscenity, as if it left a foul taste in his mouth. "Somehow, our enemies have found us out."

"It's easier to find a virgin in a whorehouse than to keep a secret in the Middle East," Glazov said, pleased at the expression of resentment his remark evoked. "Did you believe your ministers and deputies were all so faithful?"

"I can deal with the Iranians," Mashhad replied, his voice as stiff as brand-new leather. "At the moment I am more concerned with the Americans and the Israelis."

"Are you backing out of our agreement?" Glazov asked. "If so, please tell me now. Ivan Baranovich can always go back home. As for Polyarni and Serpukhov—"

"We are proceeding as agreed," Mashhad assured him. "Still, we might be forced to relocate the plant if there is danger from outside."

"Of course, as you see fit. Security is your domain."

Glazov wasn't concerned with the expense incurred by Baghdad, just as long as he was paid on time. He'd be out of business, though, if the Israelis or Americans got wind of what was happening and launched a preemptive strike to cripple Iraq's nuclear capabilities. If things got out of hand, he might even find himself in physical jeopardy.

No, thank you.

In his last full decade with the KGB, Glazov had operated from the safety of Dzerzhinsky Square, manipulating agents in the field as he, himself, was once manipulated by others. Rank had its privileges, and one of them was sitting in a cozy office while your operatives went out to risk their lives upon command. Iraq was a departure from the norm, in that regard, the first time he had actually been on-site in years, but times had changed. The Komitet was dead and buried—for the moment, anyway—and men of courage had to make their own way in the world.

In fact, he thought, it might be time for him to take a closer interest in the work of Serpukhov, Polyarni and Baranovich. A visit from their chief might help inspire them, hurry them along, and it would have the added benefit of getting him away from Al Mawsil. Mashhad was breathing down his neck these days, and Glazov would be happy for a change of scene.

"I will be traveling this afternoon," he said. "A visit to the lab, I think. It will be good for me to greet Baranovich and check up on the others."

"So."

Mashhad had covered his surprise, but not before it registered. Glazov was pleased with the effect. It almost made the interrupted dream worthwhile.

"Perhaps," Mashhad suggested, "I should join you. As you say, security is my concern. It would be wise for me to double-check the site. Do you agree?"

The smile felt brittle on his face, but Glazov kept it there. "It is your country, after all."

Mashhad was smiling now, more like a grimace on his long, lean face.

"And so," he told the Russian, "shall it ever be."

Cizre, Turkey

IT WAS WARM inside the small café, the first taste of a scorching day to come. They took a window seat and ordered breakfast—yogurt, dates, fresh rolls and butter, cheese, washed down with steaming mugs of strong, black coffee. Bolan watched the street outside while Sascha took the door behind him, checking out the patrons as they wandered in.

The drive from Malatya had left them both fatigued. At every turn the soldier half expected some new sign of conflict, bodies littering the highway or another burned-out car. Would it be Katzenelenbogen next time, with a bullet in his heart or brain?

But they found nothing, met no one as they continued on their way. Dawn lighted the countryside in hues of pink and gray, full daylight overtaking them before they reached the town where they were scheduled to connect with their Iraqi guide.

Cizre stood beside the Tigris River, facing the Syrian border in southwestern Kurdistan. Iraq lay fifty miles away along the river, somewhat farther if you traveled overland. The area had seen a flood of refugees since Operation Desert Storm's conclusion, as Saddam Hussein resumed his genocidal war against the Kurds. This day, though, it would have been difficult for anyone to tell a killing ground lay close at hand, perhaps with bodies rotting in the sun that very moment. Cizre was awake, but barely so. Mack Bolan and Sascha Lentz attracted little attention as they found the café where they were supposed to meet their guide.

Or so it seemed, at any rate.

They had been seated for approximately fifteen minutes when he felt an urgent nudge from Sascha's foot beneath the table. Bolan read the message in her eyes but didn't turn around at once. Instead he sipped his coffee, let his free hand slide beneath his open jacket, fingers grazing the Beretta in its shoulder sling. Across the table Sascha had one hand inside her purse, the P-5 automatic primed and ready.

Bolan felt the new arrival at his elbow, turned to face a slender man of five foot six or seven, with jet-black curly hair above a somber face. He glanced at each of them in turn. He wouldn't know their faces, but the Turkish-language paper lying folded on a corner of their table was the recognition signal.

"I believe you wish to travel south," the new arrival said.

"If we can find the proper guide."

"Of course. I have experience in that regard." His English had a stilted tone, as though it had been learned from a textbook.

"We should talk about it when you have the time," Bolan said, finishing his portion of the password.

"There is no time like the present."

"Please, sit down."

The new arrival pulled a chair up to their table, ordered coffee from the waitress and declined a menu. When they were alone at last, he introduced himself.

"My name is Esfahan Razi. I was expecting more of you."

"We traveled separately. The others should be coming soon."

"How many?"

"Six of us, in all."

The Arab wore a thoughtful frown. "There will be many more against you."

"That's a chance we'll have to take."

"I hoped there might be airplanes, bombs." Razi sat back and shook his head. "Instead they send me five men and a woman."

Sascha bristled at the Arab's tone, but Bolan spoke before she had a chance. "I take it you don't care much for Saddam Hussein."

"I am a Kurd. This butcher kills my people by the thousands, uses them to test his gas and other weapons. With my own hands I would kill him, if I had the chance. Instead I help you to destroy his weapons."

"Let's just hope we get that far," Bolan said.

"There are ways," Razi replied. "And it is not so far."

"How many miles?" Sascha asked.

The Kurd regarded her with something close to curiosity, then turned back to Bolan. The expression that he saw on Bolan's face persuaded him to answer Sascha directly.

"Across the border, sixty, sixty-five. From here perhaps 120 miles."

"Your people watch the site?"

"We built the site. Saddam sometimes refrains from killing Kurds if they work well enough as slaves."

"Do you have men inside?" Bolan asked.

"And women." Razi replied. "A number of the servants manage to report what they have seen from time to time. They told us when the Russians came, supplied descriptions, listened when the names were spoken. It was not so difficult to guess what the Husseinis have in mind—or who will be among the first to suffer if they should succeed."

"How are we traveling?"

"I have a tour bus that will provide sufficient cover to the border. Once across, we switch to jeeps for the remainder of the journey."

Bolan saw no point in probing after details, so he let it go. Across the border, all their preparations went for nothing if their luck ran out. A chance encounter with Iraqi troops, the passage of a spotter plane, and they were done.

He blanked the prospect from his mind. Whatever happened, they would deal with each contingency in turn.

Bolan sipped his coffee as he settled back to wait for Phoenix Force.

Bitlis, Turkey

"HERE."

Ali Birjand was pointing toward a tiny stucco house that barely would have qualified for cottage status in the States. The yard was barren dirt, worn smooth by generations of pedestrians. There was no fence, but two dogs lolling in the yard were tied with hanks of rope around their necks, secured to an iron ring planted in the soil. The house seemed lifeless as they passed, its curtains tightly drawn.

They drove around the back, parked the Mercedes in an alley at the rear, locked it and walked to the street. The dogs were waiting for them, on their feet and snarling now, until they recognized Ali Birjand and stood at ease. His knock was answered by a portly man whose hair had mostly disappeared on top, with compensation in the form of a luxuriant mustache and beard.

Inside, another man stood watching them, a folding-stock Kalashnikov tucked underneath his arm. Birjand shook hands with both men, waved Katz toward a threadbare sofa and began to speak in rapid Arabic. Katz understood enough of it to know his escort was relating the events since they had met in Ankara, with emphasis on the attack between Kayseri and Malatya. There were questions when he finished, taking up another quarter hour while the strangers satisfied their curiosity.

The bearded man took over next, with Katz pretending not to understand a word he said. In fact, some of it managed to elude him, but he gathered they wouldn't be leaving for an hour or so, at which time they were driving south. A formal escort would be waiting at the border to ensure safe passage to their destination on the other side.

Terrific.

Estimating they were still at least a hundred miles north of the border, Katzenelenbogen had begun to feel that he could calculate his life in hours now. None of his escorts knew him yet, or knew the man he was supposed to be, but once across that line...

"You will not need the pistol now, I think."

Birjand moved toward him, holding out an open hand. Reluctantly, still covered by the AK-47, Katz withdrew the Browning from its shoulder rig and gave it up.

"The other one as well."

He reached inside his jacket, to the rear, and palmed the second automatic, placing it in the man's outstretched hand. He was defenseless now, beyond the damage he could render with his feet, his left hand and the metal claw. It was a naked kind of feeling, like the dreams where one imagines going out in public and forgetting to wear clothes.

"You shall be safe with us," Birjand informed him.

"I can only hope so."

The display of hardware had surprised Birjand's companions. Both of them were eyeing Katz with new respect and something like suspicion, the rifleman shifting his weapon to get a better grip. Whatever they expected of a Russian rocket scientist, Katz had a feeling that he didn't fit the bill.

"How long before we leave?" he asked.

"Perhaps an hour. There are still arrangements to be made."

"And at the border?"

"A military escort will be waiting. You will be treated with a grateful nation's full respect."

At least until he was spotted as a ringer, Katzenelenbogen thought. Beyond that point, it would be blackjacks, thumbscrews and electrodes all the way. Unless they killed him outright in a fit of rage.

No, he decided, they'd definitely grill him first. A Russian egghead was expected, and a battle-scarred Israeli warrior was about to surface in his place. That would require some explanation, and he only hoped that Striker's team would keep their rendezvous before the questions grew too painful.

Much depended on the skill and preference of his interrogators, Katz decided. Brute force had its limitations, dulling nerves and bringing on unconsciousness if overused. Finesse was called for, and the best results were something gained with chemicals. No man could beat the modern range of psychoactive drugs for very long, without specific antidotes. The best that he could hope for, barring timely rescue, was a team of crude interrogators who relied on brawn in place of brains.

It was a game of buying time, with no real hope that he'd have a chance to run amok and damage the facility himself. Unarmed, outnumbered even if he found a weapon, Katz would be cut down in seconds flat. But if the others kept their date on time...

"Come with me," Birjand was saying. "We shall have our breakfast now."

Katz nodded, rose and followed him into the kitchen.

The condemned man ate a hearty meal.

Cizre, Turkey

BOLAN WAS A BLOCK AHEAD when Manning fell in step behind him, keeping pace. It wasn't difficult, despite the sidewalk bustling with pedestrians en route to this or that domestic errand. Bolan was a good six inches taller than the nearest competition, and the woman at his side would have been noteworthy in any crowd.

Manning knew the others would be keeping track of his every move. The Citroën was waiting two blocks back, with James at the wheel and Encizo beside him in the shotgun seat. McCarter had the north side of the street, and he was hanging back a block or so, well clear if anything went wrong.

In front of Manning, Bolan and the woman disappeared inside a haberdashery. It was the move he had been waiting for, and Manning saw the alley just ahead, a narrow breezeway set between a barbershop and grocery. Glancing back to verify McCarter in his place, the tall Canadian turned right and put the busy street behind him.

It was cooler in the alley, shaded from the sun, with none of the graffiti or discarded trash you would associate with such an urban setting in the States. Some fifty feet in front of him, another wider alley ran behind the shops, for garbage pickups and deliveries of goods. One hand was tucked inside his nylon jacket, covering the P-220 automatic in his waistband, as he cleared the breezeway, turning sharply to his left.

A slender, swarthy man had joined Bolan and the woman. Manning let himself relax a little, checking out their contact as he closed the gap, accepting Bolan's outstretched hand. The warrior's grip was firm, like always.

"Katz?" Bolan asked.

Manning shrugged. "We passed his leavings on the highway. Nothing else so far."

McCarter reached the alley just as Bolan was about to introduce their guide. The Citroën nosed in seconds later, cutting off retreat as a precaution, but the Arab still seemed perfectly at ease. His name was Esfahan Razi, at least today, and following his introduction to the Phoenix Force warriors, he suggested they adjourn to a more private place. He had a small apartment near the river, where they wouldn't be disturbed.

A nod from Bolan made it right, but Manning kept his guard up as he climbed into the Citroën, beside McCarter. Circling the block, they fell in line behind the Porsche 944 and followed it through winding streets until they reached a neighborhood of seedy flats that lined the Tigris. Looking at the neighborhood, it was difficult for Manning to visualize his surroundings as the original cradle of Western civilization.

So much for progress.

Razi lived upstairs, and he led the way with almost jaunty steps. Bolan and Sascha followed on his heels, the men of Phoenix Force behind them, with McCarter bringing up the rear. The flat was small and stuffy, but they left the windows shut for privacy. Razi made coffee while they all found seats, their numbers filling up a parlor that had been designed for two or three, expanding to the open dining nook. When everyone was seated, coffee mugs in hand, their host began.

"We have a journey of about 120 miles ahead of us," he said. "On this side of the border you are tourists. I shall be your guide. No one will question this. It is impossible for you to cross the border at a normal station with your weapons, though, so we must find another way."

"You have a way in mind?" James asked.

"I do. The smuggling trade between Iraq and Turkey has established many routes ignored by the authorities. With the annihilation of my people by Saddam Hussein, those routes are also used by refugees and rebels. I have passed that way myself, perhaps a dozen times. There will be comrades waiting on the other side with vehicles to see us through the desert."

"What about patrols?" McCarter asked.

"They are a risk, of course," Razi replied. "We will avoid them if we can. If not, our fate depends on speed and accuracy. An alarm would ruin everything."

"You have a map of the facility?" Bolan asked.

"Drawn by allies on the staff." Razi took a folded paper from an inside pocket of his blazer, knelt beside the coffee table and unfolded it as seven pairs of eyes moved closer, circling the hand-draw iagram.

"This way is north," he informed them, pointing, "and the gate lies here. A fence runs around the camp, barbed wire on top, with sentries on patrol. These buildings on the south are living quarters for the staff. Administrative functions are performed in this block, on the west." His finger moved across the map. "Maintenance here. The compound motor pool. The laboratories."

"Anything in terms of floor plan?" McCarter asked.

The Kurd shook his head ruefully. "My people are not allowed inside the laboratory proper. Security, you understand."

"We have to get there, first," Bolan said. "If we make it through the wire, we'll find a way inside the lab."

CHAPTER NINETEEN

Tigris River Valley
Tuesday, 1830 hours

The bus was a rattletrap, battered and scarred, the body rusted through in places, but it did the job. They made a curious collection, Sascha and her five companions taking seats throughout the bus, with Esfahan Razi behind the wheel. They had changed into comfortable hiking clothes, complete with high-topped boots. Their luggage consisted of duffel bags packed with their weapons and sets of desert camouflage fatigues for changing once they crossed the border.

First, however, they'd have to get that far.

It was an hour's drive from Cizre through the open countryside, occasionally passing army trucks along the way. The Turkish military kept patrols in place since Operation Desert Storm, attempting to control the flood of Kurdish refugees escaping from Iraq. The makeshift camps and shantytowns spaced out along the highway demonstrated that they were fighting a losing battle.

Razi said nothing as they motored past his displaced people by the hundreds, crouching in their tents or cardboard hovels, cooking over open fires, sometimes with metal buckets used in place of pots and pans. The camps played out as they drew closer to the border, fugitives avoiding proximity in case Saddam Hussein unleashed artillery or sent his army in pursuit. It was approaching dusk when they pulled off the highway and followed a dirt road southward for perhaps a mile, the old bus creaking as it wallowed over ruts and potholes. At last Razi nosed the bus into a deep limestone gully and killed the engine, leaving keys in the ignition as he took his duffel from its place behind the driver's seat.

Another man was waiting for them as they disembarked. Sascha hadn't seen him when they pulled into the gully, and she scanned the steep walls more closely now, on the lookout for other surprises. Razi and the stranger exchanged several comments in Arabic, then the second man boarded the bus, brought its engine to life and began to back out of the canyon, fat tires churning up a cloud of dust as he went.

"We walk from here," Razi informed them. "Once across the border, there are vehicles. First, change."

It was no time for modesty. Stripping down to her plain cotton underwear, Sascha donned her camouflage fatigues in two minutes flat. The others had more gear to grapple with, and she was finished well ahead of them, the Walther P-5 automatic snug inside a holster on her hip. She would have liked a larger weapon—a Galil assault rifle, perhaps, or at least an Uzi like Belasko carried—but at least her hands were free, and she'd leave the heavy fighting to her newfound comrades if they should encounter danger on the trail.

Inside the compound, she decided, close-range accuracy would be paramount, and she could always pick up extra weapons from the dead.

Unless she was among them.

"This way."

Razi struck off on foot along the canyon, his companions falling in behind him in no particular order. Sascha walked beside Belasko, out of habit from their past two days together, silently admitting to herself that she felt better with the tall man close at hand. She didn't know the others yet, might never have the time, but she had come to trust the American with her life.

They had been walking for the best part of an hour when the canyon dipped in front of them, the slope becoming steeper. Razi stopped short and waited for the group to overtake him, pointing to the south where darkness lay across the land.

"The border," he said. "Two hundred yards. We must be quiet now."

Without another word he turned and led them down into the shadowed valley, picking over rocks and twisted roots as they descended. In a few more moments they had left the light behind.

THE JEEPS WERE WAITING for them half a mile inside Iraq. Two drivers waited with the vehicles, but Razi dismissed them and they melted into the darkness.

It was agreed that Razi should drive the lead jeep, Bolan riding shotgun, Sascha and McCarter seated in the rear. Encizo drove the second vehicle, with James and Manning as his passengers and fire support.

"We cannot use the headlamps," the Kurd said, when they had stowed their gear and settled who would ride with whom. "But God shall provide. The full moon is a blessing."

"If you know the way," Encizo muttered.

"And I do," Razi assured him. "We shall play—how do you say it in the West?—follow the leader."

Bolan glanced around the circle of familiar faces, understanding what the Phoenix Force warriors felt. A stranger they had known for barely half a day was leading them through hostile territory, toward a firefight with opposing forces several times their strength. It was a crapshoot, with at least a hundred different ways that it could blow up in their faces, but they seemed to have no choice.

It still might be a trap, deliberately obscure, but they'd have to take the chance. If anything went wrong, the Executioner himself would guarantee that Razi didn't survive to gloat about his clever ploy.

The pallid moonlight showed an eerie landscape etched in black and varied shades of gray. The Kurd drove cautiously, no more than forty miles an hour on the flats and barely half that speed as they negotiated rocky hillsides, rolling over washed-out riverbeds. There was no road, per se, but with the jeeps locked into four-wheel drive they made fair time. At that rate, it would be approaching midnight when they reached their destination, and the hour suited Bolan's purpose well enough.

There would be time to park and scout the compound, make his mind up whether they should crash the gate or try to breach the fence more quietly, for an oblique approach. It would depend upon the sentries and security devices, what they found on-site, and there was no way he could make up his mind in advance.

He thought of Katz, somewhere ahead of them by now. How long would he be able to preserve his cover? Would he even make it to the site alive? If things went sour, Bolan knew the tough Israeli would give a fair account of himself, but that knowledge was small consolation for the loss of a friend.

Bolan concentrated on the here and now, scanning the moonlit desert with narrowed eyes, watching for unexpected gullies or boulders, alert to the possibility of ambush.

When it happened, even so, the moment took him by surprise.

A searchlight blazed, blinding him. A harsh voice called to them in Arabic, some kind of a command. He cursed and was about to pull the trigger on Razi for leading them into a trap when the Iraqi grabbed his AK-47, lurched up in his seat and fired a burst in the direction of the light.

A member of the ambush party shouted back with something that could easily have been a warning or a curse. The light exploded, raining sparks, and they were left to live or die by moonlight as a dozen hostile weapons opened up from thirty yards away.

James reacted on instinct, rolling out of his seat in the second jeep and dropping to a crouch behind the vehicle, taking advantage of its marginal cover. Numerous weapons were finding the range, including one that sounded like a .50-caliber machine gun. It was mounted high, some kind of armored vehicle, but James caught only a glimpse before incoming fire drove him back under cover.

He heard the jeep taking hits all around him, full-metal jacket by the sound, and it flashed in his mind that they might wind up walking the last sixty miles.

Assuming they were still alive.

And at the moment James wouldn't have bet the farm on that, if he had been a gambling man.

The best thing about being trapped in a corner, he decided, was the freedom it gave you to let your mind go, considering options a rational man would dismiss out of hand. The smartest thing to do in any killing situation would be cut and run, but the topography ruled out retreat as a viable option. The jeeps were poor cover at best, but the landscape behind them was wide open, a perfect shooting gallery for their enemies.

How had they stumbled on the ambush unobserved? Another hasty glance showed James a line of rocky hills some distance to the east, and closer in a ridge with stunted trees along its spine. Unless you knew the men and vehicles were there, it was the perfect blind.

Coincidence? Was the encounter random chance, a stray patrol, or had their Kurdish guide been working both sides of the street? There was no time to think about it, as James popped up and fired a short burst from his Vz.58 in the direction of his enemies. More muzzle-flashes answered, hot rounds sizzling around his ears.

He had to gain position on the snipers somehow, and his only chance involved a risk that James would have preferred to leave for someone else. Like Superman, for instance, if the man of steel would kindly drop in for a moment when they needed him.

Without a superhero, though, the job came down to any soldier with the guts and skill to pull it off.

There was a shallow cut across the landscape twenty yards to James's left. The intervening space was open ground, but if he reached the gully he'd have a modicum of cover, following its curve northeasterly until he came around behind the ridge. Behind his enemies.

It was a long shot with the heavy odds against him, but he had to try.

"Some cover," James hissed to Encizo, crouched nearby. "I'm out of here."

Without a question the Cuban left cover and sprayed a burst of rifle fire along the ridge. Manning was out of earshot, but he saw the move coming and added his Beretta submachine gun to the chorus, unloading a full magazine as James made his break.

It was just like playing football in high school, except this time the opposing players carried guns and they had more than touchdowns on their minds. He ran a zigzag pattern, crouching low, and he was ready for it when the .50-caliber cut loose, its hot rounds eating up the ground behind him. Too damn close. They'd have him in another second if he didn't jump.

James dropped his rifle, landed with a jolt on hands and knees, collapsing as the .50 raised a futile dust storm overhead. He scooped up the Vz.58, and, after checking it for damage, began to worm his way along the gully.

He felt the ridge before he saw it, registered as changing elevation and a different texture in the soil. The gully rose a little, but it also cut the ridge, a gap of six or seven feet that beckoned to him like an open door. James dug his toes in, putting on some extra speed.

His enemy was there before him, springing out of cover with an automatic weapon clutched in his fists. It stood to reason—they had seen where he was going, after all—but James wasn't prepared to let it go at that. His Vz.58 spit a short precision burst, 7.62 mm rounds punching through the man-shaped silhouette and blowing it away.

One down, and he could kiss surprise goodbye.

The Phoenix Force fighter staggered to his feet and hit the gap at speed, his boots nearly losing traction as he turned hard right to flank his enemies. They knew that he was coming, some of them at least, but there was nothing else for him to do.

He held down the automatic rifle's trigger and went for broke.

ENCIZO HAD SWERVED his jeep when the floodlight blazed in front of them, veering offtrack to disperse potential targets, and the vehicle was sitting ten or fifteen yards due north of Bolan's jeep. From all appearances, it would be sitting there until doomsday, since the tires were shot to hell and several dozen rounds had rattled off the engine block.

Crouched behind the vehicle and wishing he had somewhere else to go, Encizo thought about James and wondered if his friend would make it even halfway to the ridge before they cut him off and mowed him down. It was a desperate move, inspired by desperate circumstances, and it pissed Encizo off that James had had the notion first. At least he had a chance to move, die standing up and face-to-face with those who killed him.

But they were far from dead, and if the crazy move by James paid off...

A scuttling sound of shifting rocks and sand alerted Encizo to movement on his flank. He pivoted in that direction, risked a glance around the jeep and saw three figures rushing forward in a V formation, charging toward the jeep.

"Heads up!" he called to Manning, rolling out and dropping to a prone position even as he spoke. His

Vz.58 was lined up on the nearest of the moving targets in a heartbeat, moonlight showing him the way.

His first three rounds ripped through the pointman, spinning him like an apprentice dervish who had yet to learn the proper steps and ritual. Encizo's target went down hard, his nearest comrade forced to leap across the body that had fallen in his path.

And that made two. The automatic rifle stuttered, lurched against Encizo's shoulder, and the jumper vaulted backward, twisting in midair. He got a burst off as he fell, but it was wasted on the desert, high and wild. His impact had the sound of deadweight settling heavily to earth.

One left, and he was firing on the run. The soldier had a rough fix on Encizo from his muzzle-flashes, hot rounds kicking dust up in the Cuban's face. Encizo wriggled backward, cursing, wishing he had been a little quicker. Now the bastard had him pinned.

Manning caught the runner with a rising burst from his Beretta submachine gun, dropping him an easy ten yards from the jeep. The .50-caliber opened up again before they had a chance to celebrate, but they had shaved the odds, even so.

For all the good that it would do them now.

Pinned down, it made small difference to Encizo whether he was covered by a dozen hostile guns or one. One bullet was enough to punch his ticket, and the enemy had ample rounds to spare.

The next burst, when it came, was different somehow. Slightly muffled, muted by an intervening wall of earth for instance. Maybe even aimed at someone else.

"It's Calvin! Shit, he made it!"

On his feet and firing, Encizo decided they might have a chance after all. Not guaranteed, by any means, but something they could go for in a pinch.

And it was pinching tighter all the time.

BOLAN WAS READY TO ROCK when the burst of fire on their flank distracted his enemies. He palmed one of the L2A1 frag grenades and lobbed it overhand toward the ridge, had a second in the air before the first one reached its target. Heavy metal thunder danced on the ridge with gouts of flame and dusty geysers spewing sand and gravel toward the sky, along with twisted bodies.

It was all the chance that he'd ever have, and Bolan seized it by the throat. He had the Uzi cocked and locked, a full mag in the pistol grip as he emerged from cover, sprinting toward the ridge. Behind him, Sascha shouted something, but her voice was lost in the explosive sounds of combat. Razi was running on his flank, already firing toward the ridge, and Bolan left him to it, thankful he had hesitated for a crucial instant when he felt the urge to cut their driver down.

A rifleman sprang up in front of Bolan, sighting toward the Kurd, and the Executioner stitched him with a burst across the chest, slamming him backward into the dust. Razi took the next one up, firing on the run and using up the last rounds in his magazine. He stopped short, ditched the clip, and was tugging another from his belt when two gunmen burst from the cover of a dusty Land Rover, closing the gap with long strides.

Bolan met them with a figure eight that dropped them in an awkward sprawling knot of arms and legs, their bodies twitching for another moment as synapses fired their dying signals from the brain. Razi had managed to reload his AK-47 now, and he was firing toward the Rover, blasting out its windows, flushing another gunman from the cover of its shadow.

The warrior left Razi to take the soldier down. His full attention focused on the armored personnel carrier nearby, its big .50-caliber machine gun blasting away at the jeeps where Sascha, McCarter and the others were returning a sporadic fire. The turret gunner was exposed, bent forward over the heavy machine gun's spade grips, bright muzzle-flashes lighting his face like a Halloween fright mask.

Bolan raised his Uzi and stroked the trigger, sending half a dozen parabellum manglers on their way. The gunner took them in a rising line between his hip and armpit, staggered by the impact, dead before he toppled sideways out of sight.

A darting shadow vaulted from the rear deck of the APC and fired a burst of automatic fire at Bolan, scarcely aiming, bullets raising dust a few yards to his left. The warrior tracked his target, leading by a good six inches, squeezed off and watched him fall.

He rushed to the APC. Its rear doors stood open, its interior compartment empty. Bolan recognized it as an American M-59, doubtless sold to Saddam Hussein in the days when he was considered an ally.

Times change.

A ringing silence fell across the battleground, except for footsteps crunching on the sand. He looked around and started counting heads, came up with half a dozen in addition to his own.

All safe and sound.

It was a miracle of sorts, or you could chalk it up to reflex, combat expertise, dumb luck—whatever. Bolan didn't know or care which was correct, but he was satisfied with the result.

The team would live to fight again, but they had far to go.

"THE JEEPS ARE finished," Sascha said to no one in particular, her eyes surveying the killing ground.

"Same here with the Rover," said James, who had introduced himself to her as Cleveland Jones.

"That leaves the APC," Bolan said, and seven pairs of eyes swung toward the armored vehicle.

Sascha was prepared to drive the minitank if no one else knew how, but there appeared to be no shortage of available chauffeurs. These men were nothing, if not versatile.

"We'd best stock up on hardware," said the man she knew as Gerry Martin.

"Right." Bolan gave directions to the others, saw them on their way before he climbed inside the APC to check it out.

Sascha recognized the vehicle as an American model, designed for a two-man crew plus ten passengers. It was a tracked vehicle, fully amphibious, powered by two in-line GMC Model 302 six-cylinder gasoline engines. Its armor was 16 mm thick, and it could travel 164 miles on a full tank of fuel, with a top speed of thirty-two miles per hour. With any luck at all...

"We've got three quarters of a tank," Bolan told her from the driver's seat.

"Enough?"

"Should be."

He checked the stockpile of machine-gun ammunition and reported back. "I'd estimate they left us 1,500 rounds."

An AK-47 stood beside the co-pilot's seat, mounted on a special rack, and Sascha claimed it for her own. There would be extra magazines outside, among the dead, but she postponed her search a moment longer, turning to her companion with a question on her lips.

"This makes it better, right?"

"It could," he answered. "Anyway, we'll look legitimate when we approach the compound. Still, if someone finds this mess before we get there, I'd expect a general alarm."

And he was right, of course. They could devote the next few hours to planting bodies in the desert, but they couldn't hide three bullet-riddled vehicles, no matter how they tried. They had a schedule to keep, and time was running out.

"What, then?" she asked.

"We go ahead," he told her, twisting in the seat so she could see his face. If he was suffering from any private doubts, they didn't show. "I don't see any other way."

They hadn't come this far to throw up their hands in defeat and walk away. The risks were great, but there was too much riding on the line for Sascha to consider turning back. The mission still might cost her life, but she had been prepared for that when she enlisted with the military, and again when she moved on to the Mossad.

"Then we should hurry," she remarked.

Without a backward glance, she suited words to action, dropping from the APC and moving off to find a corpse whose ammunition belt would hold spare magazines for the Kalashnikov. Two minutes did the trick, supplying her with loaded bandoliers and several hand grenades.

The tools of war.

Before the night was out, she knew that she would need them all to stay alive, and still it might not be enough.

So be it.

She was ready for the worst her enemies could do.

As for the worst that *she* could do, it would remain for them to see.

CHAPTER TWENTY

West of Nineveh, Iraq
Tuesday, 2030 hours

Leonid Glazov sipped a glass of wine, listening distractedly while Polyarni and Serpukhov discussed their day's work in the lab. They were making progress, clearly, but the details were beyond him and he made no serious attempt to follow their discourse, letting the technical and scientific terms slip in one ear and out the other. They were earning money for him, even as they sat there on the couch with vodka glasses in their hands, and that was good enough.

He still felt stiff and weary from the morning's drive, a hangover from traveling in military vehicles that were seldom built for comfort. A hot shower was out of the question, given the average daily temperature in northern Iraq, but Glazov planned to take advantage of the site's fringe benefits that evening, when they retired to their separate rooms. He had his eye on a particular desert flower named Tayma, touted by Amal Mashhad as a talented masseuse...among other things. If Tayma couldn't work out Glazov's kinks, perhaps she could teach him some new ones.

The Russian checked his watch again and frowned as he caught himself at it. Ivan Baranovich would be there in his own good time. A watched pot never boiled, as the Americans would say. Right now, the rocket scientist was making tracks across the desert, well inside Iraq and drawing closer by the moment. The attack in Turkey was a futile gesture by Tehran. This time tomorrow—or pehaps the next day, if he felt like resting from his trip—Baranovich would be online, contributing his expertise to the existing team.

More income for the men who pulled the strings. Another step toward striking sparks that would ignite the Middle East and so restore the rightful rulers of the Soviet Union to their cherished and well-deserved positions of influence.

Soon, now.

It wasn't hypothetical, these days. Glazov couldn't have named a day when it would happen, but the change was coming, certainly before year's end. The only flaw would be Saddam Hussein, if he provoked the West to strike before his brand-new arsenal was ready. There was madness in the man, he might be capable of anything. Yet even a premature explosion would be better than no blast at all. In Moscow and Minsk, the machinery was in place for a reversion to the tested, proved ways of governing an empire. There were doors to open, buttons to be pushed, but it was all formality, the kind of details relegated to subordinates. Once the machine was put in motion, there could be no turning back.

Polyarni was debating some fine points of fusion with his scientific comrade, leaning closer, prodding Serpukhov's knee with a bony index finger. There was color in his cheeks, the sort one normally associated with a discussion of sports or women, suggesting agitation or at least substantial interest. Glazov wondered how such men survived outside their sterile labs, deciding they wouldn't last long without an apparatus to support them. They were hothouse flowers, doomed to wither from exposure to the hard, cold world outside.

Or, in their present case, the hot, dry world.

But they were thriving here, from all appearances. They had their test tubes, Bunsen burners, microscopes and centrifuges—anything they asked for that oil money could buy. Hussein might be a lunatic, but he wasn't a miser when it came to paying for the objects he desired.

In some ways, Glazov thought, the scientists were better off in Iraq than they ever had been in the Soviet Union. Except that this time, when they finished with their work, they'd become expendable.

Too bad.

There were still many weapons specialists and rocket scientists around. When the empire was back on its feet, their services would be required and they wouldn't refuse. Some wouldn't leave their homeland in the first place; others could be lured back, no matter what it took. As for Baranovich, Polyarni and Serpukhov...well, he'd miss them in a way—and welcome them with open arms if they should manage to escape the coming firestorm—but their sacrifice would be for Mother Russia in the end.

Leonid Glazov, himself, didn't intend to make that sacrifice. He'd welcome Ivan Baranovich to the facility, make sure the three of them were perfectly compatible over the next day or two, and then he'd leave—a business meeting with superiors at home that couldn't be postponed. He'd leave Berdichev in charge at Al Mawsil, send for him later...or perhaps not.

Glazov took another sip of wine and smiled. His day was coming.

Soon.

IT WAS WARM AND LOUD inside the armored vehicle. The average military planner denigrated niceties like insulation to reduce the noise of engines throbbing underneath the floorboards, and you had to raise your voice to ask a simple question while the APC was rolling over sand and gravel, heading east.

McCarter had the wheel, with Razi beside him, pointing out the way. As they drew closer to their target, they'd have to use established roads, a matter of appearances, and they were counting on Razi to see them through if they were challenged on the radio. He wouldn't know the latest military codes, of course, but they'd have to play that part of it by ear.

As for the flip side of the coin, if they were stopped and challenged face-to-face...well, they'd simply have to tough it out.

Bolan rode in back, positioned on a bench beside the armor-plated access doors. It took him back to Vietnam, the few times he had traveled any distance in an APC, but he had no time for nostalgia at the moment. They were approaching contact with the enemy—three hours, give or take—and the Executioner meant to be prepared.

It was a mental thing, as much as physical. They had more hardware now than he had ever counted on: .50-caliber machine gun, extra small arms, magazines, grenades. He had no doubt the APC would get them past the compound's gate and well inside the wire. From that point, though, it would be each man for himself.

Each woman, too.

He glanced at Sascha on his left. She seemed relaxed, an AK-47 gripped between her knees, grenades on webbing and a loaded bandolier obscuring the outlines of her body underneath the camouflage fatigues. She was a soldier first and foremost, but the Executioner still had his private qualms about the use of women in a killing situation. They were capable enough, except for certain moments when a burst of pure brute strength was needed, but Bolan had come up through a different school. In his day women were protected—or deprived; it all depended on your point of view—from bearing arms in combat, as from certain occupations deemed too risky for a member of the "weaker sex."

He understood the fallacy of such outdated thinking, but there was within himself a strong protective urge toward females that the changing mores of society couldn't eradicate. If he was watching out for Sascha when they hit the compound, it could get him killed, endanger every other member of the team. The challenge, if he chose to think of it as such, would be to let her stand or fall alone, depending on her own specific skill and training.

"How much farther?" Manning asked.

McCarter consulted Razi, then called back over his shoulder, "Seventy miles, give or take."

They wouldn't be making the APC's top speed of thirty-two miles per hour on desert terrain, an idealized rate of travel clocked on open roads in test conditions. Twenty-five would be more like it, but the pinpoint timing wasn't critical.

Except, perhaps, to Katz.

"So, what about the fuel?" James asked.

McCarter didn't turn around this time. "We'll make it," he responded, "but we won't be driving back this way unless we find a handy service station."

Bolan frowned. Withdrawal was a problem they had recognized from the beginning. Even with the jeeps it would have been a gamble. Getting out was always a consideration, but he brought his mind to bear on first priorities. They had a job to do, at any cost, and once that mission was accomplished, anything they managed for themselves was gravy.

Sascha leaned in close to him and tried her best to keep from shouting as she spoke. "You're troubled."

Bolan shook his head. "Just thinking."

"Care to pass it on?"

"It's hardly worth it. I suppose you'd say I'm running odds and angles."

Razi had briefed them on the site's defenses to the best of his ability. It was a military compound, ringed by wire, with sentries on the fence. He didn't have a head count on defenders, but he knew they came and went without apparent patterns to their movement. Sometimes there were armored vehicles around the site, and sometimes not. There was a helipad, but it was mostly used by unarmed choppers, for extraction or delivery of personnel.

"We have our duty," Sascha told him, echoing the soldier's thoughts.

"How long have you been doing this?" he asked her.

"I was born in Israel," she reminded him. "I've been a soldier all my life."

"Let's hope you live to be an old one," Bolan said, before he settled back and closed his eyes.

HIS TIME WAS RUNNING OUT, and Yakov Katzenelenbogen knew it. Riding in a military column, with an APC and jeep in front of him, the same behind, he felt like the selected filling in a sandwich, aimed directly at a giant's gnashing teeth.

Ali Birjand had ridden with him all the way. Their border crossing to Iraqi territory was a mere formality, the frontier guards prepared for their arrival. Two miles on the other side, beyond the range of Turkish spies, they had been met by uniforms and armor. Katz was treated with respect, a valued guest and ally, settled in an air-conditioned staff car with Birjand beside him and a stocky sergeant at the wheel. Unlike his comrades, trekking overland, they didn't shun the highways, but they still had miles ahead of them before they reached their destination.

Soon.

A crackle from the staff car's radio informed their driver that the compound was in sight. Katz couldn't see it yet, his view obstructed by the APC that led the column, but he felt his stomach tighten at the prospect.

What to do when they arrived?

It was a question he had pondered from the first, discussed with Bolan and his fellow Phoenix Force warriors back at Stony Man. Unarmed, the best that he could hope to do was punch or kick the nearest soldiers, try to seize a weapon...and for what? The futile gesture wasn't Katzenelenbogen's style. If he achieved no more than buying time, at least he had to do that much and give his friends a chance to close the gap, take their positions for a killing strike.

There was an outside chance that he wouldn't be burned immediately on arrival. It was slim, he realized, but if the welcoming committee was composed entirely of Iraqis, he might get away with it until another Russian showed his face.

The staff car was decelerating, and he caught a glimpse of chain-link fences topped with razor wire. No floodlights illuminated the compound, but the very darkness would enhance security. If hostile forces tried an air strike, there'd be no blazing target in the middle of the desert. They'd have to do their homework, sweat a little, and he wondered if the site had any antiaircraft capabilities built in.

Forget about it. Katzenelenbogen's comrades were confined to surface travel. At the moment they had more to fear from hostile aircraft than the Russians and Iraqis did.

The compound's gate had opened up in front of them, the APC already well inside, immediately followed by the jeep. Katz counted sentries as the staff car followed, spotting four around the gate with AK-47s at the ready. Two more moving out of sight behind some buildings on his left, and there were bound to be at least a few more tucked away at strategic points around the camp's perimeter. He guessed a dozen, multiplied by three for normal shifts, and rounded off to forty for an even number. Call it six-to-one odds, if he was able to fight when his comrades arrived.

The tank was a surprise. Parked behind a block of what he took for barracks, it was visible enough for him to recognize the Russian T-72. Twenty-five thousand pounds of rolling death, the tank sported a 125 mm cannon on its turret, with a 7.62 mm coaxial machine gun and a .50-caliber machine gun mounted to provide antiaircraft fire. Its three-man crew was protected by layers of reactive armor, incorporating explosive charges and chemical fillers to defeat various kinds of antitank rounds. The ideal top speed of thirty-seven miles per hour was academic, since the T-72 rarely had to move for anybody.

Dammit!

Bolan and the Phoenix Force team would be expecting infantry, but heavy armor was a different story. At least, Katz told himself, the tank would be restricted in its movements by dimensions of the compound. Likewise, cannon fire would be restricted by the risk of damage to surrounding structures, one of them presumably incorporating nuclear facilities. Blasting away with the big gun at close quarters would be tantamount to killing houseflies with a shotgun—in the house.

Katz told himself that Bolan and the others would devise a plan. Together they had more experience at playing lethal games by ear than any other group of warriors Katzenelenbogen knew. How many battles had been won, between them, on the strength of sheer audacity and nerve?

Still, they weren't immortal men of steel. It troubled Katz to think that he might somehow be the source of their undoing. Risking life and limb was one thing. Risking others...

The staff car was slowing, the lead jeep and APC pulling off to one side as their driver proceeded toward a structure on the south side of the compound. Glancing back across his shoulder, Katzenelenbogen saw the other jeep and APC break off and join the others, soldiers standing down.

The staff car stopped in front of double doors, its driver switching off the engine and the lights. As if on cue, a pair of men emerged to greet them, waiting while the staff car's wheelman circled back and opened Katzenelenbogen's door. The Israeli lingered for a heartbeat, then grudgingly stepped outside.

An Arab stood on his left, inscrutable and silent. On his right, a thickset European with a face Katz recognized from briefings back at Stony Man.

"Perhaps you would be kind enough," Leonid Glazov said, "to tell us who you are and what has happened to Ivan Baranovich?"

DRIVING WITH THE HATCHES open to improve on ventilation in the APC, McCarter still felt cramped and somewhat claustrophobic in the driver's seat. The land was relatively flat, and he had been required to double back for half a mile on only one occasion, losing time as he circled to avoid a steep-sided gully. The rest was slow but easy going; still, McCarter couldn't shake a sense of apprehension that had nagged him since the ambush.

They were headed into danger, that much was a given, but the worst part was uncertainty. So far, they didn't have a head count on their enemies, and nothing but a vague idea of the defensive weapons and security devices they'd face upon arrival. Granted, they were more secure inside the APC than in a pair of open jeeps or scuttling through the night on foot, but the alternative perception was to view them all as sitting ducks for any marksman with an armor-piercing rocket.

Glancing at his watch and back at the odometer, McCarter guessed they had at least another hour and a half to go before they reached their destination. They were running parallel to an established highway now, some half a mile due south, relying on the night to hide their dust trail and protect them from Iraqi scouts.

So far, so good.

Upon arrival, it would be a "simple" case of crashing through the gate and taking out the sentries they could reach, unloading in a rush and making for the lab. Of course, they'd be working from the sketch supplied by Esfahan Razi, a secondhand report supposedly prepared by spies whom none of them except the Kurd had ever met. Mistakes, deliberate or otherwise, would cost them precious time, perhaps their lives. Suppose Shiraz was wrong about which building housed the lab, for instance?

McCarter reined in his imagination, concentrating on the moonlit desert and the APC's controls. He hadn't driven armor for a while, but it came back to him like pedaling a bike or making love. Once learned, it was a skill you never quite forgot.

There had been little use for armor in the SAS or with Phoenix Force, but versatility was critical. McCarter also had a pilot's license, qualified on all British and American prop aircraft up to four engines, in case he ever needed to take wing in an emergency.

The thought of flying brought his mind back to their getaway, assuming any member of the team survived that long. The APC would be no help in that regard. It would be running low on fuel as they approached the compound, and its sluggish cruising speed would place them at the mercy of pursuers equipped with any vehicle faster than thirty miles per hour. Even armor wouldn't help them in the middle of the desert, underneath a broiling sun, when they were cut off and surrounded with their ammunition gone.

McCarter wasn't frightened by the thought of death, but neither did he relish it. If there was any way to walk away from the engagement once their job was done, he meant to find it. They could steal a smaller, lighter vehicle perhaps... and then, what?

Any way you sliced it, they'd be at least a hundred miles inside Iraq, disowned by their respective governments, with nothing but the weapons in their hands to see them through. It was a challenge, but it wouldn't be the first time Phoenix Force had battled hopeless odds.

He shifted gears and thought of Katz, already at the site by now. They had been deliberately vague on Katzenelenbogen's duties once he entered the hostile camp, knowing in advance that there was no way to script the moment. With luck he might squirrel away enough information to pinpoint the lab or the surviving Russian scientists. It could be useful once they found him.

If they found him still alive.

The APC was grinding up a gentle slope, treads biting deep into the sand and gravel of the desert floor. It would have been much simpler all around, McCarter thought, if Operation Desert Storm had lasted two or three days longer, mopping up Saddam Hussein instead of leaving him in power with a cocksure attitude of personal superiority. Their move tonight was no solution to the problem, either, but at least it would retard the butcher's effort to ignite a regional—or global—holocaust.

And when he really thought about it, that alone was worth the sacrifice.

"Another twenty minutes," McCarter said to the team at large, "and we'll turn north to meet the highway."

"Fair enough." The voice was Bolan's, coming to him from the rear deck, thirteen feet away.

Returning to the highway meant a geometrical increase in risk, but they had seen for themselves that the open desert wasn't always safe. At least if they met any opposition this time, they were traveling in an official vehicle, and it would take a larger weapon than a .50-caliber to pierce their armored skin.

Ideally, though, they could avoid a confrontation with the enemy until they reached their final destination. Clashes on the highway meant delays, expenditures of vital ammunition, plus the ever-present risk of injury or death to members of the team. A nice, clear runway to the killing ground was what McCarter wanted now.

The killing would come soon enough, and instinct told him there would be enough to go around.

Beside him, Esfahan Razi seemed perfectly at ease, relaxing in his seat with eyes half closed. McCarter reckoned they could trust him now, with his performance in the ambush situation noted, but he had expected something more in terms of visible emotion from the man.

Perhaps, McCarter thought, he found himself relieved of worry now that they were truly on their way. The battle had been joined, and there could be no turning back. Razi's people were among the chips in what was shaping up to be a high-stakes game.

But they could only play the hands that they were dealt, whatever happened next.

McCarter frowned and hoped that Bolan had a few spare aces up his sleeve.

CHAPTER TWENTY-ONE

West of Nineveh, Iraq
Tuesday, 2315 hours

"I think we will start over once again at the beginning," Amal Mashhad said. "Your name?"

The one-armed man was seated in a straight-backed metal chair, stark naked, with his arms and legs immobilized by leather straps. The chair possessed no cushion, and its legs were bolted to the wooden floor. It couldn't be inverted, turned, or even shaken very much without assistance from a lug wrench.

"Name?" The stranger's voice was parched, a rasping on the nerves. "Why don't you check my passport."

"I have done so, as you realize. Ivan Baranovich might be alive today, although I have my doubts. Of one thing I am certain—you are not the man we have been waiting for."

The one-armed stranger forced a crooked smile. "You mean this isn't Tel Aviv? I told that guide—"

The rest of it was swallowed by a rising shriek, the nude man straining at his bonds, spine arched, his toes and fingers tightly clenched. Behind his chair, the Iraqi sergeant observed a signal from Mashhad and withdrew the bare electrodes from their contact with the metal chair.

A smell of ozone lingered in the room, along with something else. Singed hair? Scorched flesh?

The subject was perspiring freely, chin slumped forward on his chest. The sweat would make for better contact next time, when Mashhad decided it was necessary to correct his attitude.

"Your name?"

The head came up, cold eyes locked on his own. If looks could kill, Mashhad reflected...but they couldn't, never would. This stranger was his private toy. He could do anything he wanted with the one-armed man, as long as he obtained the necessary information first.

"Fuck y—"

The sergeant caught his signal, moved the copper wires a fraction of an inch and smiled at the result. Mashhad stood back and watched for six or seven seconds, knowing that it must feel like a lifetime in the chair.

"Let's try another question, then. Your name is unimportant in the larger scheme of things." Mashhad spoke Russian to his captive, wondering how many other languages the stranger understood. Without a clue, his nationality itself remained in doubt. "Who sent you here?"

"Your people brought me. You were right there when we—aarrgghh!"

The voltage made him dance, within the limits of his bonds. His muscles strained beneath the skin, outlined in stark relief. The stranger's lips drew back from a sardonic mask of misery.

"We have no shortage of electric power here," Mashhad advised him. "This unpleasantness can last all night, if you insist."

It took a moment for the stranger to respond. His voice was smaller, far away. Mashhad bent closer, turning one ear toward the captive's lips.

"Again?"

"I'd hate . . . to pay . . . your power bill."

"A sense of humor. That is good. It indicates you still have some desire to live. If so, you will cooperate. Refusal at this point means certain death."

"And if . . . I talk? What then?"

"You will be treated fairly, given food and medical attention."

Did they ever really buy this nonsense? Sometimes, yes.

"I don't know...where to start," the stranger said.

"Where every story starts," Mashhad replied. "At the beginning."

Silence, while his captive took a moment to collect disjointed thoughts. Sweat dripped from chin and forehead to his chest, formed shiny rivers there and plunged south toward the forest of his groin.

"In the beginning, God created—"

This time it required no signal. Kneeling just behind the chair, Mashhad's technician brought the wires around and pressed them home. The one-armed stranger twisted, jerking as the voltage rippled through his flesh.

"I do not waste my time on fools," Mashhad informed his prisoner. "You are a spy and saboteur. This fact alone is grounds for execution in Iraq. If you refuse to help me trace your sponsors, I have no more use for you alive."

They often broke at this point, with a death threat heaped on top of pain. The one-armed man made no attempt to face Mashhad, but when he spoke again his voice was strong and clear.

"Let's do it, then."

Mashhad stepped back a pace, surprised. This man wasn't a Muslim, thus he had no guarantee of paradise. Some men accepted death without assurances, but this one...

He could feel the sergeant watching him expectantly. Mashhad glanced at the man's face and shook his head. Not yet.

There was more to this man than he understood, a secret waiting to be cracked and analyzed. If he couldn't discover what it was, the failure would be his...along with the responsibility for any consequence that flowed from that initial failure.

Even so, he had been truthful when he told the man they had all night. Tomorrow, too, if need be.

"Let's begin again," he said. "From the beginning."

"HE'S TOLD YOU nothing yet?" Glazov asked.

Standing in the middle of the room, hands clasped behind his back, Amal Mashhad looked sullen. "He has been...resistant."

"Your interrogators need more practice."

Glazov was amused to see the Arab bristle at his criticism. "They are experts," Mashhad replied. "I have no quarrel with their performance."

"Yet you lack results. Why not use drugs?"

Mashhad glanced down as if embarrassed. "I will have to contact Baghdad for the proper items."

"Ah."

That made it clear, of course. Mashhad would balk at making his superiors aware of any problem while the situation was in flux. Ranking officers had been cashiered or executed for less, under Saddam Hussein's regime, and Mashhad was clearly unwilling to admit any flaw in his current operation. With so much at stake, it was what the Americans would call a no-win situation for Glazov's Iraqi counterpart.

Which worried the Russian not at all.

His chief concern was still the People's Revolution and the setback it would suffer if his operation in Iraq was stymied in the preparation stage. Glazov cared no more about Amal Mashhad than any other third-world flunky. Each and every one of them were pawns in a dramatic game, with international power hanging in the balance. If the game plan was derailed at this stage, with the warheads nothing more than sketches on a drawing board, then Glazov and his sponsors would be forced to start from scratch.

Assuming that he ever got the chance.

It would be difficult to paint his failure as a minor setback for Petrovski and the others, waiting back in Moscow. If he failed, there would be drastic repercussions, up to and including orders for his own elimination. Glazov, in his years of duty with the KGB, had ordered liquidations and participated in a few himself. The victims weren't always foreign spies or traitors in the ranks. For every target slain outside the USSR there was one or more eliminated on his native soil for failure to complete a mission, bungling some transaction set up by the government, or simply having too much guilty knowledge stored inside his head.

"There might be risks involved in keeping silent," he advised Amal Mashhad.

"Another hour," the Iraqi said. "If he has not begun to speak by then, I will request the drugs."

"One hour."

Glazov's flinty eyes revealed more than his tone of voice. The stare he turned on Mashhad spoke volumes, telling the Iraqi that he wouldn't stand for negligence or any kind of subtle treachery. If necessary, Glazov would reach out to Baghdad on his own. A simple call to Berdichev would put the wheels in motion. They could wake Saddam himself, if necessary, and advise him of the situation, all the risks involved. Mashhad would come out looking worse by far if news of the imposter came from Glazov or his deputy.

Mashhad excused himself, and Glazov had no reason to delay him. It was in their mutual best interest if the spy was broken soon, rather than later. For the life of him, Glazov couldn't imagine how the switch had been effected. It was clearly done in Budapest, and he'd have to grill his agents there, but first it was essential that he reach Petrovski. Never mind the hour or the inconvenience. They were looking at a crisis, possibly disaster, and he couldn't keep it to himself.

The worst of it was simply that a switch meant someone knew about the plan, perhaps in its entirety. It could be the Israelis, the Americans, or someone else. In any case they had been able to remove Ivan Baranovich and substitute a ringer, shuttle him across the continent and land him in Iraq.

To what effect?

It was absurd to think that one man, quickly recognized and taken prisoner, could damage the facility. His clothing, likewise, had revealed no signaling devices that would help an air strike target the Iraqi compound. Was he being followed from a distance somehow? Did their enemies already know about the camp and its location?

Glazov muttered an obscenity and crossed the room to fetch his suitcase. It contained the compact scrambler, easily attached to any telephone, which he employed each time he was required to call Petrovski. If his room was bugged, so be it. The Iraqis already knew what was happening. The scrambler would prevent third parties from deciphering his call, and that included enemies in Mother Russia, those who had betrayed the People's Revolution in the recent past.

He couldn't shake a feeling of impending doom. A stranger in their midst, perhaps with others on the way. It made no sense at all unless the one-armed man had been selected, somehow, as the vanguard for a raiding party. He had told Amal Mashhad as much, but there were insufficient troops on hand to mount a sweep around the desert site. For all he knew their adversaries could be creeping through the sand dunes even now, and there was nothing he could do to turn them back.

The phone call, first. It would be difficult, but it was unavoidable.

If he was still in charge an hour from now, there would be time for him to plot a course of action. And if not...

He made a mental note for one more call, the second one to Berdichev at Al Mawsil. They should be ready for a rapid exit if it came to that. If nothing else, at least they might survive.

THEY COULD SEE the compound now. From half a mile away, the buildings were a dark smudge in the moonlight, nothing to announce that they were occupied or that the occupants were watching out for uninvited visitors.

Mack Bolan stood beside the APC with Sascha on his left, the others ranged around him. The armored car's engines were idling, the exhaust chugging solidly, like the panting of some prehistoric beast.

"They keep it dark," James said.

"No point in advertising," Manning answered. "Someone up there might not like them."

"Through the gate, just like we planned?" McCarter asked.

"It's still the quickest way to go," Bolan said. "Any way you run it down, we're short on time."

"You think he's broken yet?" James asked.

The ensuing silence was oppressive, each man in the strike force picturing their friend as they had seen him last, imagining what they might find in the Iraqi camp. Imagination was the worst of it, perhaps, but each of them had been there, more than once. They understood the grim realities of their profession inside out.

If Katz was still alive, they'd do everything within their power to bring him out. If not, God help the men responsible.

God help them anyway, in fact, for all the good that it would do.

They still had no clear picture of the odds, but it would make no difference now. The die was cast, and they were going in with all guns blazing.

He glanced at Sascha, caught her profile in the moonlight, hair swept back from her face and held with an elastic band. The AK-47 looked especially lethal in her hands, as if a child were carrying the weapon, but he knew that she could handle it and take care of herself.

"You think we ought to split it up?" James asked.

"This close," the Executioner replied, "I don't like waiting while a second team gets in position."

"There's the other problem, too," Manning added.

"Right."

They didn't have to spell it out. If Katz was blown, almost a certainty by now, he could have spilled the basic outline of their plan to his interrogators. The Iraqis would have numbers, and they'd be on full alert, perhaps with sweeps of the surrounding desert under way. No troops or military vehicles were visible from where he stood, but they could easily be waiting in a gully or behind that craggy mass of limestone on the northern flank.

The best way was the simplest, relying on whatever vestige of surprise that still remained. The APC would give the compound sentries second thoughts, and it would also get them through the gate. Its turret-mounted .50-caliber would provide suppressing fire until the ammunition was exhausted, or until such time as it was knocked out by a rocket or grenade. Beyond that point, the Executioner couldn't predict a sequence of events with any accuracy. Combat had a way of tossing expectations out the window, leaving each participant to watch out for himself.

"Inside the wire, we scatter," Bolan said, reiterating the instructions that would have to pass for strategy. "Hit your targets hard and fast. Watch out for Katz and keep your heads down."

It was far from a precision game plan, but they had their targets spotted on the map supplied by Esfahan Razi. McCarter would be staying with the APC as long as possible, the Kurd assigned to man the .50-caliber and raise hell with the barracks, pinning down whatever sentries he could see. Bolan and Sascha would make for the lab, destroying anything and everything they could in the allotted time. Manning had drawn the administration block, assigned to take out any brass who might be hanging out around their offices at midnight. James was down for the communications wing and generator housing, hopefully eliminating any threat of outside help. Encizo would be targeting the compound's motor pool, with one eye out for vehicles that might prove useful in a swift retreat.

They had a chance, but Bolan pitied any fool who wagered his life savings on their prospects of survival. If they scrubbed the site it would be good enough. Emerging with their little troop intact would almost take a miracle.

No praying man, the Executioner would put his faith in steel and human skill this time, but he wouldn't reject assistance from the Universe if it should come his way. A savvy warrior used whatever weapons he could lay his hands on in a crunch.

And they were coming to the crunch right now.

"Let's do it," he said, and turned back toward the waiting APC.

CHAPTER TWENTY-TWO

The Compound
Wednesday, 0027 hours

"Coming up!" McCarter snapped, the two words barely audible as they accelerated, rumbling toward the chain-link gate. "They're scrambling."

Esfahan Razi stood ready, just below the open hatch that granted access to the .50-caliber machine gun mounted topside. Bolan and the others huddled on their benches, braced for impact with the fence.

And it was no real contest, when you thought about it. Clocking thirty miles per hour when it hit, the APC weighed something over forty thousand pounds, against the flimsy gate's top weight of twenty-five or thirty. Tissue paper would have done as well, in terms of a defensive barrier.

They felt a jolt and heard a rattling, scraping noise beneath the tracks, the gate transformed into a welcome mat. Razi was up the metal ladder in a flash, and Bolan heard the heavy weapon open up, spent brass making music on the APC's hull.

McCarter had them well inside before he tapped the brakes and slowed their progress to a crawl. Bolan slammed an open palm into the lever that controlled the exit hatch, burst through it, sprinting as he hit the ground.

Outside the sanctuary of the APC lay chaos. At a glance the buildings he could see matched their location on the rough map held by Razi, but getting oriented in a combat zone was very different from plotting movements on a piece of paper. Angry voices shouted back and forth across the camp in Arabic, the .50-caliber was hammering at targets to the east, and other weapons had begun returning fire.

He marked the buildings that Razi had labeled as the laboratory, feeling Sascha close behind him as he ran. Disruption or destruction of the site was their primary goal; if they could find and rescue Katz, it would be frosting on thc cake.

The compound had been dark when they arrived, but suddenly it blazed to life, as bright as day. Strategic floodlights bathed the camp in thousand-candlepower brilliance, like an unexpected sunrise. Bolan squinted in the sudden glare and heard a curse from Sascha on his flank. One of the lights exploded in a twinkling shower as the APC's big machine gun took it out, but there were plenty left to make the raiders highy visible.

A pair of sentries ran to intercept them, breaking from the shadow of a building hard on Bolan's right. More laboratory space, if he could trust the map. Both soldiers carried AK-47s, and they started firing from a range of forty yards, their bullets raising spouts of dust and whining angrily around the warrior's ears.

Without a break in stride, the warrior stoked his Uzi's trigger, stitching a burst of parabellum manglers right across the taller sentry's chest. The impact jolted Bolan's target backward, yanked him off his feet and dumped him on the backside in the dirt. At that, the sentry's rifle kept on firing with a lifeless finger on the trigger, emptying the magazine toward distant stars.

The other sentry skidded to a halt and snapped his rifle up for better aim. A burst from Sascha's AK-47 cut his legs from underneath him, dropping him directly in her line of fire. Another short burst finished it, and they moved on.

Two down, and Bolan still had no fix on the odds.

The warrior had no way of knowing if the entrance to the laboratory block was locked, and he wasted no time finding out. A short burst from his Uzi tore the lock apart, and there was no resistance as he shouldered through the doorway. Sascha, bringing up the rear, glanced back and fired an automatic burst at someone in the yard.

They were inside. The trick, from now on, would be taking out as much equipment as they could in record time and slipping out alive.

And it would be the last part of the trick, Bolan thought, that was toughest to perform.

AT THE INITIAL SOUND of gunfire, Leonid Glazov thought his world was coming to an end. The Moscow conversation had been short and far from sweet. Petrovski was relying on his agent in Iraq to save the day at any cost. There must be no disruption of the master plan. Glazov would do whatever he deemed necessary to insure the plot's success. Mistakes at this stage of the operation would be grounds for termination.

Glazov had been masterful, exuding confidence he didn't feel, assuring his superior that they could get along without Ivan Baranovich for now. Another rocket scientist could be recruited from among the unemployed, perhaps less famous than Baranovich, but adequate enough to satisfy Saddam Hussein. One of Baranovich's students, possibly—Dobrinyn, maybe Malenkov.

The possibilities were endless.

As for any danger to the project, Glazov played it down. Someone was spying, tracking scientists who left the Russian motherland, but that had been expected. Was it not a Western Press release that led to fabrication of the plot originally? It was no surprise that Washington or London, even Tel Aviv, would keep a close watch over Russian experts moving toward the Middle East.

Of course, replacing one of those with an imposter would be something else again. Baranovich also had an escort, killed in Turkey by Iranians, but who had *really* died in the exchange. Was it another spy, or had the real escort sold out to foreign enemies?

No matter now. The man was dead, and his accomplice would be right behind him. Just as soon as he was broken by Amal Mashhad.

Glazov was ruminating on that prospect, wondering how long the full interrogation would require, when automatic weapons opened fire outside his quarters. Dropping to the floor instinctively, he wriggled to a window, risked a glance outside, and saw some kind of armored car parked in the middle of the compound, a machine gun spitting tracers from its turret mount. Dark figures were unloading from the rear at double time, while the Iraqi sentries tried to pull themselves together and return effective fire.

The Russian cursed and scuttled backward from the window toward the bed. He had an automatic pistol in his suitcase, tucked away beside the scrambler with a pair of extra magazines. It took a moment's awkward fumbling, Glazov half afraid to raise his head above the level of the mattress, but he found it, palmed the gun and dropped the surplus clips into a pocket of his coat.

He hadn't seen enough to judge the full size of the raiding party. Half a dozen men, at least, but there might be more armored vehicles outside, perhaps a mobile army bearing down upon the camp. He couldn't—wouldn't—place his trust in the Iraqi forces. Neither could he save the compound by himself, but he could try to save Piotr Serpukhov and Vladimir Polyarni. With the human merchandise intact, Glazov might salvage something even from defeat. Saddam Hussein would bear the cost of any damage to the site, but with the last two scientists alive and well, Glazov could pick up with the operation in a new locale at any time.

How long since he had carried out a mission under fire? It made no difference to a true professional. He could recall the first man he had killed, and every one thereafter. Distance from the deadly game hadn't depleted Glazov's skill at playing with the best.

He hesitated at the door, peeked out and found the corridor deserted. With his pistol cocked and ready, Glazov stepped outside and shut the door behind him. There was no point advertising he had gone, in case someone came looking for him.

That was paranoia talking, he decided, but precautions didn't harm. He moved along the corridor in the direction of an exit that would take him outside. It was a short jog to the quarters occupied by Serpukhov and Polyarni, where he would herd them to safety—at gunpoint, if need be.

And where was safety at the moment? Glazov couldn't say with any certainty, but he'd find it. A survivor from his early days around Dzerzhinsky Square, he still remembered how to look out for himself.

He reached the exit, listened for a moment, waiting as the nearest sounds of gunfire drew away. Somewhere across the compound, an explosion rocked the night.

No time for hesitation.

Glazov hit the hard-pack running, shoulders hunched beneath the floodlights' glare.

THE COMPOUND'S MOTOR POOL consisted of an open shed some sixty feet in length. Its corrugated metal roof cast shadows over half a dozen jeeps, a vintage M3A1 half-track and a flatbed truck. This was the working fleet, reserved for military personnel.

So far, Encizo hadn't fired a shot. The motor pool was left unguarded, possibly by soldiers who had rushed to join the battle on the far side of the yard. From where he crouched between two dusty jeeps, the Cuban had a clear view of McCarter's APC, its turret-mounted machine gun spitting tracers in an arc that swept the nearest barracks, clearing window-frames and drilling through the flimsy prefab walls.

Somebody was catching hell in there, he thought, imagining Iraqi soldiers waking from a solid sleep to find their quarters had become a shooting gallery. There was a spark of flame inside, and then another—tracers starting fires in bedding, uniforms, most anything at all. Across the compound, sentries blasted at the APC with automatic weapons, scoring hits that would be wreaking havoc on McCarter's ears.

Encizo left them to it, concentrating on his own job while the battle raged. He might not have much time, and he couldn't afford to waste another moment.

When they left the compound—if they left—the Stony Man warriors would require some rugged transportation capable of higher speeds than the commandeered APC. To Encizo, that meant a pair of jeeps on standby, while the others were disabled, but he couldn't act precipitously while the battle raged around him. Any moment he might be spotted by the sentries, drawing fire. If he disabled four jeeps now and later saw the others damaged by incoming rounds, his comrades would be left on foot, without a prayer.

Which meant he had to watch and wait, lie low and bide his time.

Delayed-action charges would have solved the problem in an instant, but their arms source back in Budapest hadn't been stocking C-4, timers, or the other gear that he'd need to rig the motor pool. Encizo had retrieved some frag grenades while scavenging around the ambush site, and they might do the trick, but he couldn't afford to wire the jeeps in advance, until he knew for sure which two his comrades would be using for their getaway.

The flatbed was a different story. Circling around behind the half-track, the Cuban produced a sturdy trench knife lifted from its onetime owner in the desert and began to slit the tires. He left one side inflated, saving time, content to see the flatbed listing like a sailboat shipping water on the starboard side.

That done, Encizo moved back to the M3A1 half-track, opened the driver's door and climbed in. He stepped across the seat, threw the hatch back and used his arms to hoist himself into position, staring down the vented barrel of a Browning .30-caliber machine gun. Down below he found an ammo box, brought it up and attached it to the weapon, making sure the belt was set to feed without a hitch. He cocked the thirty, braced himself and swept the open yard in search of targets.

There!

Three uniforms just broke from the cover of a toolshed, jogging toward the APC from Razi's blind side. Encizo gave them a few more steps, making sure there were no more to come, then lined up the MG's sights on their leader, holding down the paddle trigger with his thumb and tracking right to left across the killing ground.

The three Iraqis literally came apart, their bodies jerking, twisting, dancing with the impact of his concentrated fire. Encizo gave them twenty-five or thirty rounds to make it stick, then lifted off the trigger, watching as they folded up like broken mannequins.

A bullet whispered past him, several feet away but close enough to make him duck and scan the compound for its point of origin. He saw the muzzle-flash, and half a dozen AK-47 rounds glanced off the half-track's sloping hood. One of the sentries had him made, and it wouldn't take long for others to decide they had an enemy holed up inside the motor pool.

So be it. If he bailed out now, they'd keep blasting at the vehicles regardless. While he lingered in the half-track, they'd have a concrete target and the jeeps parked yards away would have a slightly better chance of coming through unscathed. And, when he thought about it, he'd also have a chance to kick some ass.

Encizo smiled and swung the Browning toward his latest adversary's hiding place.

"Let's rock," he said, and held the trigger down.

KATZ KNEW BETTER than to let the sounds of combat raise his hopes unreasonably. He was still stark naked, strapped into his metal chair and aching head to foot from the abuse he had endured the past three hours. Twice, unconsciousness had rescued him before his strength and courage failed, allowing to spill whatever secrets he had locked inside his brain. The second time, his captors had been slow reviving him, and they had wandered off somewhere to grab a cup of coffee or discuss new strategies while he recuperated on his own.

But it would be a respite, nothing more.

Katz knew they'd be coming back to finish it, wring answers from his lips or silence him forever. In his present state he couldn't even beat them to the punch with suicide. He had no options to the screaming death they chose for him.

And then all hell broke loose outside.

He had already given up on keeping track of time, afraid that something had delayed the Stony Man team or stopped them altogether. He'd die exactly where he was, and there was nothing he could do about it, save for holding out as long as possible before he told his captors everything he knew.

With any luck, when they returned, the sergeant might get angry and kick in too much voltage. Maybe Katz would have a chance to ride the lightning, and to hell with spilling anything.

When the machine gun opened up, assorted small arms close behind, he knew that it was going down. Somehow the others had arrived and breached the camp's perimeter, but there was still no guarantee they'd be able to fulfill their mission, much less live to set him free.

So he was waiting, wondering if footsteps in the corridor outside would mean a friendly face next time, or someone sent to finish him. There would be no time for interrogation in the middle of a raid, but Katzenelenbogen's captors might decide that they were better off without him. The attack itself would answer many of their questions, making Katz superfluous.

It was stuffy in the room, and warm. His arms and chest were slick with perspiration, and he tried to make it work to his advantage, testing the straps that held him fast. His left arm was hopeless, pinned at the wrist, but they had less to work with on the right. The strap on that side had been buckled just above his elbow, and by twisting, straining until his vertebrae were on the point of cracking, Katz discovered he could move his arm. One slow inch at a time he worked it until, nearly exhausted, it was free and he could rest, the half arm slack and hanging at his side.

Small favors.

How do you attack a buckle with a stump? If he was wearing his prosthetic arm, Katz could have freed himself in seconds flat. But this way...

Try it!

Gathering his strength, Katz twisted in the metal chair, his legs held fast below the knee, burns shrieking at him from his buttocks, thighs and back. No matter. If he twisted far enough and dropped his shoulder on the left, he found that he could reach the strap that pinned down his left arm.

Now what?

The strap was snug around his wrist, the buckle on top like a curious wristwatch. It was tight enough that he couldn't withdraw his hand, nor could he work the binding farther up his arm, to loosen it or place the buckle within biting range.

The straps weren't a fixture of the chair, per se. They were attached once someone took a seat, but they could move—slide up and down the arms or legs, for instance—if they had sufficient slack. Katz thought if he could slide his left arm back a few more inches, twist his elbow outward to prevent it being trapped, he just might have a chance.

It came by fractions of an inch, Katz pausing frequently to rest and listen for a sound of footsteps in the corridor outside. So far, the action in the courtyard seemed to have his jailers fully occupied. If they could only stay that way for ten or fifteen minutes more...

When it was time to use his lips and teeth, Katz twisted farther to his left, bent almost double from the waist, joints popping as he folded in upon himself. Sweating freely, cursing as he strained his neck, Katz knew that he'd have to make it or give it up and simply wait to die.

AMAL MASHHAD was huddled with a group of his subordinates when the attack began. Frustrated by the one-armed spy's resistance to interrogation, he had called a temporary halt and summoned those in charge of operational security.

He might not know who sent the spy or paid his wages, but Masshad was clear on one thing. There was no way that a solitary operative could realistically expect to trash the site or slip out and report his findings once he was discovered on the grounds. A native rebel working maintenance could come and go, perhaps, but this one? Never.

That, in turn, meant he had been dispatched as a diversion, the advance man for a larger force that might arrive at any time. And when it came, Amal Mashhad was confident that it would only have one goal in mind.

Scorched earth.

The Jews had done it once before, in 1981, with the facility near Baghdad. Tel Aviv reserved the right to terrorize her neighbors on a whim, if she detected or imagined any threat. This time, of course, there was a threat, and it wouldn't surprise Mashhad to learn that the Israelis had a strike force in the air right now, complete with bombs and rockets, bent on wrecking everything that he had worked for in the past twelve months.

The worst part of it was that he couldn't defend the camp against an air strike. They had no defensive missiles, nothing in the way of antiaircraft guns, because Saddam Hussein had opted for economy and secrecy. The compound was supposed to seem innocuous, to avoid arousing any dire suspicions while the men inside were busy building nightmares.

All in vain, once they had been discovered by their enemies.

Mashhad was dictating instructions to his subordinate officers when the shooting began outside, a heavy machine gun rattling its death song in the night. Small arms responded, the sentries returning fire, and Mashhad rushed to the nearest window, uniforms crowding close behind him for a glimpse of the action.

An armored personnel carrier with Iraqi markings was parked in the middle of the compound, its turret-mounted .50-caliber machine gun sweeping back and forth along the eastern fence and barracks. Other muzzle-flashes lighted the night as guards broke desperately for cover, firing on the run. By moonlight, on his left, Mashhad could see the front gate standing open. No, on second thought, the gate was down, ripped from its moorings, uniformed bodies sprawled out on either side.

He bellowed at his troops, the officers retreating from his fury as a group, boots hammering the wooden floor. He watched them go, already moving toward his desk and lifting out the pistol he kept tucked inside the upper right-hand drawer. Because he always kept it loaded, with the safety off, there was no need to check before he tucked it down inside his belt.

His enemies were well inside the camp, but there was still a chance to turn them back. He wasn't ready to surrender yet, by any means.

Mashhad would wipe them out, and he'd start with their accursed spy.

He found the sergeant outside his office, waiting with an AK-47 slung across one shoulder and another tucked beneath his arm. Mashhad relieved him of the latter weapon, feeling better with the rifle in his hands.

"I want the prisoner," he said. "Go fetch him now, and bring him to the conference room." The sergeant snapped a crisp salute and went to do as he was told.

Moving toward the conference room, devoid of windows where a stray round might slip through, Mashhad began to plot his radio dispatch to Baghdad. For his purposes, the battle should appear both desperate and heroic.

A heroic victory.

And if a certain Russian was among the friendly dead, so much the better for Amal Mashhad.

CHAPTER TWENTY-THREE

Calvin James had drawn the target labeled on Razi's map as the communications center of the compound. He was halfway to his destination when the floodlights blazed around him, dazzling in their sudden brilliance, leaving him exposed with nothing in the way of cover close at hand. The .50-caliber machine gun mounted on the APC cut loose at one light, blowing it away, but there were easily a dozen others mounted at strategic intervals around the compound. There was no way he could kill them all and still cope with his enemies, his mission.

Twenty yards to go, and James was running all-out when the front door of the building he was headed for flew open, soldiers spilling out. He counted three, and there was no more time for thinking as he squeezed the trigger on his Vz.58 and let the automatic rifle do his talking for him.

Number one went down immediately, crimson spouting from a ragged line of holes across his chest. The soldier's weapon flashed, too late and well off target, spraying bullets over James's head and off into the night. There was a muffled sound of boot heels drumming on the ground, covered in moments by the other noise of combat.

On his left the second gunner stumbled, tripping on the rounds that ripped his abdomen, a stunned expression on his face. He seemed too young to be in uniform, much less in combat, but James had no time to analyze the situation or lament a young man's passing with his own life riding on the line. It was a kill-or-be-killed situation, and he didn't plan to come out second best.

And number three was almost good enough to tag him, even so. The submachine gun in his hands was rising, spitting death, when James caught him with the tag end of a looping burst and slammed him back against the nearest wall. Gravity took over from there, and the soldier slid down into a seated posture, leaving traces of himself behind.

The way was clear, and the Phoenix Force warrior burst through into the silent building. Dim lights burned in the corridor and none in rooms on either side. He knew what he was looking for and started kicking doors along the hallway, left and right. An office here, a storeroom there. He encountered no opposition as he made his way along the corridor.

He got it right the third time, slapping at the wall switch, facing a sophisticated radio arrangement with computer terminals on either side. A burst from James's rifle finished it, but he made sure with a grenade that he had lifted from a soldier at the ambush site. Retreating in a sprint, he dropped another can inside the office doorway as he passed.

He cleared the threshold in a leap and dodged aside, already crouching as the first grenade went off. The building was a prefab structure, thrown up in a hurry, never meant to cage destructive force inside. A large piece of the roof blew off, and James heard the windows shatter, squatting with his eyes closed and the Vz.58 clutched tight against his chest.

The second blast was closer, shrapnel punching through the flimsy wall in front and whispering across the compound. Two more of the hated floodlights had been mounted on the roof, and both of them went dark with the explosions, dropping shadows over a quarter of the yard that he could see.

Fringe benefits, you bet.

Next door, the compound's generator still kept chugging in its separate quarters. James scuttled off in that direction, nearly deafened by the close-range blasts, still conscious of the steady fire around him. Bullets slapped the wall above his head, and he responded with a burst that caught a sentry in the open, spinning him around and dumping him facedown in sand already moist with blood.

He reached the generator hut and found it open, no latch on the door. Inside, a heavy unit labored to provide the camp with power, four-stroke motor chugging steadily, the generator humming. James used the last rounds from his rifle's magazine to blast the motor off its mount, reloading as the power plant shut down.

No point in taking chances, so he left a frag grenade behind, emerging into darkness as the floodlights died. He made it halfway to the smoking wreckage of the old communications center, ducking as a blast ripped through the shed behind him, flinging jagged chunks of corrugated steel in all directions.

Done.

His basic contribution to the effort was complete, but he wasn't clear yet, or even close. Survival was the top priority, and that meant taking out as many of the opposition as he could, before they had to cut and run.

And it could still go wrong a hundred different ways.

James closed his mind to ugly options and went hunting in the dark.

KATZ WAS WAITING in the metal chair, head slumped, chin resting on his chest, when he heard footsteps drawing closer in the corridor outside. He had already tried the door and found it locked, whereupon he resigned himself to lying in wait as the only alternative. If no one ever came for him, at least it had to mean his tormentors were dead.

But he heard someone coming now.

He had considered hiding out behind the door, prepared to leap from ambush when his enemy appeared, but that would only get him killed if there was more than one. Instead he opted for the chair, the arm straps loosely buckled to preserve appearances, leg leather cast off in a corner where it wouldn't be immediately noticed.

Lacking any clothes and weapons, Katzenelenbogen thought it was the best that he could do.

A key turned in the lock, the door swung open and he raised his head a little, putting on the pained expression of a man who was about to reach the end of his endurance. One man stood in the doorway, and he recognized the sergeant who had dealt with the mechanics of his torture while the honcho asked his questions, nodding when he wanted voltage in the line.

The sergeant was by himself, and he would do just fine. If only he stepped close enough.

"No more," Katz rasped, his voice a beaten thing. "I beg you."

The sergeant wasted no time on an answer, if he even understood the plea. Advancing on his prisoner, he held an AK-47 in his right hand, pointed at the floor and reached out with the left to loosen one of Katzenelenbogen's bonds.

"You come," he said in heavily accented English.

By the time his fingers reached the buckle, recognized a crucial something out of place, the time to save himself had passed. Katz brought up his right foot with stunning force between the sergeant's legs, a satisfying crunch on impact as the genitals were hammered flat. The next sound that emerged between the Iraqi's lips was high and shrill, a cry of agony.

Katz whipped his arms free of their bonds, his left hand going for the rifle while his right stub cracked the sergeant hard between the eyes. His adversary staggered, wheezing, clutching at his wounded privates, barely offering resistance as the folding-stock Kalashnikov was twisted from his grasp.

The Israeli swung up the rifle without a moment's hesitation, jammed its muzzle tight between the gaping lips and fired a single round at skin-touch range. Percussive impact slammed his tormentor backward, spraying blood and bits of tissue in an abstract pattern six or seven feet across.

He kept the automatic rifle handy while he stripped its owner's corpse. The sergeant was a man of average size, which made him large for an Iraqi, if a trifle small for Katz. The khaki pants would zip, but Katzenelenbogen left the button at his waist undone so he could breathe. The shirt was tight across the shoulders, but a mighty wrenching motion solved that problem when a seam let go in back.

The boots were hopeless, but he put the heavy stockings on regardless, anything to give his feet some insulation from the rubble he might find outside. The sergeant also wore a belt pouch, with three spare magazines inside, which Katz appropriated.

All done.

He wouldn't pass for an Iraqi under normal scrutiny, but with the sounds of battle emanating from outside, he thought it just might work. Ironically, if he was too convincing, he'd run a risk of being shot by someone from the Stony Man team.

It was a risk that he'd have to take.

In fact, it was his only chance of getting out alive.

THE ADMINISTRATION BLOCK was Gary Manning's target, and he chose a side door, dodging into shadows where the overlapping floodlights didn't reach. The door was locked, but Manning cleared it with a burst from his Beretta submachine gun, kicked it in and went through in a fighting crouch.

A hallway, dimly lighted, stretched out in front of him, doors closed and standing mute on either side. He waited for a moment on the threshold, half expecting some response to his explosive entry, moving on when there was none. He checked each room in passing, offices and storage dark and silent now. He wouldn't waste his frag grenades on desks and filing cabinets unless...

The single shot was muffled, almost lost amid the racket from outside, but it was different somehow. For a start it had been fired inside the building where he stood, somewhere ahead of him, but Manning couldn't gauge the distance from a single shot. If it should be repeated, he'd have a better chance, but in the meantime he'd need to have a closer look around.

He had begun to move again when someone poked his head out of an office two doors down, on Manning's left. The man glanced left and right, gave out a yelp as he beheld the Phoenix Force warrior, then jerked his head back like a turtle hiding in its shell.

Too late.

The glimpse had been enough for Manning, after memorizing mug shots at the Farm. He recognized

Piotr Serpukhov on sight and knew exactly what he had to do.

It all came down to this. Search and destroy.

He reached the door in six long strides, stood well off to the right and dropped into a crouch before he reached out for the knob. A twist and shove, his arm drawn back as pistol shots exploded from the office, bullets ripping through the flimsy door chest-high.

So Serpukhov or someone else inside the room was armed. No problem. Manning palmed a frag grenade and freed the safety pin. The door was still ajar, and the big Canadian hit it with a solid backhand, broadening the gap. Another bullet whistled through and smacked the wall directly opposite, but it was wasted effort on the shooter's part.

It was a backward toss, but Manning didn't have his eye on accuracy. If the office ran true to form, it would be fifteen feet by twenty at the maximum. A desk or other furniture might well absorb the blast, but he was counting on the frag grenade for a diversion, more than anything.

He let it go, ducked back before another pistol round could tag his arm, and heard the lethal egg impact on something solid, dropping to the floor and rolling with an awkward, wobbly sound. He hit the deck and stayed there, counting off four seconds in his mind before the detonation. Shrapnel filled the air, some of it coming through the doorway, other pieces slicing through the wall and whispering above his head.

He came erect and rushed the smoky doorway while the blast was still reverberating through the corridor. Inside the office, crouching low, he homed in on the muffled sound of voices gasping, cursing.

Russian voices.

Manning found them in the corner, partly shielded by a filing cabinet. Polyarni knelt with one arm braced against the wall, a pistol in his free hand, pointed at the floor between his knees. A ragged gash along his hairline streaked the Russian's face with crimson on the right side, while the left was chalky white. Behind him, Serpukhov was seated with his back against the wall, knees drawn up to his chest and held there by the circle of his arms. The warhead builder's hair stood out in crazy tufts, and blood was leaking from his nose, but he seemed otherwise unharmed.

Polyarni stiffened at the sight of Manning in his combat gear, approaching through the haze of smoke. He muttered something in his native language, got a garbled answer back from Serpukhov and raised the pistol in a trembling hand.

It would have been a relatively simple thing for Manning to disarm the Russian, wing him with a parabellum round if necessary, but he hadn't come in search of prisoners. These men had been recruited by Saddam Hussein to set the world on fire, and they would do the same again for someone else if they survived.

It was damage control, plain and simple. No options.

He fired the Beretta in a burst that pinned both men against the wall and held them there, limbs thrashing for an instant, finally relaxing as the bolt locked open on an empty chamber and the final empty cartridge casing rattled on the floor at Manning's feet.

All done.

No check for vital signs was necessary. Manning dropped his empty magazine and snapped a fresh one into the Beretta. He put the smoky killing room behind him, scratching off two targets from the hit list he had carried in his mind the past four days.

He froze, his weapon rising, locking into target acquisition on a uniformed commando, thirty feet away. His index finger tightened on the trigger, ready to unleash a hail of parabellum rounds before the adversary's AK-47 had a chance to speak, but something stayed his hand. Perhaps it was the soldier's shock of iron-gray hair, his silhouette and posture, or the fact that one arm had been severed just below the elbow....

Katz!

They recognized each other simultaneously, rushing forward, talking all at once until they caught themselves and took a break.

"Are you all right?"

"I'm getting there," Katz said. "Yourself?"

"I tagged Polyarni and Serpukhov."

"We'd better move it, then. I'd like to hang around, but I don't care for the environment."

As if to punctuate his words, a new explosion rocked the far end of the building, dark smoke boiling in the corridor.

"This way."

And it was only smoke, the tall Canadian decided, that accounted for the burning in his eyes as he led Katz outside.

A PAIR OF SENTRIES had been stationed at the entrance to the lab. Mack Bolan caught them whispering together, watching one direction while he surfaced from the other, squeezing off an Uzi burst that dropped both soldiers where they stood.

Behind him, Sascha watched the corridor both ways while Bolan stepped across the leaking bodies, tried the door and found it locked. A short burst tore the latch apart and he was in, fluorescent ceiling fixtures humming into life once Bolan found the wall switch.

"Clear."

It was a first-rate job, he had to give them that. No physicist, he recognized the gear regardless: an oscilloscope, the giant centrifuge, bank of microscopes, computer terminals, a vacuum chamber with robotic arms inside, for safely handling radioactive material.

They didn't have a nuclear reactor yet, by any means. No sign of any warheads waiting for assembly. The Russian team was weeks or maybe months away from turning out a finished bomb, but there was no time like the present to prevent their going forward with the plan.

Some plastique would have been a help, but Bolan could make do with his grenades. Inside the vacuum chamber, several leaden boxes housed the current batch of isotopes, but simple detonation of grenades wouldn't be adequate to start a chain reaction in the lab. As for contamination if the boxes shattered or were spilled, he didn't plan to be around the place that long.

And the Iraqi cleanup crew could watch out for itself.

A sound of running footsteps in the hallway brought them both around, their weapons tracking toward the open doorway. An Iraqi soldier stood there, gaping at his fallen comrades for a moment, glancing up in time to see his enemies before converging streams of automatic fire ripped through him, blowing him away.

"I'll check it out," Sascha said, moving toward the door while Bolan turned back to the lab equipment, estimating how to cause the most potential damage in the least amount of time.

If anything within the lab was critical, it had to be the centrifuge and vacuum box. Those items were the heart of any nuclear experiment, and shattering the vacuum box would also free the isotopes within, potentially contaminating any personnel who passed this way without protective suits. The notion left a sour taste in Bolan's mouth, but he was playing hardball, and the object was to win.

"How is—"

Before he could complete the question, Sascha fired a short burst from her AK-47 back along the corridor, in the direction they had come from. Another automatic weapon answered, Sascha standing firm and firing back as Bolan moved to help her.

"Gone," she snapped when he was at her side. "An officer, I think. I missed him, dammit!"

"Never mind. I'm closing down their show."

"I'll keep watch here."

He slung the Uzi, unclipped two frag grenades and walked back to the bank of lab equipment.

"Ready when I give the word," he said.

"You'll have to catch me," Sascha promised.

Bolan pulled the pins on both grenades, the safety spoons secured by his grip until the final instant. Opening the centrifuge, he stood with one hand poised before its yawning mouth, the other cocked and ready for a pitch in the direction of the vacuum box.

"On three."

The answer was a shuffling footstep, Sascha stepping across the threshold, ready for her sprint to safety.

"One."

It would be in the fan if the Iraqi officer should double back and pin them in the laboratory.

"Two."

Forget it. There was nothing they could do now, but to pitch both grenades and run like hell before they detonated.

"Three!"

In another heartbeat, he was pounding down the corridor with Sascha several feet in front of him.

The double blast was something of an anticlimax, most of it contained by lab equipment and the intervening walls. A flash fire chased them briefly down the corridor but soon lost interest, burning out on Bolan's heels, and they were slowing by the time they reached the exit, balancing the risk of gunfire in the yard against the possibility of leaking radiation from the shattered lab.

Another blast, and all the lights in the camp went out. James had found the generator.

"Ready?"

Sascha switched a bright smile on and off. "As ready as I'll ever be."

They raced out into the darkness, running for their lives.

AT FIRST McCarter thought the hand grenade had merely detonated in the sand outside his APC. The vehicle had shivered, rocking from the impact of the blast, but it was built to take abuse. He didn't realize the gravity of his situation until he jammed the stick into reverse, eased off on the clutch and felt the left-hand track digging in by itself, the right-hand side frozen.

He tried again and got the same result. By now the APC had circled to its left some sixty-five degrees, and it was going nowhere fast. The .50-caliber was firing shorter bursts, conserving ammunition now, and a moment later Razi, the slim Kurd, ducked in and shouted at him.

"There! Look toward the fence!"

The floodlights had shut down a moment earlier, but they could still rely on headlights from the APC. McCarter's mouth fell open, and he felt his blood run cold. For God's sake, how could he have missed a tank?

It was the angle, he decided. Having backed around in something of an arc, they had a different viewpoint—and the tank was moving now. Not swiftly, yet, but it was creeping forward from the shadow of a barracks building that had helped conceal its bulk. He saw a tardy crewman scrambling for the turret, wrenching at the open hatch, and then Razi loose with his machine gun, tracers looping through the night to find the man and make him dance.

McCarter briefly reviewed what he knew about the Russian T-72. It carried a three-man crew for starters, minus one and counting, and weighed close to thirteen tons, sporting a 125 mm gun with a maximum range of 2.5 miles. Not that the gunner would need that kind of range this night. Sixty yards was more like it. Call that point-blank range for the gun that was already turning, an inch at a time, to aim in their direction.

Razi was blasting with the heavy machine gun, hot rounds striking sparks against the armored hull and turret. Penetration was a lost cause, but he kept on firing, giving the tank crew hell, until a burst of automatic rifle fire from somewhere on their flank sent bullets pinging off the APC.

The Kurd cried out and lost his footing in the turret, tumbling down behind McCarter with a thud. The Briton tore himself away from the controls and periscope to check on the man, finding blood pouring from a fist-size wound behind one ear.

A glance back at the periscope, and he could see the big gun coming into target acquisition. It felt like looking down a mine shaft or an old, abandoned well.

No time to waste. He leaped across the corpse, hit the back doors running, tumbled from the APC and landed on his face. Adrenaline was pumping through McCarter's veins as he got to his hands and knees, a desperate scramble, putting ground between himself and the preliminary target of his enemies.

The muzzle blast was loud, a clap of thunder, but it was nothing compared to the explosion generated by an armor-piercing high-explosive round that ripped through the crippled APC. The shock wave picked McCarter up and slammed him through an awkward somersault, so that he wound up lying on his back thirty feet away from where he started. Smoke and dust were everywhere, with twisted chunks of blackened metal raining to the ground.

At first the Phoenix Force warrior thought he was dead, then he realized that the blast had merely deafened him. A moment later, he discovered even that was wrong.

For he could hear the tank advancing now, its engine growling, big treads finding traction on the sand. The juggernaut was coming for him, bent on finishing the job and grinding him to bloody pulp beneath its tracks.

BOLAN WAS EMERGING from the laboratory building when the APC exploded fifty yards away, its ruptured fuel tank spewing gasoline in incandescent streamers. Part of the disintegrating tread lashed out and snaked across the open yard like some gigantic flatworm, thrashing in the seconds prior to death.

He glimpsed McCarter, lying on his back and obviously stunned, some distance from where the wreckage of the APC lay burning on its side. The Russian tank was grinding closer, veering to avoid the shattered carcass of its latest kill, and leaping firelight showed the Executioner an open hatch atop the turret.

"Stay right here!" he snapped at Sascha, moving out before she had a chance to speak.

He didn't run directly toward the tank. Instead he dodged around the behemoth's blind side, picking up his pace the last few yards until he had velocity enough to make a leap from six feet out and catch a metal handgrip on the starboard side. For something like a heartbeat, Bolan's legs swung perilously near the churning treads, then he was clear and scrambling up the broad back of the tank, its diesel engine sending powerful vibrations through his legs.

How long before the metal monster crushed McCarter where he lay? No time for guesswork now, as Bolan palmed and primed a frag grenade—his last one—reaching up to stretch his arm across the broad curve of the turret toward the open hatch. He dropped the lethal egg and slammed the hatch behind it.

Four seconds passed, give or take, and he was airborne when the frag grenade went off inside the tank. Its shrapnel couldn't penetrate the heavy armor, but the blast set off an instant chain reaction, 125 mm artillery rounds detonating in rapid-fire, tearing the juggernaut apart from within.

Bolan hit the ground running and never slowed, sprinting with his shoulders hunched, expecting shrapnel or a bullet from the dark perimeter to bring him down at any moment. Scooping up McCarter on the run, he dragged the shaky Phoenix Force warrior into cover in the shadow of the laboratory complex.

"Look!" McCarter blurted, pointing, blinking dust out of his eyes.

Across the compound, Gary Manning and a battered man dressed in an Iraqi uniform were just emerging from the compound's office block. A second, closer look told Bolan that the tall Canadian's companion had to be Yakov Katzenelenbogen, on his feet if not exactly safe and sound.

"Razi?"

McCarter shook his head. "He went up with the APC."

That still left Calvin James and Rafael Encizo, but their time was swiftly running out. In fact, it might already be too late for an escape.

As if in answer to his thoughts, a horn began to blare from the direction of the motor pool, its bleating interspersed with bursts of .50-caliber machinegun fire.

Encizo!

Bolan glanced across the compound, caught a glimpse of Katz and Manning on the move, responding to the Cuban's signal. Sentries on the south side of the compound were continuing to spray the yard with automatic fire, but they'd have to move despite the risk, or stand and die for nothing where they were.

"You up to running?" Bolan asked McCarter.

"Try me."

"Right. On me."

The Executioner broke from cover, racing toward the motor pool, and offered up a silent prayer that there would still be two good friends behind him when he got there, safe and sound.

CHAPTER TWENTY-FOUR

Encizo had two jeeps running when they reached the motor pool, their engines ticking over quietly, exhaust plumes rising from the pipes in back. James was with him, manning the big machine gun on the half-track's turret, holding back their enemies with cover fire. The team was still intact, except for Esfahan Razi, but they had no time for a fond reunion in the middle of the killing grounds.

"Take these." Encizo raised his voice to make it heard above the steady gunfire. "We'll be right behind you in the armor. Wait a second once you clear the gate, okay?"

"You've got it," Bolan told him, sliding in behind the wheel of one jeep, Sascha in the shotgun seat. McCarter took the other vehicle with Katz and Manning, pulling out ahead of Bolan, rear tires spitting sand.

The half-track would be slow on open ground, a detriment to rapid flight, but Bolan knew Encizo never meant to go that far. He had a different plan in mind that could, with any kind of luck at all, delay pursuit and give them just a bit of time to spare.

Another moment and he had the jeep in gear, then rolling, following McCarter's tracks. They used no headlights, needed none to guide them with the leaping flames on either side. They had to run a gauntlet from the motor pool to the gate. Along the way, lone sentries fired at random, with a huddled clutch of gunners here and there, most of them hasty on the pull and jerking triggers when they should have squeezed. The jeep was taking hits, regardless, some of them too close for comfort. The Executioner returned fire with his Uzi, driving one-handed while Sascha sprayed the shadows on their right.

He flicked a glance in the direction of the rearview mirror and saw the half-track lumbering along behind them, gaining speed. James was in the turret, laying down a screen of cover fire along their backtrack while Encizo drove the armored car. The M3A1 had a long extended bumper with an automatic winch in front, almost a ramming prow, and that was how Encizo used it when he came to any obstacles. The burned-out APC was rudely shoved aside, and when a foolish sentry tried to block the half-track with his body, he was mowed down in his tracks.

McCarter reached the open gate and drove through, someone in the back seat covering with what appeared to be an AK-47. Katz or Manning? Bolan didn't know or care, as long as both men were alive and well enough to flee the compound with their comrades. He stopped short of being optimistic in the present circumstances, but at least they had a chance. Encizo's ploy would buy some time, but they'd have to use it well.

He reached the portal, braking as he rolled across the flattened chain-link gate, a dust cloud overtaking Bolan as he rumbled to a halt outside the fence. Behind him, he could hear the half-truck drawing closer, Encizo shifting down, preparing to make his move.

The blockade was simplicity itself. He swung the armored car hard right and hit the brakes, a broadside skid of sorts. Three inches short of twenty-one feet long, the half-track blocked the gate effectively from side to side, a ten-ton obstacle that the Iraqis would be forced to circumvent before they could give chase.

James was busy with the .50-caliber, firing back into the compound, when Encizo bailed out on the driver's side, a shouted warning on his lips. The former Navy Seal unloaded then, without delay, and he was running on Encizo's heels when a grenade went off inside the half-track's cab. It struck a sympathetic spark beneath the hood, somehow, and Bolan watched the heavy engine go ballistic in a heartbeat, catapulting out into the sand.

A moment later, James and Encizo were both on board, the jeep in motion, following McCarter through an arid wasteland, navigating by the pale light of the desert moon.

All clear, but they had far to go, and Bolan knew his enemies wouldn't give up easily. It would be seven guns against the pack, perhaps against an army, with the final outcome still in doubt.

But they had done the job, by God. The rest of it was gravy, seeing who would live or die.

AMAL MASHHAD WAS beside himself with anger. The laboratory lay in smoking ruins and his Russian scientists were dead. The nameless prisoner had managed to escape, killing Sergeant Dazvin in the process, and had fled with the attackers. Mashhad himself had narrowly missed death in the administration building, forced to run and hide like some despicable coward.

He raged at his surviving soldiers, cursing them as they labored to clear the gate, pulling the disabled half-track with jeeps while uniformed sentries pushed from behind. It gave by inches, twenty thousand points of battered, blackened steel surrendering to physics and the power of determination.

Glazov stood beside him, looking grim and somewhat dazed. The Russian had emerged without a scratch from the engagement, but he understood the risks inherent in survival. Everything that he had promised and been paid for had been wiped out in a short half hour. There was no way to report the raid with their communications gear destroyed, but Baghdad would be furious to say the least. Mashhad might very well be executed for his failure to defend the prize, but he wouldn't be going down alone.

If they could catch their enemies, take onc or two alive for questioning, he might yet salvage something from the grim debacle. It didn't seem likely, granted, but Mashhad could think of nothing else to do. If they sat still and let the raiders get away, it would be even worse when he was summoned to account by his superiors.

Mashhad knew all the stories circulated in regard to what went on in Baghdad when Saddam was in a rage. One man, they said, had been immersed in acid, slowly, screaming piteously as his body was dissolved by inches. It wasn't an isolated case, nor was it necessarily the worst expression of Saddam's ferocity when he was riled.

All things considered, then, Mashhad would rather take his chances in the desert. If he won, at least they might determine who had blitzed the compound, punishing the individuals responsible. And if he died in the attempt, well, he'd take a bullet over acid any day.

The half-track was in motion, creeping to one side. Behind Mashhad, his staff car and another jeep stood ready with their engines idling, drivers at the wheel.

With two jeeps working on the half-track, that made four vehicles operational, a dozen soldiers left to follow him in the pursuit of their attackers.

With the helicopter, he could easily have run them down by now and strafed them from the air, but he had sent the chopper back to Al Mawsil that morning, and he had no radio with which to summon aid. His adversaries had a fair head start, almost ten minutes now, but he'd hunt them down at any cost.

At last a portion of the gate was clear, enough at any rate for their procession to slip through. "You ride with me," he snapped at Glazov, brooking no denial as he started shouting orders at his troops. A few more seconds, and they had the jeeps uncoupled from the half-track, soldiers piling in and falling into line behind the staff car.

Not too late, Mashhad assured himself. He would not let it be too late. At least a hundred miles of desert lay between the compound and the Turkish border. Anything could happen in the time it took to drive a hundred miles, and at the other end, his enemies would have to circumvent Iraqi border guards to make good their escape.

Mashhad got in the car with Glazov on his right, a soldier on the Russian's other side to wedge him in. The staff car crept around the half-track, gaining speed along the roadway, headlights blazing in the night.

THEY WERE FORTY MILES due north of the Iraqi compound, less than halfway to the Turkish border, when the engine blew. It started with a wisp of steam and escalated swiftly to a frantic knocking underneath the hood. When Bolan stopped to check it, he could smell the stench of overheated wiring, and he found his explanation in a solitary bullet puncture on the starboard side.

"Well, hell."

"No problem," McCarter said. "We can double up and load the other vehicle. Katz won't mind someone sitting on his lap."

But it would slow them with all the extra weight, and there'd be more fuel consumption, when they needed every mile per gallon they could get.

"How many survivors did we leave back there?" he asked of no one in particular.

"It's hard to say," Katz answered. "Working from the troops I saw, you've got to figure forty, forty-five on-site, including clerical."

"So if we caught a break and tagged two-thirds of that," James said, "it still leaves twelve to fifteen guns."

"You want to stand and fight?" Encizo asked.

"I'd rather hear an option," Bolan told him.

But there were no options to be had. The proposition came down to a simple choice of fight or flight, and if they had to do their running in a badly overloaded jeep...

"I like those boulders," Katz decided, pointing to a craggy outcrop fifty yards downrange. "You want to check them out?"

"It couldn't hurt."

In fact, the upthrust boulders formed a kind of minifort, albeit open on the north and east. If they were circled by the enemy, they'd be lethally exposed to flanking fire. Still, it was better than the open ground. It just might work, if they could find themselves a twist.

It came to him like that and put a frown on Bolan's face.

"I need a volunteer," he said.

LEONID GLAZOV KNEW the kind of trouble he was in, and how could he escape? The pistol in his pocket was a useless toy, compared with all the weapons that surrounded him. Suppose he killed Mashhad and the remaining soldiers in the car without one of them shooting him. What then? He'd be sitting in a staff car full of dead men in the middle of nowhere, with two jeeploads of armed Iraqi warriors behind him.

Dead end.

Better to follow Mashhad for the moment and try to salvage something from the wreckage of his grand design. He had no opportunity to warn Petrovski or obtain advice from his superior, for what it might be worth. At best he was consigned to what the Americans would call deep shit.

But could he find a safe way out?

They had been burning up the road for fifteen minutes when the staff car's driver slowed, drawing an angry rebuke from Mashhad before he pointed out tire tracks leaving the pavement, running north on a more direct course. Two vehicles by the look of it, if Glazov was any judge.

"Proceed," Mashhad ordained. The driver clearly had misgivings, doubts about his vehicle's ability to cope with the terrain more suitable for four-wheel drive, but he kept silent, bearing down on the accelerator. Grit and stones played a percussion tune against the undercarriage of the car, and Glazov braced himself for the inevitable moment when they plunged into a hidden ditch.

Another fifteen minutes, still miraculously mobile, and they saw the jeep ahead of them. Its hood was hoisted like an open mouth, tendrils of smoke or steam rising from the ruined engine.

"Wait!"

The staff car slowed, then stopped. Mashhad craned forward, staring through the windshield at the open flats still ahead. Some fifty away and slightly west, a clutch of boulders thrust up from the desert floor like a malignant tumor. Glazov eyed the rocks, then swept the darkness, searching for the ruby pricks of taillights in the distance.

Nothing.

"One jeep lost." Mashhad was almost talking to himself. "Where did they go?"

Glazov didn't reply. It was self-evident that they'd have to check the rock pile, for the sake of thoroughness, before they headed north again. The driver knew it, too, and he was ready when Mashhad made up his mind.

"Go that way."

In another moment they were past the jeep, shaving the distance to twenty yards, then fifteen, the staff car moving at a crawl. When they were barely ten yards from the rock pile, automatic gunfire erupted on their flank, from somewhere near the end of the procession, bringing Glazov's head around. He couldn't see the muzzle-flashes yet, but it made little difference. Headlights blazed in front of them, a vehicle in motion on a hard collision course, and several weapons cut loose from the stony crags.

Glazov's blood froze as he watched the trap swing shut.

STRETCHED OUT beneath the dead jeep and breathing vapors from the ruined engine, Gary Manning was reminded of the soldier's basic admonition—never volunteer for anything. His post was probably the worst of any in the makeshift ambuscade, with no real cover, no mobility beyond his own two legs, but someone had to do it and the tall Canadian felt equal to the challenge.

If he blew it, they could only kill him once.

He had replaced the compact submachine gun with an AK-47, which had better range and knockdown power for the job he had to do. It was a waiting game and something of a gamble, lying underneath the jeep until their enemies arrived on the scene, then hoping no one spotted him before they moved on to inspect the nearby rocks. If one of the Iraqi soldiers glimpsed an elbow or a foot, or just decided he should spray the jeep with bullets for the hell of it, the game was up.

All things considered, Manning almost felt relief when he saw headlights in the distance, growing larger by the moment. Three vehicles traveling in single file, and that was another relief. There were no trucks among them, which limited the number of hostile troops. Fifteen or twenty tops, depending on the way they packed their rolling stock.

When they were close enough to see him, Manning lost his worm's-eye view. He heard the engines idling, had already recognized a staff car leading jeeps, and waited for the crunch of boots on gravel that would tell him he was trapped. How many could he take down, firing from a prone position, in the time before they riddled him with bullets or dispatched him with a hand grenade? Say two or three, if he was very lucky and their own luck didn't hold.

If it came down to that, he reckoned it would have to be enough.

Another endless moment passed, and then the lead car pulled away in the direction of the rocks. He waited, heard the jeeps roll past in turn, the numbers falling in his mind. He had the distance calculated, paced off in advance, and knew precisely when to make his move.

It took a second and a half to wriggle clear and raise his weapon, sighting on the rear jeep in the short parade. He had the AK-47 set for automatic fire, his finger tightening around the trigger, rattling off a burst from fifteen yards away.

And suddenly, on cue, all hell broke loose.

ENCIZO HAD THE WHEEL, and James was riding shotgun when the play went down. They heard a blast of fire from Manning's plug position, other weapons kicking in from fissures in the rock, and the Cuban revved up the jeep, a speed shift as the back tires dug in, spitting sand.

They had been shielded from the enemy as he approached, concealed behind the mass of rugged stone, but there was no more cover as they roared across the open desert, headlights blazing, locked on a collision course with what appeared to be a military staff car. James saw two jeeps bringing up the rear, caught a glimpse of Gary Manning covering the back door from the shelter of their own abandoned jeep, then he had to think beyond the heartbeat, instinct taking over in a rush.

He had the Vz.58 in one hand, Manning's short Beretta submachine gun in the other, and he felt a bit like Dillinger or Jesse James as they approached the convoy, pushing close to forty miles an hour now, both weapons blazing in his hands. It was a trifle long on drama, but it got results, the staff car swerving as its windshield frosted over, shattered, spraying pebble glass around the passenger compartment. James saw the driver clasping one hand to his face before the face and hand exploded, then he left the veering car behind to face the jeeps.

It was a bit like jousting, but you didn't simply bruise your ass and ego if you lost the round. He felt a bullet whisper past his face, another close behind it, and his weapons answered, muzzle-flashes going off like strobe lights in the night. On past the second vehicle and racing toward the last in line, his shoulders hunched against the impact of a killing round that never came, arms rigid with the elbow locked to keep both guns on target.

Empty.

They were past the second jeep and swinging through a wide U-turn, with James reloading on the move. Manning was on his feet and firing from the shoulder now with measured bursts. Their orders were to spare at least one vehicle, if possible, but see the job done right no matter what.

On the return trip, they were running into friendly fire. Their comrades held the high ground, sighting on the hostile troop, but there was no such thing as absolute precision in a firefight. Any one of their companions—Bolan, Katz, McCarter or the woman—might unleash a careless burst, and that would be the end of Calvin James.

But he'd take the chance.

"Haul ass, amigo!"

In the driver's seat, Encizo flashed a grin and braced his automatic rifle on the bench rest of his own left arm, prepared to fire one-handed when they overtook their prey.

"I'm hauling, bro'. Just watch your own."

And then there was no time for conversation, only time to kill.

KATZ SAW the damaged staff car veer off course, decelerating, with its windshield shattered and a dead man slumped behind the wheel. His instinct told him those he sought would be inside the car, already scrambling to unseat the lifeless driver and discard his corpse before the engine died.

So little time.

Katz broke from cover, heard the woman shout a warning after him, out there was nothing she could tell him of the risks involved that he didn't already know. He had to watch the stones beneath his feet to keep from falling, experiencing a momentary loss of contact with his enemies before a final jarring leap that brought him to the desert floor.

The staff car hadn't stalled completely, rolling at a snail's pace with the engine laboring, twenty yards from where Katz stood. He caught a glimpse of frantic movement in the car and fired a chest-high burst from his AK-47 that raked the vehicle from back to front, window glass exploding with a crash.

It might have been the driver's body shifting or some bungled action by another passenger that did the trick. In any case the staff car gave a sudden lurch, surged forward, stalled. Its engine died.

A door flapped open on the side facing Katz, and he was ready when a chunky man in uniform emerged, stumbling on his exit, going down on one knee. Before the soldier had a chance to use his weapon, Katz unleashed a burst that slammed him back against the car and dumped him in the dust.

His door swung shut.

It was enough to make the other three survivors scramble out the driver's side, away from Katz. He followed them, reloading on the move—not an easy task without his prosthesis—and had his AK-47 ready when a figure broke from cover at the rear end of the staff car, sprinting desperately as if the open desert offered shelter from impending death.

The Russian, Glazov. Jerking headlights framed his profile for an instant. Katz led his moving target with the AK-47, fired a 6-round burst and watched the former KGB man drop. He didn't rise.

One down and two remaining.

Katzenelenbogen circled cautiously around the staff car, going wide, expecting an attack with every step he took. Behind him, in the open, squealing tires and automatic-weapons fire attempted to distract him, but he kept his focus, going for the kill.

A slender man in bloodstained khaki came to meet him, pumping pistol rounds at Katz in rapid fire. Katz hit the deck and rolled out to his left, already firing as he came up, with the AK-47's muzzle angled high. He took the soldier's head off in a burst of gray and crimson, dropping him out of sight behind the car.

And that left one.

Katz rose and took his time about it, moving on the balls of his feet, circling the vehicle to find his target seated on the ground, blood leaking from a chest wound.

The Phoenix Force leader didn't know Amal Mashhad by name, but he'd hold the slim Iraqi's face forever in his mind. The man was injured, but he wasn't dying—not unless the shot had angled downward, clipping major arteries along the way. In that case, though, he should be dead already, and the man's eyes were very much alive.

So, too, were the hands that held a pistol in his lap.

The image of his former captive standing there unhinged Mashhad. He twisted from a seated posture, rising to his knees, the pistol wavering in front of him. He braced it with his free hand, seeking target acquisition, lips pulled back into a snarl.

Katz gave him half a magazine from less than twenty feet away. The man's flesh and clothing rippled, spouting crimson as the 7.62 mm rounds ripped through him, jerking him around and draping him across the back seat of the staff car, with his twitching legs outside.

Behind him, there were scattered gunshots fading into silence. Katzenelenbogen turned and faced the killing ground, suddenly aware that the battle could have gone either way. He might be all alone, surrounded by his enemies.

In fact, one of the military jeeps was lying on its side, a body pinned beneath it, others scattered on the sand where they had been cut down attempting to escape. The other had run out of steam when bullets found the driver, and its passengers had been no match for Bolan and the Stony Man team.

All dead.

Katz moved back toward the rocks and found Bolan and Sascha Lentz coming down to meet him. McCarter was already checking out the second jeep, crooning to the stalled engine, bringing it back to life.

"We're in business," he reported, gunning it.

"All present and accounted for," Manning said as he joined his comrades.

Katz counted heads to reassure himself, eyes coming back to Bolan's face. "We're finished here, I think."

"Looks like."

"Still got a long drive back," James said. "I wouldn't want to hang around this neighborhood too long."

"Damn right," Encizo agreed.

"We'd better move it," the Executioner said.

And so they did.

EPILOGUE

Stony Man Farm
Friday, 1140 hours

This time, the War Room's atmosphere held nothing of the tension evident a short week earlier, when those now seated at the conference table had convened to hear their fates pronounced. Among the missing, Leo Turrin had remained in Washington, while Yakov Katzenelenbogen was recuperating from his superficial burns in Maine, at a little hunting cabin on the coast. The ocean would be good for him, he had decided, not to mention the female companion who had accompanied him to the East Coast retreat.

The others settled in around the table, filling empty spaces, waiting for Brognola to begin. The big Fed was unusually animated, smiling as he made small talk with Barbara Price and Aaron Kurtzman, waiting for the other members of his audience to sip their tea or coffee—Coca-Cola, in McCarter's case—before he spoke.

"I hope you've got the jet lag whipped," he said by way of introduction, passing off a glance exchanged between the Executioner and Barbara Price. "It goes without saying you all did a hell of a job, but I'll say it anyway. Well done."

McCarter's eyelids fluttered. "It was really nothing that your average superheroes couldn't do."

"Your modesty's too much," Brognola quipped. "In case you haven't heard, the UN Security Council is meeting today, voting on new sanctions against Iraq. Inspectors on the scene confirm nuclear research in progress, and Saddam's raising hell about Iraq sovereignty."

"What else is new?" James asked.

"The Russian response, for one thing," Brognola replied. "They're moving to dissociate themselves from what went down. We've got eleven resignations from the current government already, more expected by the weekend. One of the reputed suspects, Josef Petrovski by name, was found dead in his dacha last night. They're calling it an accidental overdose of sleeping pills."

"It works out all the way around. Nobody really wants a trial on this. The problem goes away, we're satisfied."

"For now," Bolan said.

"Right. For now."

And that, as everyone around the conference table knew, would be the problem. There was no such thing as final, lasting victory in the unending war these soldiers fought. A respite now and then, perhaps—some R & R between engagements—but the larger war went on. It had been raging long before Brognola's birth or Bolan's fledgling trip to Vietnam, and it would certainly outlast them both.

Too bad. And yet...

"Now's all that matters," James remarked to no one in particular. "I mean, now's all that matters *now,* if you get my drift."

"You're drifting, that's for sure," Encizo said, and the solemn mood was broken, smiles around the table as they started up the old accustomed banter, chiding one another for imagined failings. Brognola recognized a classic form of tension release, and he welcomed the diversion.

"Anyway," he said in closing, anxious not to drag it out, "we're clean on this one. That's official from the Man, with plenty 'attaboys' to go around."

His eyes met Bolan's, and the big Fed felt a sudden chill, the message loud and clear. The war could wait a day or two, but it would still be out there. Waiting. Hungry. Ready to devour a soldier who got careless, letting down his guard.

It didn't hurt to celebrate, as long as each and every one of them remembered that they might not be so lucky next time out.

And that would always be the catch.

Next time.

"This meeting is adjourned," Brognola announced. "I've got a flight to catch, and I imagine you've got things to do. I'll be in touch the first part of next week, if nothing pops."

A weekend didn't seem too much to ask, but he had given up on betting long shots.

Bolan walked him out, a driver waiting for the short run to the airstrip. Standing on the shady porch with sunshine close enough to touch, Brognola asked him, "Is there something on your plate right now?"

"A few things I should look at. San Francisco. Houston. Montreal. I'll let it simmer for a day or two."

"It couldn't hurt," Brognola said.

"I guess that's right. It couldn't hurt."